BLACK TIE

HOT Heroes for Hire: Mercenaries: A Black's Bandits Novel

LYNN RAYE HARRIS

Printed in the United States of America

First Printing, 2019

For rights inquires, visit www.LynnRayeHarris.com

Black Tie

ISBN: 978-1-941002-44-5

Prologue

TWENTY YEARS AGO…

THE BOY HUDDLED under a dingy blanket on the couch and tried not to cry. It was bitter cold in the trailer and had been for days now. The weather had turned overnight, and his mother didn't have enough money to fill the propane tank or pay the electric bill. So he pulled on every shirt he owned—four of them—and his only two pairs of pants. He had two pairs of socks, both with holes, but he put those on his hands and feet. Then he curled into a ball and waited.

He sniffled and looked at the empty Saltine box. He'd long since finished them off and his belly rumbled in the silence. Where was his mother? When was she coming home?

He didn't know. He never knew. He lied to his

teachers when they asked and said she was working, but Mama didn't have a job. Or not the kind he could talk about anyway.

He must have dozed for a while because the key scraping in the lock woke him. It was dark out. He held his breath and listened.

A tinkle of laughter reached his ears and hope soared. That was her. That was his mother.

He sat up but he didn't push the blankets off. The door fell open and Mama tumbled through, a man coming in behind her, his big shape blotting out the light from the street.

"Baby," the man said. "It's freezing in here."

"It won't be for long," Mama said in that throaty purr she reserved for the men she brought home. She reached out and tugged him toward her bedroom.

She didn't call out for the boy, probably didn't even know he was there. And the boy knew not to say anything.

If Mama took the man to the bedroom, they'd have money to eat. Maybe, if Mama took enough men to the bedroom, they could pay the bills and have light and heat.

The boy listened for a while, and then he didn't. He put his head under the covers and waited. Eventually, he heard the heavy tread of footsteps echoing across the creaking floors. The door banged open. It did not shut.

He waited, listening for Mama's voice. Listening

for the man in case he returned. It was hard to hear anything over the pounding of his heart in his ears, but when he was certain the man hadn't returned, he pushed the blankets back warily.

The door stood wide open, the interior of the trailer even colder than it had been before.

"Mama?" the boy called. Softly, because he was afraid. He was always afraid.

There was no reply. The man might have given her drugs and she might have passed out. Wouldn't be the first time.

The boy stood, his legs aching with cold and cramped muscles, and tiptoed over to the door. He tugged it shut when he didn't see any cars outside, then he went down the hallway to Mama's room.

"Mama?"

She didn't answer. She lay on the bed, but she wasn't beneath the covers. The moonlight shafted through the broken blinds and across her body.

She was naked. The boy hurried over and tugged the blanket up to cover her. He'd known better than to take her blanket when he was so cold, though he'd wanted to.

"Mama?"

She didn't move a muscle. There were dark spots around her neck. He'd seen them before, though usually it was only one or two. These were bigger. Almost like hand prints.

He poked at her. She'd be mad at him for waking

her up, but he had to do it. He was scared and he needed to hear her voice.

But Mama didn't wake. She didn't stir.

It took him a long time to realize that she never would.

Chapter One

Avignon, France

TALLIE GRANT WAS USED to people staring, but she didn't like the way the man was looking at her. Her eyes often caused stares and comments from strangers. Sometimes she wore colored contacts to prevent it, but she hadn't put them in today.

She wished she had.

She'd grown up with one blue eye and one hazel eye, and she was used to it by now. The stares. The questions. The comments and unsolicited opinions.

But she was working and she didn't have time for rude idiots today. She quickened her pace as she strode through the flea market in Avignon. She was looking for a few very specific pieces for her clients and she didn't need to get distracted. The sooner she found what she was looking for, the sooner she could fill the shipping crate she'd reserved with French antiques and head back home to Virginia.

But this man unnerved her, probably because she'd first seen him at dinner last night when she'd been sitting at a sidewalk cafe. He'd stared but he hadn't said anything. To see him again, here, when she'd been talking to a vendor about a Louis XIV cabinet was somehow unnerving.

She wasn't unaccustomed to international travel, and she'd certainly encountered her share of odd people along the way. She should stride up to him and ask him what he wanted. That would probably shock him and he might go away if he knew she was onto him. Her eyes notwithstanding, French men were sometimes a little too bold in their appreciation.

Still, there was something about the scrutiny that unsettled her. Probably it was just the remnants of her conversation with her mother last night.

Mary Claire Grant was a perfectionist in every sense of the word. And Tallie wasn't quite perfect enough. This was her first solo trip to buy for her mother's interior design firm and Mary Claire was micromanaging every single detail.

"Don't pay too much, Tallulah," she'd said when Tallie told her about an exquisite Normandy desk she'd spotted.

"I know, Mother," she'd replied, hating that her mother always called her by a name she thought old-fashioned and pretentious. She'd been Tallie since she was in diapers. Her older sister, Josephine, unable to pronounce Tallulah, had always called her Tallie. It stuck.

Except for her mother, who'd stubbornly gone back to calling her Tallulah after Josie died in a car accident last year. Tallie swallowed the sadness she still felt when she thought of her sister.

Josie'd had so much going for her. She'd been bright and beautiful and very talented. Josie had been the true heir-apparent to the design business, the one with all the right ideas, while Tallie struggled to please their mother with her own designs.

Josie's designs were always received with delight. Tallie's were nitpicked to death until Mary Claire was satisfied. That hadn't been Josie's fault, though she'd always told Tallie that her drawings and idea boards were already good without their mother's input.

God, she missed Josie. They should be here together, perusing the markets of France and discussing all the treasures they found.

Tallie shot a look over her shoulder, trying to see if the man was still there. Still staring at her as he pretended, badly, to look over some linens on a table.

Relief rolled through her as she failed to spot him. She got her fair share of attention from men, though Josie had always gotten more. Tallie was five-two if she was an inch. Five-five in heels. She had no boobs to speak of. She was an A-cup, for pity's sake.

Josie had been five-eight like their mother and generously proportioned in all the right ways. Tiny waist, big boobs, curvy hips. Tallie didn't have much in the way of hips either.

She did have a pretty face, though. And hair that somehow always looked fabulous—or so her bestie said. But Sharon loved her and always told her she looked amazing, so how much could she be trusted?

Tallie finished up at the flea market, purchasing several items that she carefully marked in her notebook. A bedroom set, a mirrored cabinet, a cabinet with elaborate carvings that someone could use in a dining room.

There were chairs and sofas and silver and dishes. Bronzes, paintings, linens, and figurines. The crate would be full in another day or two and she would arrange for shipment. Then she would be on the way home.

It was starting to rain when she hailed a taxi for the ride back to the hotel. She'd worn a jacket today but the rain was chilly and she didn't feel like walking. A taxi pulled to the curb and Tallie opened the door to climb inside.

She shook the rain from her blond head and patted her face with the scarf she'd wrapped around her neck that morning as she gave the driver her hotel's address.

"*Oui, mademoiselle,*" he said, but the car didn't move. She consulted her notebook again, determining which market she'd hit tomorrow. But still the driver didn't accelerate.

Tallie started to ask him what the problem was

when the front passenger door opened. The man who'd been watching her earlier plopped into the seat and slammed the door.

Tallie's heart beat hard for a moment. She reached for the handle, reacting on instinct rather than any overt evidence of danger.

The door didn't budge. The car suddenly accelerated, throwing her back against the seat.

"Stop the car," she yelled in French and English both—but the driver ignored her.

The man who'd climbed in beside the driver turned and gave her a hard, evil look. He snatched her purse from the seat beside her before she could react, taking her identification and her phone with it. "Shut up. Now," he ordered.

Panic filled her. Tallie grabbed the door with both hands and tried to open it. She didn't care that they were rocketing down the street at a speed that would probably kill her if she jumped. She only wanted out.

But the door didn't open. "Let me go. *Please,*" she begged.

The man ignored her. They both did.

"She will bring a high price," the passenger said in French. "And we will get a huge bonus, my friend."

"Maybe we could sample the goods before we turn her over, eh?"

"No. Unmarked and unspoiled. That's what they want. Besides, we'll have plenty of money for whores when they see this one. She's unique."

The driver made a noise. "Not where it counts she

isn't. Stupid rich men. If I had that kind of money, I'd not spend it buying a woman."

"Be glad they do or you'd be driving a taxi for real."

The two men laughed. Tallie watched the city speed by. And then she started to cry.

Chapter Two

THE GATHERING OF MEN IN A CRUMBLING VENETIAN palazzo was exclusive, the clientele wealthy beyond the average person's wildest dreams. Brett Wheeler took in the glittering chandeliers made of glass blown on the island of Murano, the mirrors on the walls, the rococo carvings and gilded statues that ringed the room with its black and white terrazzo floor, the tiles set almost like a chessboard, and felt a wave of disgust flow over him.

He didn't have the kind of wealth that should land him in this crowd, but he wasn't Brett Wheeler tonight. He was a Texas businessman with too much money and no morals. And he was here to buy a woman.

That's what they were all here for. The sale of female flesh. The men who'd gathered were the kind of people who thought they were entitled to whatever they wanted. However they wanted it.

"Another Scotch, sir?" a uniformed waiter asked in accented English as he made the rounds of the tables.

"How about a bottle of water, buddy?" Brett drawled.

He'd had three Scotches, all dumped discreetly when he was able to do so. Of course he'd had a few sips for show, but nothing to impair him.

"Yes, sir."

The waiter disappeared and Brett let his gaze wander over the room and the men who were milling about with champagne and stiffer drinks. Assholes, all of them.

Brett almost wished he was still holding a glass of Scotch so he could have a sip. These men made him think, uncomfortably, of things in his life he'd rather forget.

He nodded to a German businessman, who nodded back in polite acknowledgement.

It had taken months of work to get this far.

Ian Black, Brett's boss, had carefully built his dossier as Carter Walker, Texas oilman and real estate magnate. Carter had a wife and a mistress back home, but he was bored and looking for something a little more exciting.

The women were supposed to be here willingly—not that he believed it was true—their bodies bartered for a share of the money that would help them pay off debts for their families or for themselves.

For the few who might have come willingly, Brett

understood that kind of desperation. The depths to which your life had to sink in order to be willing to do anything to survive. He'd been that desperate once.

He hadn't had to sell his body for money, but he'd known others who had.

He pushed those memories away and kept searching the gathering.

He would bid as part of his cover, but winning wasn't his objective. His objective was to learn as much as he could about the auction, and the others like it that took place in exclusive venues such as this one.

To note who attended. Who bid. Who won.

And to be invited back for another event where he could learn even more.

Black Defense International worked around the globe, on many causes, but Brett knew that the subject of human trafficking was one of Ian's hot buttons. Just like it was one of his.

Not for the first time Brett wished he was miked, but everyone here had to pass through a very thorough security scan. He had earpieces because Carter Walker wore hearing aids—and he only had them in case something went wrong and he had to make contact. They were so small as to be invisible anyway. But if anyone asked, that's what they were. He had his phone as well, because real hearing aids were controlled through it, but any attempt to make a call would be intercepted.

It was that kind of a gathering. And it should be,

considering some of the men he saw lingering in the ballroom. They were prominent businessmen, government officials, sheikhs, magnates, and mobsters. Ostensibly here for a charity event, though everyone in the room knew what they were really here for.

Brett swallowed a wave of disgust. Why these men should want to buy women for their personal playthings when they could just as easily get all the free pussy they wanted, with the kind of money they possessed as an attractant, was beyond him.

But here they were, ready to pay exorbitant sums for the right to own a woman's body.

The waiter reappeared. He opened a cool green bottle of San Pellegrino and poured it into a cut crystal tumbler. "Here you are, sir."

"Thanks, buddy," Brett said, deepening his accent as he did so.

He was a Texan, but he'd spent enough time away from Texas that he'd finally lost most of the drawl that had marked him for so long. Still, he could call it up when he needed it.

Tonight, he needed it. He'd almost worn a cowboy hat with his tuxedo, but he'd felt that was carrying it a little too far. And it was too identifiable. Nobody would forget a man dressed like that.

Just like he wasn't going to forget the sheikhs in their turbans and flowing robes.

A beautiful woman in a sparkling dress glided out onto the stage that had been placed at one end of the ballroom. Her hair was red, but not a natural red—

he'd bet his last paycheck on that. She had long pink nails and big eyes that were accented by thick eyelashes—also fake. She took the microphone in her hands and caressed it suggestively.

"Good evening, gentlemen," she finally purred. "Welcome to the finest party you'll attend all year."

There were murmurs of appreciation throughout the room. There were no women present, other than the one on stage at the moment.

"We have a wonderful charity event planned for you tonight. As you know, we've scoured the land for the prettiest ladies we could find, and they've agreed to participate in our little bachelorette auction. You will be bidding for a date, gentlemen."

She paused and arched an eyebrow as if daring someone to disagree with that understatement. "Any further arrangements are between you and the young lady, of course. You have your paddles. Raise them to bid. When the auction is finished, someone will come to your table. You'll be required to provide payment before you can begin your *date*. Once your payment has been confirmed, you and the young lady are free to go wherever you choose."

She shook her hair and laughed as if she were amused with herself. "And now, gentlemen—are you ready for our first bachelorette?"

A cheer went up from the crowd. The curtains on the stage glided open. A young woman in a diaphanous garment that hid next to nothing stood in the spotlight. Her dark hair was piled on her head and her lips were red. She was exquisite, and the bidding started enthusiastically before rising to ridiculous heights.

Brett raised his paddle a few times, to cement his cover as one of these men, though the heat of anger curled in his belly even as he did so.

When he'd taken this assignment, he'd known full well what he was in for. Didn't mean he liked it though.

But he had to keep his focus on the bigger picture. The money that flowed from these events had thus far been untraceable. He was here to find out as much as he could.

He'd had to pay an entry fee—they all had—but Ian's IT team hadn't managed to follow the transfer to the final destination.

Which meant they didn't know who was behind the auctions, or what they were funding.

Young woman after young woman stood on the stage, in various phases of dress and undress meant to appeal to a variety of tastes. Some of the women trembled visibly. Some stood on the stage with utter defeat written on their features. Others were lethargic and vacant-eyed, though to the untrained eye they seemed shy and maybe even virginal.

They'd been drugged, which ratcheted up the tension in Brett's gut. His mama had used drugs. Whether to dull her senses to the men who used her body, or simply for an escape from poverty and never-ending toil, he'd never know.

The curtains opened again and the last woman stood on the stage. She was no more than a girl, really. A teenager.

Blonde, pale, and slender, she wore platform heels that rocked every once in a while as she tried to hold her balance, and a white lace nightgown that skimmed her body and ended a little higher than mid-thigh.

Her golden wheat hair was pulled up into two short pigtails that gleamed beneath the spotlights. Her creamy skin made her seem ethereal. Her eyes appeared to be different somehow, but he couldn't tell what it was that made them different at this distance.

Nevertheless, she was strikingly pretty—and utterly terrified.

He could see it in the way she shook, the way her gaze searched the crowd, seeking a friendly face. A face she could plead with, perhaps. Brett's senses went on alert. Of all the women tonight, this one seemed the most afraid. The most confused.

"Gentlemen," the hostess purred. "We have a special treat for you tonight. The lovely bachelorette standing before you, our last of the evening, is unspoiled. Utterly unspoiled. See how innocent she is? How pure? And there's a bonus as well. This lovely young thing has one blue eye and one golden. Very rare, gentlemen!"

A murmur went over the crowd. Brett could feel the excitement in the room like a palpable thing. He stared at the girl, his heart twisting. Poor kid. Poor, poor kid.

"Place your bids for this prize so that you may guide our sweet innocent into a world of pleasure. We will start at two hundred and fifty thousand dollars."

The bidding erupted with paddles shooting into the air and animalistic shouts from some of the men. Brett watched the petite blonde blink rapidly, her gaze darting around the room like a cornered rabbit.

He wanted to act, but he couldn't save them all. He knew that. He'd known it when he'd taken this assignment. He'd mostly taken it for his mother's memory. Because nobody else had done a damned thing to help her when she'd needed it. They hadn't even cared that she'd been murdered.

That's why he had to be here. If he could help dismantle this sick event and bring the organizers to justice, then he was in all the way.

As the bidding intensified, he told himself to walk away. To turn his back, get his coat, and slip into the Venetian night. He could find a quiet canal and puke his guts out, then he could head back to his hotel and call Ian.

He could wash the putridness of this night away in a hot shower, or he could go for a run through empty streets until he was ready to drop from exhaustion. Anything to clear his mind of the images currently crowding it.

But the girl stood on the stage, looking younger and more vulnerable than any of the previous ones had, and his heart throbbed. Her gaze met his—or it felt like it did—her eyes pleading with him.

Do something. Help me.

Brett felt something hot flare in his belly. "Goddammit," he growled.

Then he lifted his paddle and joined the frenzy.

THE ROOM WAS FREEZING. It wasn't an important detail, not compared to everything else Tallie was going through, but it was probably the most normal thing about the situation.

She was standing on a stage in a glittering room filled with men in black tie—and some in long robes—wearing next to nothing and tottering on her high heels. She was groggy, but not so groggy she wasn't aware of her surroundings.

As much as she wanted to open her mouth and say something—anything—she couldn't make her lips work. Her throat wouldn't form the words, her mouth wouldn't release them. It took everything she had to stand in place and not fall.

The woman with red hair stood nearby, calmly reciting numbers into her microphone. The men in the audience raised paddles and then the lady asked for greater and greater numbers with each paddle being raised.

Tallie peered into the room beyond the stage. But the spotlights shined directly in her eyes, not enough to make her squint, but enough to obscure the faces in the crowd.

Think, Tallulah.

But what could she do? She told herself to move, to fall if that's what it took, but her body didn't obey. She simply… stood.

How many days since she'd climbed into the taxi? Three? Four? She didn't know. She'd heard enough to know the men intended on selling her to someone. But then they'd drugged her and everything became a blur.

She had an impression of lying in a moving vehicle for hours while men spoke to each other in a language that wasn't French, or even European in origin. She didn't think those were the original men who'd taken her because they had spoken French in the taxi.

At a certain point the new men had blindfolded her, removed her from the vehicle, and taken her onto a boat. That was how she'd ended up here, wherever here was.

The light shifted, one of them fading until she could see faces. She swept her gaze over them in a panic—until she connected with one man in particular.

He seemed angry somehow. For her? Hope flared in her soul even though she had the barest evidence on which to base it.

"Please," she thought. *"Oh please. Do something."*

The spotlight that had burned out shined in her

face again as someone repaired it—and the man was gone. Her heart thumped.

The fog of whatever they'd given her was strong, but she could still find herself within it.

I am Tallie Grant. I'm an American. I'm an interior designer. This is a dream. I'm going to wake up soon and this will all be over…

"Very nice, gentleman," the red-haired woman purred. "We are down to three very determined bidders. Who will give me one million dollars?"

Chapter Three

If Brett had been a different kind of man, he'd be sweating under his tuxedo. Not because he was about to spend a million dollars of Black Defense International's money to rescue a teenager, but because he was going against orders to do so. And not just any orders, but orders issued by Ian Black.

He shot a cool look in the direction of the two men bidding against him. One was the German from earlier. He looked coolly furious as he kept raising his paddle.

Determined.

Brett knew that look, and also knew the man's reputation.

Heinrich von Kassel wasn't the sort who liked losing, especially when he'd made up his mind about something. He spent time at the casinos in Monte Carlo, and he was known to wager huge sums on games. It was rumored that he'd put his own daughter up as a prize when he'd run short on funds one night.

A man who would do that would probably do anything.

The other man was more of a mystery. He didn't appear as determined as Von Kassel. It almost seemed like he was bidding just to drive up the price.

Brett considered giving in. Letting Von Kassel or the other man win and then finding a way to steal the girl away later. If it was Von Kassel, then Brett could break into his hotel, immobilize his people, and take her before Von Kassel could do anything about it.

But what if the other man won? Brett didn't know who he was yet, and had no idea where the man was staying or if he could find the girl in time.

No, the best way to save her was to win the auction, the expense be damned.

"Gentlemen?" the auctioneer asked. "Who will give me one million dollars for this lovely blonde goddess? She is like a fairy queen, so small and perfect. And she can be yours if you desire her enough."

"One million dollars," Brett said firmly.

Von Kassel didn't say anything. He didn't raise his paddle again. But the look he shot Brett dripped with malice. He didn't have the money.

The other man seemed to consider it. He also turned to look at Brett, but it was a more considering look than Von Kassel's. Perhaps he was trying to decide if Brett, aka Carter Walker, had enough money to keep driving up the price.

He must have decided that Brett did because he shook his head and dropped the paddle.

The auctioneer tapped her golden gavel against the podium. "Going once… going twice…"

She paused for a long, long moment while Brett ground his teeth together and waited for someone else to jump into the fray at the last possible second. Or for the mystery man to change his mind.

"Sold to the gentleman at table twenty-two!" The gavel came down and the auction was final.

Brett had just bought his first human being.

"DAMMIT, MAN," Ian Black spat into the phone. "This wasn't the way we planned it."

Brett stood on a terrazzo overlooking the Grand Canal and watched water taxis and gondolas slip through the dark waters below. He had a cigarette in his hands, because Carter Walker smoked—and Brett Wheeler did sometimes too, especially when his nerves were jangled by long buried memories. He took a soothing drag and held the smoke in before letting it rush out again.

"I know."

"Why did you do it? You told me you could handle this."

"I *can* handle it," Brett growled, spinning to make

sure no one else was near. "I am handling it. This is another opportunity to follow the money trail. Besides, I've gone as far as I can here. They don't let anyone see too much of the operation. But tonight puts me on their radar as a serious buyer. There'll be more opportunities now. More chances to learn who's behind it all."

He couldn't see Ian but he could hear the wheels grinding away in his boss's mind. Finally, Ian let out an explosive breath.

"I hope you're right because we've got no choice but to play it your way now. Jesus H. Christ."

"I'm right. Paloma has already suggested as much." The redhead had introduced herself to him after the conclusion of the auction. Her smile had filled him with disgust. Her touch, when she'd brushed her fingers along his sleeve, had nearly made him shudder. He hadn't, but just barely.

Ian tapped the keys on his keyboard. "She's been working for the organizers for the past year. She liaises between them and the men who find the girls. Then she runs the show, from the sets to the guest list to how the women are presented."

"Yeah, she's a real winner," Brett said bitterly. Any woman who was willing to profit off the misery of other women was somehow worse in his mind than the men who did it. Might not be fair, but that's how he felt.

"She knows things. Don't let your disgust cloud your judgement."

Brett dropped the cigarette and ground it beneath his foot. "Not about to, boss."

"So you've bought yourself a virgin. Now what? You can't just let her go."

No, he couldn't. It would blow his cover entirely to free the girl right away. He had to keep her for the time being, and he had to learn who she was. Where she came from.

"After I know who she is, I'll make a plan."

"She might have come from a bad situation. Sending her back won't change anything. She'll probably wind up on the auction block again. Or worse."

He thought of Heinrich von Kassel and how angry he'd been to lose. He wouldn't lose a second time, of that Brett was certain.

No, somehow he had to make sure this girl didn't end up in the auction ever again.

"What about the others?" Brett asked, still seeing the young women who'd stood on the stage one after the other.

"We'll track them down. I have your list of the men you recognized. We'll identify the others."

Ian didn't say more, but Brett knew that Ian intended to make sure every woman who'd passed through the auction tonight would regain her freedom. The beauty of Ian Black was that he didn't care how it happened, either. He wasn't going to adhere to anyone else's idea of justice: the idea that the men who'd dared to buy human beings should merely lose their prizes and nothing more. If they could be punished, they would be punished. Brett liked that about the bossman.

"Good."

Ian snorted. "We'd have freed her, you know. You didn't have to bid."

"Yeah, but how long would it have taken? She's young. Too young. And it might have taken too much time to identify her purchaser."

"We're on the path you chose now. Get back inside and take care of business. The money will be there."

The call ended and Brett returned to the palazzo's ballroom. Paloma smiled as he walked in.

"Ah, Mr. Walker. Your payment has gone through. Shall I send your prize to your address?"

Carter Walker owned a small palazzo on the Grand Canal, but of course it was really Ian's. BDI had lodgings around the world, some of them in incredible places like this one. The beauty of the place didn't quite make up for the nastiness of the assignment, though.

"Thanks a lot, ma'am," he drawled. "But I'll take the girl with me. No sense troubling you further."

Paloma's eyes sparkled. "Yes, of course. You are eager to enjoy your treasure. I quite understand. She should give you no trouble. She has had a mild sedative for her nerves, but it will not affect your plans."

"Wonderful," Brett said. "When will you have another event? I'd love to be on the guest list again."

Paloma squeezed his arm as she blinked up at

him. "Oh, you most certainly are on the list, Mr. Walker. As to when, I cannot say. Someone will contact you."

Brett forced himself to smile. When he turned on the charm, women rarely resisted. And as much as this one disgusted him, charming her was a good idea.

"Call me Carter."

"Carter, then."

"Will you be holding the event here again, or somewhere else?"

Paloma shrugged. "It changes. I don't know until I'm told. But rest assured that all preferred guests will be notified."

Brett knew better than to keep pushing. "Ah, well, I'll look forward to it then."

"And I will look forward to seeing you."

She offered her cheek for him to kiss. He did so, then kissed the other one in the Italian way.

"*Ciao*, Carter."

Paloma handed him off to a uniformed man who took him down to the dock where a gondola waited. Inside the gondola, the blond-haired girl lay against the cushions. He thought she might be asleep, but she stirred when he stepped into the craft. Bright eyes stared up at him as he settled in beside her on the plush seat. He got the impression she wanted to speak but couldn't seem to do so. The drugs, no doubt.

The gondolier pushed off from the dock and plied the waters of the canal smoothly and efficiently. Soon, they were coming alongside the dock of Ian Black's palazzo.

A dark shape stood on the edge of the canal, waiting for him. When the gondolier brought the craft to a stop, Colton Duchaine stepped forward.

"I see you stopped for takeout," he said wryly.

"Shut up and help me," Brett said, gathering the girl in his arms. She was limp but her eyes blazed with fear as she searched his face.

He hated seeing that fear but he couldn't reassure her yet. Not in front of the gondolier, who might be on Paloma's payroll and report everything back to her.

He handed the small form of the girl up to Colt, gave the gondolier a generous tip, and climbed onto the dock. The gondolier rowed away, whistling a tune.

Brett wanted to take her from Colt's arms, but he didn't. Instead, he led the way toward the wrought iron gate that protected the interior courtyard. He slipped a key in the lock and let them inside. It was a short journey to the top floor where their rooms were. The palazzo had a caretaker, and servants when required, but it was late and everyone had gone home for the night.

Colt set the girl down on a plush couch and stepped away. She huddled inside the cloak she'd been given, her gaze darting between them.

"How'd the boss take it?" Colt asked.

"How do you think?"

Colt snorted. "Not well. What'd you spend?"

"A million."

Colt choked. "Dude—what the fuck? Really? You paid a million dollars for this poor girl?"

"They said she was a virgin. It was either me or Von Kassel—or some other asshole whose identity I don't know. I think he could have spent the million, but I don't think he wanted to. Von Kassel didn't have it, thank God."

"Got it." Colt's eyes flashed. "In my mind, you did the right thing."

"The right thing would have been getting every single one of them out of there tonight."

"Yeah, I know. But we'll get them. You know the boss is working it right now. He has spies everywhere."

"I know. I still don't like it though."

Brett hunkered down in front of the girl. On closer inspection, he realized she wasn't as young as she looked. She'd seemed like she was about seventeen or eighteen, but she was probably closer to twenty-five. It was the way they'd dressed her, in that silly virginal garment with her hair tugged up into two short pigtails. They'd wanted her to look like a teenager.

Her pupils were dilated, but the irises were still striking. One blue, one golden hazel. He'd thought it might be contacts that they'd used to produce the effect, but it appeared to be her genuine eye color. There was no ridge of a contact anywhere.

"Heterochromia," he murmured. "It's real."

"Pretty striking," Colt added.

"It is. Poor girl. That's probably why they took her." He shook his head. "I thought she was about seventeen on that stage."

"Fuckers."

"Yeah."

"Can you speak yet?" Brett asked her. "Tell me your name? Do you even understand English?"

With some effort, her mouth dropped open. "T… Lee," she whispered.

"Lee?" he asked.

"That's what I heard," Colt said.

Her eyes shimmered. "Ta…Lee."

He couldn't quite make out that first part. "Okay, Lee. It's okay," Brett told her. "Go to sleep. We'll talk when you wake up."

She continued to stare up at him, her eyes wide and wet. He didn't think she trusted him, but the drugs weren't going to give her a choice in the matter. Her eyelids drooped.

When she finally closed them, two tears slipped down her cheeks.

Chapter Four

TALLIE DREAMED, BUT THE DREAMS WERE DISTURBED. In them, she ran down a dark hallway, the sounds of footsteps behind her. Her heart beat hard, her blood pounding in her ears. Fear was a living thing, nipping at her heels.

She ran faster, around sharp corners, always trying to get away. Behind her, the sounds of pursuit intensified. A dog barked, tracking her scent, and she knew they would catch her before very long.

Once, she woke up, drenched in sweat, the room silent. Something stirred and a glass of water appeared.

"Drink," someone said. A male voice.

She wanted to shrink from it, but she was thirsty. So she drank with the help of the man holding the glass. Then she collapsed again and fell into another disturbed sleep.

When next she woke, sunlight streamed from tall

windows, spearing across the room like spokes in a wheel. Tallie pushed herself onto an elbow. Her mouth was dry and her head spun, but she felt like herself for the first time since this nightmare had started.

It was like waking from a three day drunk to realize the world was still there. Still waiting for you.

"Hello?" she said, mostly to test her voice but also to find out if anyone lurked nearby. No one answered and her pulse kicked up. If she could just get out of this bed, walk across the room, and maybe find her way outside....

Somebody would help her if she could get away. She had to get away.

Tallie pushed herself upright. Her head throbbed with a headache. There was a glass of water on the nightstand. She reached for it—and then she hesitated. What if they'd been drugging her through the water?

She put the water back and dropped her feet to the floor. It was cool beneath the soles of her feet. Stone. She heard a noise and her heart skipped—but the noise was coming from outside. From the yard, maybe.

It sounded like more than one voice. Was that an engine? Were there people out there, just beyond these walls? Her heart beat a little bit harder at the thought. People meant rescue.

Tallie shoved a hand through her hair. It met resistance. She felt around in her hair, found the ties that formed pigtails—and memories came flooding back.

The woman with red hair. The stage with the bright lights.

One million dollars.

One million dollars? For what?

For her.

The men who'd taken her from the street outside the market said she would fetch a high price. It was stunning to contemplate, but she'd been sold like a racehorse at an auction. To a man who'd paid one million dollars for the right to own her.

Anger and fear flooded her throat with acid.

She'd been abducted in broad daylight, in France, and sold like a commodity. She thought of flying through Atlanta and seeing the signs about human trafficking in the airport. The signs that told people what to look for, and assured those who were being trafficked that they could get help.

She'd been trafficked. She wouldn't have thought such a thing was possible. She was American, not a child, and not helpless. But they'd taken her and they'd sold her like an animal.

Tallie shuddered. What kind of person would pay money for another human being?

Not the kind of person she wanted to know.

She had to get out of here, before someone returned and found her awake. She got to her feet, tottering on weak legs. She had no shoes, no clothing beyond the white silk nightie she still wore.

Panicked, she felt for her panties. They were still there too. Of course that didn't mean some lecherous jerk hadn't molested her while she was drugged, but she didn't feel like there'd been genital to genital contact. What kind of man would put her panties back on if he was willing to rape her in the first place?

She stumbled toward the open door that seemed to lead into a bathroom. First she had to pee, then she was getting out of here. Tallie stopped at the mirror, stunned at what she saw. The pigtails. The juvenile makeup that was smeared from sleep.

She jerked herself away from her reflection, did her business, and then thought about taking a shower. The shower was huge, walk-in, and it was filled with toiletries. There were towels. She reached inside and turned the taps.

She could do this fast. Just a quick shower to dissipate the fog inside her brain and wake her the rest of the way up. She needed to think clearly and that wasn't happening just yet. A shower would change that.

She closed the bathroom door and locked it, just in case—and nearly moaned at the sight of a thick robe hanging on the back of the door. That would be a lot better to escape in than a silk nightie.

Tallie got beneath the spray. It was hot. She poured shampoo into her hand, then realized she still had the pigtails. She tugged at the ties until they came loose, then lathered her hair almost manically.

She scrubbed her face, her body, shampoo getting

into her eyes and stinging. At some point she realized she was sobbing.

Pull it together, girl!

Tallie gulped down the tears and scrubbed harder, then she stood under the spray and let the soap rinse away. She turned the heat down and opened her mouth, drinking the barely lukewarm water until she no longer felt thirsty.

Hurry!

Tallie twisted the taps, grabbed a towel, and dried as fast as she could. Then she wrapped the robe around her and pressed her ear to the door. Listening for movement.

When she was certain nobody was there, she pulled the door open and stepped through. She hurried to the outer door and did the same thing. But when she tugged on the door, it didn't open.

She pushed the handle again and again, but it was locked. Tallie pressed her cheek to the door and cried silent tears. And then something inside her burst and she beat the door with her fists, screaming weakly for help.

It wasn't until she heard a key in the lock that her fear grabbed hold of her again. Tallie stumbled backward, looking for something she could defend herself with.

She was still looking when the door opened and a man walked in.

THE GIRL STOOD in the middle of the room, wrapped in the white robe that'd been hanging in the bathroom, her hair wet and her face scrubbed free of any trace of makeup. Her skin was red, either from the heat of the shower or from the scrubbing, and her remarkable eyes watched him with fear and disgust.

Brett held out a hand. "It's okay, Lee. Nobody's going to hurt you."

She frowned. He didn't know if she even understood him, but he didn't make any sudden movements so she'd know he was safe.

"Who are you?" she asked, her voice scratchy.

Brett's senses piqued. It was hard to tell when she'd said so little, and all of it rusty, but was she American?

"A friend," he said.

"A friend? If you're a friend, then let me out of here. I want to go home."

Definitely American. Jesus.

"You have to tell me who you are."

She nibbled her lip and tugged the ends of the robe's belt tighter around her. "I-I'm Tallie—Tallulah—Grant. I live in Williamsburg, Virginia."

So that's what she'd been trying to say when she was drugged. *Tallie.* He'd heard the first sound, but it had been so weak that only the second sound was audible. He and Colt had both thought her name was Lee.

"Are you hungry, Tallie?"

"I want to go home."

"I know that. And you're going home. But first, you have to eat."

"My mother—I was in France, buying antiques for our business. *Her* business. They took me from the market. She'll be worried. I need to call her."

"I'll make sure she knows you're safe."

Her eyes shimmered with tears. He could see her fighting not to cry. She didn't understand what was going on, but he couldn't let her start calling people just yet. And he couldn't put her on a plane back to Virginia either. Not yet.

"You aren't letting me go. You-you bought me. I remember you from that place."

Brett closed the door behind him and eased into the room. He didn't approach her, though she swayed where she stood. Still weak.

"You remember?"

"I—" She swallowed and looked down, as if realizing that she might be in danger if she knew too much. She was a thinker. He liked that.

"It's okay, Tallie. I need to know what you know. I was there, you're right. And I did buy you. But not to own you. You're still your own person. You don't belong to anyone but yourself."

"Then let me go."

"I can't do that yet. It's too dangerous."

She swayed again. He started for her, but she scrambled backward, a hand held out as if to protect herself from him. He stopped moving.

"Stay away from me," she growled.

"You need to sit down. Before you fall down."

"You drugged me," she accused.

"You were drugged, but not by me. You've spent the past twelve hours sleeping it off. I imagine you've got a headache by now. Eating will help."

She reached the edge of the bed. Her hand sank onto it gratefully, as if she were holding herself up. "I just want to leave. Let me go. Please."

Brett's heart twisted. He hated that he couldn't do what she asked. "I will, Tallie. When it's safe. But you're going to have to trust me right now." He made a decision. "My name is Brett. I'm from Texas originally, but I live in Maryland these days. I travel a lot for work, so I guess it's better to say I stay in Maryland when I'm not working."

She frowned but didn't say anything. She was trying to decide whether or not to trust him.

"I'm working now, which is why I can't let you go yet. Buying you was a job. And if I let you leave, people will know it wasn't real. They'll know that I'm not who I said I was—and they'll know who you are. That could be bad for both of us."

He'd told her much more than he should have, but he hated seeing fear in her eyes. Ian would think he was losing his touch if he were here right now.

Maybe he *was* losing his touch. Hell, working a human trafficking mission was probably the worst damned thing he could have done. It brought up old wounds that had never fully healed.

And never would.

"This is work?"

"Yes."

"Where are we?"

"Venice. You're currently in a palazzo on the Grand Canal. It's safe. My boss owns it."

And everyone who worked in it was on the BDI payroll. Ian paid them handsomely for their silence. They'd been vetted and cleared—and they didn't ask questions.

She cocked her head. "That explains the sounds then."

He nodded. "Water taxis, gondolas, tourists. They're all outside these walls."

She wrapped her arms around herself. She seemed to relax for the first time since he'd walked into the room. "I hear them laughing sometimes. Enjoying themselves. People have no idea what goes on beneath their noses, do they?"

He'd certainly found that to be true in this line of work. "No, not always. Probably a good thing, really."

She sank onto the edge of the bed, as if giving up the fight to remain upright. "I am hungry."

She pushed a hand through the short strands of her wet hair. It came to her shoulders, darker blonde when wet, but it was already starting to turn golden as it dried. No wonder Paloma had saved her for last.

Brett didn't think she was a virgin, but he wasn't going to ask. That had been a fabrication to get more money. If a buyer realized the truth and complained, Paloma and her people would have denied it. They'd have continued to swear she was a virgin no matter what.

"Signora Ricci is preparing breakfast for you. How old are you, Tallie?"

"Twenty-six."

There was a knock on the door. Brett went and opened it. Signora Ricci bustled in, carrying a tray with covered dishes and a silver coffee pot with two small cups.

"*Buonjouno,* Signor. Signorina," she said as she went over and set the tray on a small table with two chairs. She poured a cup of coffee, humming while she did so. "Sugar?"

"No, thank you," Tallie said.

"Milk?"

"Yes, please."

Signora Ricci splashed in some milk and handed Tallie the cup. She took it politely, but Brett could see her hesitation. She was afraid to drink it in case they were drugging her.

Signora Ricci wasn't stupid. She looked at Brett. "Signor?"

"Yes, please. With milk." He normally drank it black, but if he didn't have the coffee the same as Tallie's she wouldn't believe it was safe.

Signora Ricci handed him a cup. "Shall I serve the signorina? Or does she prefer to do it herself?"

"I think she wants to do it herself," Brett said as he watched Tallie struggle with what he assumed were her manners. Southern girls and their damned etiquette. She didn't want to be rude, but she still didn't trust them fully.

"Very well. I will leave you then."

"It's perfectly safe to eat," Brett said when she was gone. "If you prefer, I'll have a bite of everything first."

He went over and sat at the table. Tallie sipped her coffee, then pushed herself up and shuffled over to join him. Her hands trembled just a little bit.

Brett uncovered the food. There were slices of salami and prosciutto, melon, eggs, and a couple of pastries thick with powdered sugar. It was a bigger breakfast than most Italians ate, but Signora Ricci was convinced that Americans liked a lot of food in the morning. Not that any of them had known Tallie was American. Signora Ricci just did what she always did when Brett was there.

Tallie didn't reach for anything, so Brett dug a fork into the eggs and took a bite. Then he ate some prosciutto with melon. Tallie watched with eager eyes. Her stomach rumbled loudly and he put the fork down. "Eat, Tallie. You're starving."

She picked up the second fork on the tray. Signora Ricci had thought of everything, naturally, and been prepared for Brett to eat too. Even though he'd eaten breakfast three hours ago.

Tallie ate delicately, though he was positive she was starving. She consumed all the eggs, one pastry—after he took a bite of it for her—salami, prosciutto, and melon. She drank two cups of coffee, and a large glass of water.

"If you give me your sizes, I'll send for some clothes," he told her.

"Thank you. I had a suitcase at my hotel in Avignon. I don't suppose you could get that too?"

"I'll get it. What about your passport?"

"It was in my purse. I'm sure they took all my ID." She shook her head. "My notebook is missing too."

"Notebook?"

"I was buying for the shop. I kept records of the antiques I'd purchased. Mother has probably arranged shipment of everything that's arrived at the port by now." She blinked at him. "What's the date? I don't even know how long it's been since they kidnapped me."

"November tenth."

Her jaw dropped. "I was in the market six days ago. Six days! And I don't remember most of the time since then."

"Because they drugged you. That's also why you're so weak now. They probably didn't feed you much either. They wanted you pliable for the auction."

Her face clouded. "I thought they were going to rape me. And then leave my body somewhere."

"Do you remember the men who took you? Could you describe them?"

"I could describe one of them. He followed me for

two days. The other—I never really saw his face. I got into a taxi and he was the driver. The other man who'd been following me also got in—and that was it. They took me to a warehouse and blindfolded me. Then they injected me with something. After that, I don't remember a lot. Impressions. A van. Two men speaking a language I couldn't quite figure out—maybe a Baltic language. There might have been other people in the van, but I'm not sure." She tilted her head as she studied him. She wasn't shrinking in fear anymore and that made him happy. "Are you a policeman or something? Are you investigating those men?"

He popped a piece of melon into his mouth. "Not a policemen. But the more you can tell me about what happened to you, the better."

"But why? If you aren't a policeman, what can you do about it?"

Brett smiled at her. "You'd be surprised."

She flushed red and he knew it was anger. "I hope you find them and I hope you put a stop to what they're doing. I hope for more than that, but it's not right to want people to suffer so I won't say what I really want."

"You don't have to say it, Tallie. I know what you want because I want it too. And believe me, if I have my way, everyone who had anything to do with what happened to you will never hurt anyone again. They won't be able to because they won't be breathing."

Chapter Five

TALLIE FELT BETTER AFTER SHE ATE, BUT SHE WAS still tired and she soon climbed into bed and fell asleep.

When she woke again, it was dark out. The sounds from outside were still there, though maybe not as plentiful as before. She lay beneath the covers and thought about the man who'd bought her.

Brett. It was an interesting name. A memorable name.

She wasn't quite sure what to make of him, but she wanted to trust him. He seemed sincere in what he'd told her, and he hadn't tried to touch her at all. Other than the fact he wouldn't let her call home or leave, he seemed quite normal.

She called up everything she could remember about him. He was tall, about six-two or three, and he'd been wearing a button-down shirt, open at the collar, tucked into dark trousers. He had dark hair, green eyes that seemed honest, and a couple of days growth of beard that made him look a little dangerous and a lot handsome.

If she'd encountered him under other circumstances, she'd have run home and called Sharon to tell her all about the hottie she'd met.

She frowned as she wondered if there'd been a ring on his finger. She didn't remember one, but she hadn't been watching his hands much. She pictured him eating food with her, and she still couldn't decide if there'd been a ring or not.

Not that it mattered. Once this was over, she would probably never see him again—not that she even wanted to.

She didn't know how long she had to stay here, but it couldn't be much longer. Then she'd go home and Brett would keep doing whatever it was he did for his job.

Not a policeman, but something like it, she imagined.

Unless she was completely wrong and this entire thing was a hoax. If he was just telling her what she wanted to hear before he did bad things to her.

Until he let her call home, anything was possible.

Even if her gut feeling told her she could trust him, she had to be wary. She got out of bed and went into the bathroom. When she returned, she spotted shopping bags sitting on the table they'd eaten at earlier. She went over and reached tentatively inside the first.

She pulled out panties and bras. She quickly slipped into some underwear, then checked the next bag. There were pants in this one. Another bag revealed shirts and a knit dress. She pulled on the knit dress with a pair of tights and added the Italian leather knee boots she found in yet another bag. There was also a pair of ankle boots, and some loafers.

Everything was high quality, and all in her size. She let out a breath, feeling almost normal now. She went back into the bathroom and found a brush. It didn't take much to make her hair behave. When she was done, she stepped back and looked at herself in the floor-length mirror on one wall.

She didn't look like a woman who'd been kidnapped and sold to the highest bidder.

Of course the outer door was locked again. She leaned against it and listened.

"Hello?" she called. "Is anybody out there? Thank you for the clothing."

A key scraped in the lock a few moments later and Tallie stepped back just in time. The door swung open and the woman who'd brought breakfast stood there. She wasn't a big woman, but she was still bigger than Tallie.

Tallie dismissed the idea of trying to push her down and run. She probably wouldn't get far if she tried.

"*Buona sera,* signorina. You are hungry?"

"I think so. Where is Brett?"

"The signore said to bring you downstairs when you were awake, if you wished."

"Yes, I do."

"Then please come."

The woman strode from the room and Tallie followed, hardly believing they'd let her out. The ceilings in the hallway were tall like in her bedroom, the floors stone. The palazzo was furnished with antiques, both French and Italian, and the walls featured carved friezes and gilding along with what looked like silk wallpaper.

This was the sort of place that her mother would hate. Mary Claire loved to mix modern and antique styles in her interiors, but Tallie was primarily old-world style all the way. She loved a room filled with oriental carpets, wooden cabinets, old oil paintings, and white couches to provide that pop of something that brought a room alive. The white stood out, but it also didn't overpower the stars of the show which were the antiques and rugs.

Tallie followed the woman down a wide marble staircase and into a room with a massive fireplace where a small fire burned. Two men sat in high-backed chairs near the fireplace. They looked up when she walked in.

Brett stood. So did the other man.

"I will serve dinner in fifteen minutes," the woman said before disappearing again.

Tallie glanced around the room, taking it all in. She wasn't free yet, but she almost felt like she was.

"You found the clothes," Brett said.

"Yes. Thank you. The sizes are perfect."

"Good." He looked at the other man. "Tallie, this is Colt. He works with me."

The other man was also tall, also good-looking. Blond where Brett was dark. "Hi, Tallie. How are you feeling?"

She was about to fall back on her ingrained politeness, but she decided to just tell the truth. What did it matter?

"Confused. Scared. A bit angry." She shrugged self-consciously. "I've never been abducted before, so I don't think I quite know what to feel."

"Understandable," he said.

"Can I go home yet?"

Brett and Colt exchanged a look. "Not yet, I'm afraid," Brett said. "A couple of days."

Despair rolled through her. What if they were lying?

"My mother will be frantic." Mary Claire might be a perfectionist, she might think Tallie needed a lot of improvement, but she loved her daughter and she *would* be worried. Tallie hated to think of her mother believing she'd lost her remaining child.

"My boss has been in touch with her," Brett said. "She knows you've been found, and she knows you're well."

Tallie blinked at them both. "And she just accepted that? Without speaking to me?"

That wasn't very likely. Her mother wasn't a

pushover. When Mary Claire made up her mind, obstacles fell to the wayside as she bulldozed right through them.

"The boss is very persuasive. She's placated for the moment, though she expects to hear from you soon."

Tallie's heart thumped. "You mean I'll be able to talk to her?"

"Of course you will." Brett came over to her side, but he didn't touch her. He just gazed down at her with those green, soulful eyes that compelled her to trust him. "You aren't a prisoner, Tallie. Not anymore. We'll be leaving here in a couple of days and flying home."

She wanted to believe him. "I hope so," she said, her throat tight.

"I know it seems like you should be able to go now, but we have to make sure we aren't being watched. It's safer for you that way."

"Watched?" Tallie shook her head. "I don't understand. Why would anyone care now that—" She swallowed. "Now that night is over?"

He frowned. She wasn't sure he'd tell her anything at all, but then he spoke. "It's complicated, but there are very bad people involved and a lot of money. It didn't end with the auction, unfortunately. I need you to trust me. I *will* get you home again. I promise."

BRETT HATED that he couldn't just send Tallie Grant on her way, but it wasn't that easy. First, they had to get her a new passport—a real one, not a fake one—and then they had to lay the groundwork to get her back home.

The hotel in Avignon had reported her missing, so Ian had to deal with police reports and claiming her luggage. It wouldn't take him too long, but a couple of days was standard.

Then there was the matter of convincing her that she couldn't talk about her ordeal. To anyone. Not her mother, not her friends, not the police.

He didn't know Tallie all that well, but he had a feeling that part was going to be the most difficult of all. She wasn't the kind of woman who was going to accept what had happened to her without wanting to fight back somehow.

She stood near, her scent invading his senses. It was the shampoo, but it was also her. Sweet. Vanilla and violet, maybe.

Her gaze darted between him and Colt. Dressed as she was in a knit dress and boots, she didn't look like a teenage girl anymore. She was small, slender, and youthful. But not jailbait, thank God.

Her hair was barely shoulder length, and it twisted and turned in golden curls that looked like she'd spent time in a salon. She wasn't wearing makeup, because he hadn't thought to ask her if she wanted any, but she didn't really need to. Her eyes were even more remarkable now than they had been earlier.

He didn't know how that was possible, but it probably had something to do with her being dressed and looking like a woman instead of a frightened child.

The golden-green and blue were striking. Just the sort of thing Heinrich von Kassel would be fascinated with. The man collected things. And some of those things were apparently human.

"I think you paid a lot of money for me," she said softly. "Why did you do that?"

He hesitated. Colt arched an eyebrow. Yes, why had he done it? It'd been an instinct, a compulsion. Once he'd lifted his paddle, he'd known he wasn't quitting. No matter the cost.

There were many things he could say, but he went with the most basic of them.

"Because you looked like you were about seventeen. And you were terrified."

She dropped her gaze. "I should thank you for saving me. I haven't done that yet."

For some reason, a current of anger ripped through him. "Don't thank me. If they hadn't made you look so young, I wouldn't have done it."

Her head snapped up and her eyes widened. She looked afraid again and he cursed himself for saying it.

Beside him, Colt murmured, "Dude, chill."

Brett drew in a deep breath. "I'm sorry. I shouldn't have said that."

A furrow appeared on her brow. "I think I understand. You wanted to help everyone, not just me. But you chose me. I'm very glad you did."

His heart throbbed one painful beat before going back to normal. He had wanted to help them all. Knowing he hadn't been able to was something he wasn't likely to soon forget.

The women would be freed, because Ian Black would make sure of it, but it was going to take a little time to get it done.

Signora Ricci appeared in the entry. "If you will please go to the dining room, dinner is ready."

They went into the huge room with the soaring ceilings and the long table that could seat twenty and took their seats at one end. Brett sat at the end with Colt on his left and Tallie on his right. Signora Ricci had lit candles, which was a little bit of overkill, but it made her happy, so whatever.

She'd placed all the food on the table so they could pass it between them, though whenever anyone's cover required it, she gathered up her staff and served a sumptuous meal course by course. Carter Walker's cover would require that level of detail should he have dinner guests, but since it was only the three of them tonight, it wasn't necessary.

"Wine?" Brett asked Tallie as he picked up the open bottle of Montepulciano.

She hesitated. Then she shook her head, her hair gleaming in the candlelight. "No, thank you."

He didn't push. Brett poured a glass for himself

and then Colt took the bottle, also pouring a glass. Tallie had water.

They ate marinated vegetables with creamy mozzarella, a seafood stew that Brett knew was one of Signora Ricci's specialties, tender beef with grilled asparagus, and pasta with a simple sauce of oil, garlic, and pepper.

There were cheeses and fruit for after the meal, and a bottle of Prosecco chilling on the sideboard. Signora Ricci would return with espressos when they were ready for them.

"Do you travel to Europe often?" Colt asked Tallie.

Brett hadn't said anything to her because he hadn't known what to say. Now he felt like an idiot.

"Yes," Tallie said. "France mostly. This was my first solo trip, though." She frowned. "I'm not sure I'll want to travel again anytime soon."

"You were buying antiques for your mother's interior design business?" Brett asked, though he already knew the answer.

She nodded. "Yes. We buy about four times a year. After we fill a shipping crate, it gets sent back home and then we sell the items in the shop, or Mom uses them in her interiors. There's a terrific markup—but she's long-established in the business and has no shortage of clients."

"Mary Claire Grant Interiors in Williamsburg, Virginia," Brett said.

"That's her. I work as an interior designer and buyer there."

"And you live in Williamsburg." She'd told him that earlier, but it was something to say.

"I do. I love Williamsburg, especially Colonial Williamsburg. It's such a wonderful place to live. So alive with history." She took a sip of water and fixed him with a stare. "You said you live in Maryland. What part?"

He probably shouldn't have said anything at all, but it was too late now. "The Eastern Shore."

"Oh, that's beautiful. So peaceful and quiet."

"It can be."

"And what about you, Colt? Where do you live?"

Colt shot him a look. "Also Maryland. HQ is there."

Colt was typically recalcitrant to talk, but Brett knew that Colt had only decided to park himself in Maryland recently. He also knew—or suspected—it had a lot to do with one Angelica Turner. Colt had met Angie when he'd been working a mission with Jace Kaiser, who'd been protecting Dr. Madeline Cole from an assassin.

Angie was Maddy's best friend. After Colt was shot during that mission, Angie had visited him in the hospital and seemed to be interested in seeing him afterward. But then she'd cooled off and nobody seemed to know why.

Colt had—with the help of Brett, Ty, and Jace—paid a visit to the man who'd tried to force himself on

Angie when she was doing some work for him. It had been satisfying to watch a blowhard like Tom Walls quake in his boots at the sight of the four of them.

But Angie still wasn't giving Colt the time of day, which made Brett wonder if his reason for camping out in Maryland had something to do with bringing her around.

Frankly, Brett didn't think she was worth that much trouble. In fact, he didn't think *any* woman was worth that much trouble. He'd go to the ends of the earth to save them, make sure they were safe and in control of their own lives, but settling down damned sure wasn't for him.

Been there, done that, got the scars to prove it.

"We have clients in Maryland," Tallie said.

Colt's phone rang and he lifted it to his ear as he stood. "Hey," he said. "What's up?"

Brett cocked an ear but he couldn't hear anything as Colt strode out the door, seeking privacy—or maybe trying not to be rude since Tallie had been talking.

"How are you feeling now?" Brett asked.

Tallie's eyes widened with fear. Brett cursed himself.

"I didn't mean how are you feeling *now*, like I expect you to be feeling sleepy because I've drugged you. I meant how are you feeling now that you've been awake for a while. Your appetite seems good."

She grasped the empty wine glass on her right.

"You know, I think I'd like just a taste of that wine after all."

He poured in a splash and she stopped him before he could add too much. She took a small sip and swallowed. Then she looked up at him, a look of regret in her gaze.

"I'm feeling pretty good, thank you. And I'm sorry for jumping to the worst conclusion, but this is a new experience for me and I guess I'm still not quite sure how to react."

"It's understandable. A lot has happened to you. And I'm asking a lot of you in requesting your trust without seeming to offer anything in return." He hoped he didn't regret this next part. "Would you like to go outside? There's a big terrace where we could sit and watch the boat traffic."

Her expression lit up with joy. "Really? Could we maybe go for a walk as well?"

He shook his head. "No walks. I'm sorry. But the terrace will be safe enough. We can have coffee out there."

She took another sip of wine. Her gaze was troubled, but finally she set the wine down and nodded. "I'd love to go outside."

Brett stood and offered her his arm. It was the gentlemanly thing to do, and he had a feeling that Tallie Grant was accustomed to gentlemen in her life.

She stared up at him, thinking. He wondered what was going on behind those remarkable eyes. He was about to drop his arm and step away when she got to her feet.

A moment later, she slipped her arm into his. Their skin wasn't touching, but he still felt a jolt of electricity. One glance at her face told him she'd felt it too. Her eyes were slightly wide, her lips parted as if she wanted to say something.

But she didn't. Neither of them did.

Brett led her outside, fighting his body's reaction to her the whole way.

Chapter Six

The night air was cool. Tallie took her arm from Brett's the instant they walked outside, mostly because she felt jumpy the longer they touched, but she hadn't realized how much heat his body provided her just by standing so close.

Still, she wasn't going to grab his arm again, so she wrapped her arms around herself and walked over to the stone balustrade instead of sitting in one of the chairs. She could feel Brett immediately behind her. Not too close, but not so far he couldn't catch her if she tried something.

Like what? Jumping off this balcony into the water below? Shouting at the water taxis gliding by with their hordes of tourists?

She could do that. Shout, that is. As soon as she heard any voices speaking English—or even French—she could scream for help. Or maybe she could just scream for help anyway. Surely a scream for help was universal?

Something stopped her, though. Brett entered her field of vision as he stepped to the edge of the balcony and leaned against the stone. He twisted his neck to look at her. A cold breeze ruffled the dark strands of his hair. The light reflecting off the water glinted in his eyes. She knew then that he had a good idea what she was thinking.

"It's not the best plan," he said. "Or maybe it is, because it will surely get back to the people who held the auction. You'll be cementing my cover as a rich asshole who buys underage girls. With them anyway, because the authorities won't enter this building."

Tallie shivered. The knit dress wasn't as warm as she'd like, but she didn't want to go back inside just yet. There was something about having the air on her face that made her feel like herself once more.

It was a thing she'd thought, in her few lucid moments, that she might never get to experience again.

"I considered it, you're right. I decided it wasn't a good idea. As far as I can tell, you and Colt are my best shot at getting home."

"We are."

His phone dinged and he took it from his pocket. The light illuminated his face as he read the text.

Handsome.

It shocked her to think of him that way. Was she

suffering from Stockholm Syndrome already? Falling for her captor?

He's not your captor, Tallie. He's your savior.

She hoped like hell that was true. She was starting to believe it was—really believe it—but she'd also believed she was safe in France, traveling alone and buying antiques for the business.

"Colt?" she guessed.

He glanced at her. "Yes. He won't be rejoining us tonight."

Her heart thumped. "Oh."

Brett arched an eyebrow. "I didn't know you liked him."

She laughed, surprising herself. "It's not that. I..." She swallowed. "I'm not sure I want to be alone with you."

He straightened, and she was reminded just how much bigger he was. Tall and muscular. Lethal strength in a very appealing package.

"I'm not going to hurt you. If that's what I wanted, I could have done it by now." He sighed and looked out over the water. Then he turned back to her. "I'm going to tell you something, Tallie. Something personal."

"Okay."

He seemed to be gathering his thoughts. "My mother was a sex worker. Because she had no other options—or didn't think she did. She sold her body for food, for drugs, for a roof over our heads. I hated the men who used her. The men who only wanted to get laid and wouldn't give a shit about her two seconds after they'd gotten off."

Tallie's heart sped as she listened to him. Heat bloomed in her cheeks. Not because she was ashamed, but because she was suddenly very aware that she'd caused him to have to tell her something painful.

"I'm sorry."

He shook his head. "Don't be. It was a long time ago and it's over now. She's long gone—but I want you to understand something. If I was the kind of man who could buy a woman for my own personal sex slave, I'd be an even worse kind of human being than the men who paid my mother for sex were. And I'm not. I hated those men. I'm nothing like them. I never could be."

Impulsively, she put a hand on his where it lay on the balustrade. His skin was warm and a little sizzle of awareness shot through her. She withdrew her hand by instinct, and then wished she hadn't.

"I believe you. And I really am sorry about your mother. No one should have to suffer that way."

His eyes glittered hard for a moment, like diamonds. She thought there might be more to the story, but he didn't say and she didn't ask.

"I'm one of the good guys, Tallie. I joined the Army out of high school, did four years, then got out went to work for this outfit. I've been at this job for six years—and I love it because I get to make a difference in the world. Attending that auction, as disgusting as it was, is part of something bigger. Those people will be stopped, I promise you."

She turned to watch the boats on the Grand Canal again. The breeze was cool, refreshing, though it also brought the scents of sea and fuel with it. She'd never been to Venice before. She'd always heard that it stank, but it didn't. Maybe it was the time of year and the fact it was cooler, or maybe it just didn't stink at all.

"It's hard to believe in this day and age that people actually sell other people. Or that someone like me—independent, American, not without means—could fall prey to them."

"I don't think most people like you will ever have to worry about it, fortunately. Typically, traffickers prey on women—and men—who are vulnerable in some way. But this is a different group of traffickers and they're looking for a particular type of woman. You're young, you're beautiful, and you have very rare eyes. You had the misfortune to attract the attention of men who were looking for more than the typical."

Heat bloomed in her cheeks. He'd said she was beautiful. It shouldn't make her blush, and yet it did. Because he was beautiful himself—and she was attracted to him in spite of everything that'd happened.

"I wear contacts when I don't want the attention. I didn't put them in after I arrived in Avignon because my eyes were irritated."

"Even if you had, they probably would have taken

you anyway. You were alone. They watched you for a while to make sure of it."

She thought of the man she'd seen following her. He had been there for a couple of days. She'd mistaken the attention for something else entirely.

"I'm not sure I'll ever be able to travel alone again. I'll always be looking over my shoulder—and I hate that because I love to travel. The antiquing trips to France make me happy. Or used to anyway."

"I'm sorry you're scared now. It'll take time, but you may find yourself ready to go again someday."

She sighed. "I've mentioned to Mom that I could lead antiquing trips. Plan a trip for a few select clients, guide them through the markets, help them choose and buy. She's always thought it would take too much effort—but I think it's the only way I'll ever go again."

"Traveling with a crowd isn't a bad idea. And after this, I'll bet your mother won't want you to leave the country anyway. Not for a while."

"No, probably not." Tallie frowned. "Are you certain she's okay?"

"According to my boss, she is. He wouldn't lie about it."

"My sister died in a car accident almost a year ago. It's been hard for her. We don't always see eye to eye, but I know she loves me. If she thought I was gone too, I don't know what that would do to her."

"She knows you aren't gone. It's for your protection that you can't talk to her right now. The people who took you know who you are. They could be watching your mother. We have to make sure they aren't before we let you return."

"But why? If I was just a random person they grabbed, why would they even care? They got their money, right? So what does it matter now?"

"It shouldn't matter at all. And it probably doesn't. We're being cautious. That's the job, Tallie. Consider everything and plan for the worst."

It made sense. She understood, even if she didn't like it. Finally, she felt like she was settling in to the things he was saying. This was caution, not imprisonment. He and Colt and Signora Ricci had been nothing but good to her. They hadn't been drugging her, and they weren't going to hurt her.

For the first time since she'd awakened in her room and felt the terror of her situation, those feelings finally faded. Not the fear of what had happened to her, or the fear of it happening again—but the fear of being here in this place. With these people.

"It's a terrifying thought that they know who I am. Where I live. I don't know if I'll ever feel safe again."

"It's not very likely they'll come for you. It's too risky when there are millions of other young women they can choose from. And they can't sell you to the same crowd again. You wouldn't fetch as much a second time."

Tallie shivered. "I know that's supposed to make me feel better, but it really doesn't. I don't know what I'm going to do when I get home, but staying by myself isn't very appealing right now."

"Do you have a security system?"

"Yes. I should probably get a dog, too. I had a cat but he died of old age three months ago. I haven't had the heart to get another pet. Maybe it's time."

Sharon had told her to get another cat right after Alfie died, not to replace him but to help ease the pain. She hadn't been able to do it at the time.

"A dog isn't a bad idea if that's what you want."

Tallie propped her elbows on the balustrade and folded her hands beneath her chin. "I don't know what I want. I just want life to be normal again. But it probably won't be, will it?"

She turned her head to gaze up at him. He gave her a look filled with the kind of quiet resignation that made her heart fall. A look that said he wanted to make it rosy for her—but that he wasn't going to.

"Eventually. But not right away."

TALLIE GRANT WAS SMART. And stronger than she seemed to know. He'd been involved in enough rescues over his career to see a variety of reactions.

Some people couldn't function for weeks. Sometimes months. Post-traumatic stress was a real concern, and Brett didn't necessarily think Tallie was immune to it.

But so far, she was handling the situation with grace and intelligence. He hadn't known what to expect when he'd determined to save her. He hadn't known who she was or where she was from or if she even spoke English.

He hated having to tell her that life was going to be difficult for a while, but she already knew it. Knew it and seemed to be making plans to deal with it.

He admired that. Recognized it as a strength, and one he shared as well. Even when he'd been eight and sitting beside his mother's dead body, he'd made plans for how to get through the next few hours. Then the next few days. Then months.

Without his ability to compartmentalize, he'd have never survived the years of foster care. He'd had terrific foster parents, and not so terrific ones. Each change in situation was like a hammer blow to his carefully constructed mental walls.

But he'd always bounced back. He'd survived, and he'd thrived by the end. He didn't dwell on the past. He forged forward. His background had prepared him for the Army, and then for working with Ian Black.

The only thing he would change, if he could, was that he wished his mother had lived and gotten clean. It might have made him a different person, but that would've been okay too.

"Thanks for being truthful with me," Tallie said.

"Why wouldn't I be?" He wouldn't if she were a weaker person, but he didn't tell her that.

She shrugged. "I think a lot of people might prefer to sugarcoat the truth. Tell me it'll all be great and I'll get over what happened in a week or two."

"You won't ever get over it," he told her. "But you will figure out how to live with it."

Her eyes glistened. He wanted to reach for her, but he thought that would be a bit too much.

"I don't even know if they… you know." She swallowed. He knew what she was trying to say.

"I don't think so, Tallie. And I'm not just saying that. The women are valuable to them, and they want the best price possible. Rape is for the client who purchases, not for the men who work for the organization."

He was angry saying those words, but she had to know. Maybe he should have tried to find a doctor, one Ian could have paid off, and had a rape kit done on her. But it'd been too risky and he hadn't wanted to take the chance.

Still, their information about the organization thus far was that the girls were not sexually abused before going into the auction. That was for after.

"The men who took me talked about it, and one of them said I was supposed to be delivered untouched. And I don't *feel* like it happened—but if I was drugged for days, they could have done anything and I wouldn't have known."

He wasn't going to deny it. She knew better.

"You may want counseling when you return home."

She blinked up at him. "I didn't think of that."

"There's time."

She went silent then, staring at the scenery.

Venice was incredibly beautiful at any time of day or night. The palaces that lined the Grand Canal were lit from below, warm light caressing their facades.

There were restaurants perched along the canal, too. Brett could hear the clinking of silverware on plates and the voices of happy tourists enjoying the beauty of the city. The water lapped the foundations as boats traveled along, and music drifted up to the balcony from the gondoliers who played recordings of traditional Italian love songs as they rowed gape-eyed lovers through the city.

"It's so beautiful," Tallie eventually said. "I never realized. Pictures don't quite do it justice."

He hated that her first time in Venice would always be associated with something terrible. Maybe it was her last time, too. She might never want to return. He didn't blame her.

"Wait until daylight. It gets even better."

"You'll let me outside then?"

"Do you promise not to scream for help?" He said it lightly, but he was serious too.

"I'm not going to scream for help. I've realized that you *are* my help."

He relaxed slightly. "I'm glad to hear it. And yes, you can sit out here for breakfast if you like."

"What about my bedroom door? Will that still be locked?"

"No. Your door was locked because we didn't know how sick you'd be from the drugs. We thought it best not to let you wander around until they'd all been flushed from your system."

"You aren't worried I'll try to escape?"

"The outer doors are locked. You can't walk out."

Her gaze dropped for a second. "Of course. But I don't intend to try. Like I said, I believe you now. And I trust you to get me home again."

He studied her features. The outside light illuminated creamy skin, a small nose, finely arched eyebrows, and generous lips. Her eyes were the star of the show, however. Even in the dim light, he could tell they were different. One was deeper than the other.

"What was it like growing up with heterochromia?" he asked softly.

She smiled. "You know what it's called. I guess I shouldn't be surprised."

He'd said the word when she'd been drugged, but she clearly didn't remember it. He was surprised she remembered anything at all, though she did seem to remember snatches of things.

"I know a lot of random stuff."

"Well, it was a bit of a nightmare, actually. Kids are cruel, you know. And of course I couldn't wear contacts then. Even when I was old enough, my parents wouldn't let me. My dad was a big proponent of embracing who you are. He had heterochromia too, though it was more subtle in him."

"He's gone?"

"Yes. Suicide, unfortunately. I guess embracing himself was a bit too much in the end."

"I'm sorry."

"Thank you. It was five years ago. I miss him every day."

He didn't miss his mother anymore, but she'd been gone for twenty years. When he thought of her, he realized how little he'd really known her.

And he hadn't known his father at all. She would never say who his father was. It wasn't until he'd gotten older that he realized she probably hadn't known. Though when she'd been clean, she'd talked of growing up in a town with parents and grandparents and a normal life. He used to beg her to take him back there. She never did, which made him wonder later if it had all been made up.

He'd tried, unsuccessfully, to learn more about her and who her family might have been. Some things were better left alone, he reckoned. That was one thing that working for Ian had taught him. You didn't always want to know the truth.

He'd stopped searching. Because it didn't matter anymore. What mattered was who he was now.

His phone buzzed in his pocket. "Yo," he said, recognizing the number as Ian's private line but not wanting to give any hint to Tallie that he was talking to the boss.

"Yo yourself," Ian said. "How's Sleeping Beauty doing?"

"Great," Brett said, eyeing her.

"I'm hearing rumblings. Von Kassel is offering big money to anyone who can retrieve Miss Grant—not that he's referred to her by name—from Carter Walker."

Brett's gut twisted. "What? Why? If he'd had it, he'd have spent it when he had the chance."

He could feel Tallie watching him, so he kept it deliberately vague. Von Kassel had tapped out before one million. He'd known he couldn't come up with it, not on that short notice, and he'd lost the bid.

"He has what he didn't spend last night. That's more than enough to pay an extraction team."

"Shit. What about the other guy? Do you know who he is yet?"

"Still working on finding that out. I've got a rush on Miss Grant's passport. You're going to need to pick it up."

"When?"

"Tonight. Make sure you're ready to go. I'll be in touch."

Chapter Seven

"Is something wrong?" Tallie asked. Brett's expression had changed during that phone call. It wasn't anything overt, but there'd been a hardening of his features. A subtle shift from the openness she'd seen earlier to a more closed off look.

He dropped his phone into its holder and gave her a smile. He had the kind of smile that probably made panties spontaneously combust. Tallie's mouth went dry and she licked her lips to moisten them. Brett's gaze honed in on that tiny flick of her tongue.

But then he tugged his gaze upward and looked into her eyes. She'd been impressed that he'd known what the genetic condition she had was called. It was rare and most people she met didn't realize there was a name for it. It wasn't just humans who had heterochromia. Animals—cats, dogs, and horses—had it too.

"Nothing at all," he said. "But there's been a

change of plans. We're going to leave sooner than expected."

Her stomach fluttered. "You mean I get to go home?"

"Yeah."

He didn't elaborate, but she told herself that didn't mean anything. What more was there to say anyway? They were leaving, and she was going home.

"Do you know when?"

"Not yet. Soon, though."

Signora Ricci walked outside with a tray bearing two small cups of espresso. "I thought you might like something to warm you up," she said.

"Thank you, signora," Brett replied. "Tallie?"

"Yes, please."

"Sugar?"

"Absolutely." Because you needed sugar in espresso or it was too bitter. He spooned some into both cups, stirred quickly and thoroughly, then handed one to her.

"There is tiramisu for later, if you like," Signora Ricci said. "Call me if you require anything further."

"Grazie," Brett said.

She took the tray and disappeared inside. Tallie sipped the hot liquid, grateful for the warmth. She was chilled, but she didn't want to go inside just yet. It felt too confining, even though the palazzo had large rooms with soaring ceilings. Walls were walls, it seemed.

"It's beautiful here, but I'd be lying if I said I wanted to stay any longer than I have to."

Brett sipped his espresso. "I can understand that. Maybe you'll get to come back some day under different circumstances."

"I hope so." And she did. She'd always intended to see Venice, but it would probably be a while before she'd return.

He gazed across the canal, then turned his head slowly and looked in each direction. It was methodical, as if he were looking for something.

"Tell me what you do back home," he prompted after his examination of their surroundings. "You buy antiques for your mother's shop. What else?"

Tallie straightened. Had she been imagining his scrutiny? "I'm a junior designer in the firm. I often work as a design assistant to my mother, but I've done a few of my own."

She didn't add that her mother didn't let her do many interiors on her own. And when her mother did, she often made changes to the design before it was final.

His attention seemed to drift again as he studied a boat passing by on the canal below.

"And what do you do back home?" Tallie asked.

He jerked his gaze to her. The question was silly when put to him, but it had the desired effect. "What do I do?"

Tallie felt herself coloring. "Yes. Here, you apparently attend illicit events and traffic in women for a cause. What do you do at home?"

He hesitated. "I go to Orioles games."

Was he deliberately misunderstanding her? Probably, she decided.

"I play guitar," he continued. "I like microbreweries, and I hang out with friends. We barbecue and play poker."

"Sounds very normal for an international man of mystery." She said it with a smile, not willing to push him farther on the subject of his job when it was clear he didn't want to answer.

He snorted. "It is. Mostly."

"Is there a Mrs. Brett?" She asked lightly, but she was intensely interested in the answer. *Mere curiosity*, she told herself.

His expression was stony for an instant before relaxing. "There was. We're divorced."

"Oh. Sorry I asked."

"It's fine. The divorce has been final for a few years now. I don't regret it. I only regret that it didn't happen sooner."

Yikes. Manners dictated she steer clear of the topic. But screw manners. Her life the past week had flipped everything she knew upside down, so why not manners too?

"You must have been in love to get married in the first place."

"I thought so." He drained the espresso. "But there's a fine line between love and hate, apparently. I found the other side of the line a lot faster than I'd have liked. Wait, no. I wish I'd found it even faster than that. Like *before* we got married."

Whoa. Tallie blinked up at him.

"You want to know what happened. Who wouldn't after a statement like that, right?"

All she could do was nod.

"There are people in this world who can hide who they truly are from you. My ex-wife is one of those people. She presented the face she thought people wanted to see, but it was all a game to her. She's a psychopath. Not a violent one, but a narcissist who pretends to care about others while hurting them for gain."

"She hurt you."

"She hurt a lot of people. She's a charming woman, very beautiful, and an expert manipulator. I thought she loved me because she wanted me to think so. But she's not capable of it. She only loves herself."

"I always thought psychopaths were serial killers and stuff."

"They can be, but the majority aren't. They're just amoral. They don't have any feelings except for themselves."

"Wow. I'm sorry I asked."

"Don't be. It's not painful—not emotionally. The only thing painful to me now is how I fell for the bull-shit. She remarried and had a couple of kids. I feel sorry for them. And for the poor bastard who married her."

"I'm not married," she said, feeling like she was obligated to say it after she'd pried into his life the way she had. "Haven't come close either."

"You don't want to get married?"

"Oh, I do. Someday. I haven't met the right person yet, I guess. I had a boyfriend for a while, but we broke up last year. He's a lawyer in a big firm and he has this idea of the things he needs to succeed. Wife, check. Two or three kids, check. Big house, check. I didn't want to be a check mark on the way to success."

"Wise choice."

"I thought so."

He pulled in a breath and cast his gaze over their surroundings again. "It's getting colder. Maybe we should go inside."

Disappointment speared into her. Not at going inside, but at the end of the conversation. He was done with it, she could tell.

"Yes, it is a little chilly."

He swept his hand out to indicate she should precede him. "After you."

Tallie cast one last look at the grandeur of Venice. And then she strode into the palazzo and tried not to let panic take over when the door closed behind them.

She wasn't a prisoner. She was going home. She just had to keep repeating it to herself until she stood inside her townhouse with its familiar surroundings.

But for the first time, there was a speck of unease inside that had nothing to do with her desire to get home. And everything to do with the man whose solid presence she could feel behind her.

Not because she was afraid of him.

Strangely enough, it was because she didn't want to say goodbye to him.

HE HADN'T SAID anything to Tallie about being ready to leave. He thought it was best if he didn't alarm her. All she had was the clothing BDI had bought for her anyway, and that would fit into Carter Walker's Louis Vuitton satchel.

Brett stuffed his clothes and equipment into his duffel, a sturdy black canvas bag similar to his Army issue duffel—though not as huge—and eyed the LV bag. Stupid how much that shit cost. His mother could have paid all the bills and fed and clothed them for six months on what one of those fancy bags fetched.

He thought of Tallie in the gray knit dress and boots, her blonde hair a riot of waves tumbling to her shoulders, her pretty eyes looking up at him sweetly, and he could picture her with the satchel. As if it was made for her especially.

She was pretty, and he'd be lying if he said he wasn't attracted to her. He hadn't been when he'd seen her standing on that stage, because she'd looked so young, but once she'd emerged showered and dressed, her hair silky and bouncy and her eyes bright, a hot, sharp feeling started in his gut and spread lower.

He hadn't meant to tell her about Julia, but she'd asked and he'd found the words spilling out. He wasn't embarrassed, and he didn't have feelings for his ex-wife—God no—but it wasn't the kind of thing you typically told a stranger. Still, she'd asked and he'd talked. Too late to take it back now.

Brett checked the time. Midnight. Colt wasn't coming back because Ian had sent him to meet with an informant in Rome. Brett hadn't told Signora Ricci they were leaving, but he knew she suspected. She'd been employed by Ian for a long time, and she knew the rhythms of BDI's operators.

When the call came, it was a little after two. Brett snapped awake, fully clothed, and snatched up his phone.

"Hey, boss."

"Morning, sunshine," Ian said cheerfully. "It's go time."

"Where to?"

"You'll get further instructions once you retrieve her passport. It's a fake for now, but the real one will be done soon enough. I'm sorry I couldn't get this one couriered to you, but there's no time."

"When is there?" he said jokingly.

Ian snorted. "True. I'm afraid you're going to have to walk across Venice with the girl, Brett. Leaving by water would draw the attention of people we'd rather not alert that Carter Walker has left the building."

"Roger that."

"Can she manage it?"

"I think so. The drugs took a long time to clear her system because she's small, but I think she's capable. If not, I'll carry her."

Ian gave him an address in the Santa Croce neighborhood and told him who he'd be meeting. Still, they both knew Brett would call to check in once he was there. Just in case.

The address was in the vicinity of the parking garage where the tourists who didn't arrive by train left their cars before finding their way to their hotels. It was a good walk from where they were in the San Marco neighborhood, but it was typically safe and always interesting. Venice at night was a different city than during the day when the hordes arrived. At night, you felt like it belonged to you alone.

The call ended and Brett shouldered his bag before picking up the Louis Vuitton. He'd have to carry this one too, but it wasn't large and Tallie didn't have a lot of things.

He made his way through the passageways to her room. He started to push the door open, then hesitated and knocked. There was light spilling from beneath the door. It didn't mean she was awake, but if she was he didn't want to burst in on her.

"Yes?" she called, sounding a little fearful.

He hated that she did. "It's Brett. Can I come in?"

"Yes."

He opened the door and found her sitting cross legged on the bed, a book she'd obviously retrieved from the library sitting on the bed in front of her. She was wearing jeans and a light sweater, as if she'd known. Not that she could have.

Her eyes widened as she took in his clothing—dark shirt and jacket, dark pants, boots—and the bags he carried. He was armed as well, but his pistol was tucked into a holster beneath his jacket.

"Are you leaving?"

"Yes." He slung the satchel down on the bed. "We both are. Need you to put what you can comfortably carry in here and get your shoes on. We're going."

She blinked. "In the middle of the night?"

"Yes. Hurry, Tallie."

She hesitated—and then she climbed from the bed and tugged open the drawers where she'd stashed her new clothing. There wasn't much, because he'd been expecting to take her home soon. She tossed everything unceremoniously into the satchel, zipped up the ankle boots, and took the coat he'd bought her off the back of the chair she'd hung it on. "Toiletries," she said, starting for the bathroom.

"Don't worry about those. There'll be more where we're going, or we'll purchase more on the way."

She stopped. "Where are we going?"

"For now, we're going to pick up your passport. I'll know more after that."

"At this time of night? Really?"

"Yeah. The boss gets things done."

She straightened determinedly. "Well, okay then. I guess I have no choice."

"Not really. There are reasons for everything we do. My priority is getting you out of here safely, so I need you to trust me and do what I tell you. Can you do that?"

"Yes."

He closed the distance between them and took her chin in his fingers so she had to look into his eyes. His fingertips burned where her skin touched his. She was like a fire in his veins, this girl.

"You need to mean it, Tallie. Your life—and mine—depend on it."

She swallowed, her pretty eyes wide. "I understand."

"I seriously hope you do. If you try to run away from me out there, it'll delay our escape. And it might tip off those who are watching us."

He could feel her shudder. "I want out of here and I want to get home alive. I'm trusting you to do that. Even though I don't really know who you are or who you work for."

He frowned. Something compelled him to tell her the truth. He didn't resist that feeling. It had saved his ass on more than one occasion.

"My last name is Wheeler. It's my real name. I work for a company called Black Defense International. We do many things, not the least of which is attempt to break up human trafficking organizations. I came here undercover to learn more. I defied orders to purchase you. I'm not about to let anything happen to you now."

Her lips dropped open, but no sound came out. He should let her go. But he didn't. He didn't want to.

Driven by an impulse he knew he should ignore, he bent swiftly and pressed his mouth to hers.

Chapter Eight

IAN BLACK LOOKED UP AS JACE KAISER WALKED IN. They were both at BDI's headquarters late tonight. Jace worked as hard as ever, but he looked different these days. He wasn't as serious, as uptight.

Oh, he was still serious. But there was an undercurrent of satisfaction that ran through his life now. Dr. Maddy Cole's presence, no doubt.

"Hey, boss," he said. "Found something interesting."

Ian sat back in his chair. "Oh yeah?"

Jace held a photo. He handed it to Ian. It was still warm from the printer. It featured a group of people on a yacht, laughing at something. Three men and three women. One of the women was a redhead. Her face was in profile, but it was the woman who called herself Paloma Bruni. She was leaning forward, her bare shoulder exposed as she reached for something.

Tattooed on her tanned shoulder was a symbol. Two straight lines with a curved line at the top and the bottom.

"Gemini," Ian said. "Well, shit."

"It's not a surprise though."

He shook his head. "No, definitely not a surprise. The Gemini Syndicate probably has a hand in just about every criminal enterprise imaginable."

Jace threw himself into a chair. "Fuckers. They take women from public places, from their families, and sell them into slavery like they have the right. Tallie Grant's abduction was blatant. She's not a woman from a bad situation, or one who wouldn't be missed."

Anger simmered deep within. Ian knew there were people out there who preyed on the vulnerable. Wooed them, brainwashed them, controlled them and sold them into slavery. It was all evil, whether it was a runaway teenager from a bad home or a successful woman like Tallie Grant.

He'd vowed to put an end to it wherever he could. There were just so fucking many of them. He wanted to kill every asshole he found participating in human trafficking. That would make him a serial killer, though. Sometimes he didn't think it would be such a bad thing to snuff out the lives of the kind of bottom feeders who sold their fellow human beings.

"It's not proof, but I'd say it's a damned good guess." Ian turned the photo over. Jace had written the names of the others on the back. The men were all wealthy. All names he recognized. "Either we've got some members of the Syndicate here, or Paloma was simply working her contacts and dangling temptation in front of their faces."

"I put Lane Jordan onto researching if any of these men paid large sums into the same bank account where we sent the money for Miss Grant."

The IT team was still working on tracing the money to its final destination, but so far they hadn't found it. Whoever'd set up the payment system was smart. And paranoid. You couldn't be too paranoid when you were a criminal.

"That's a good start." Ian pushed a hand through his hair. "Jesus there are some sick people in this world. With that kind of money, you should be able to attract all the women you desire. Or men, I suppose. It'd be a lot cheaper than paying the kind of money Brett paid for Miss Tallulah Grant."

"No kidding. I've certainly seen enough young and gorgeous women with fat old rich men. Money is catnip to a certain type of person."

"Yep."

Jace tapped his fingers on the arms of the chair. "Speaking of the Syndicate… any word from Calypso lately?"

Ian tamped down any emotion lest it show on his face.

Calypso. Now there was someone who got to him

more than he liked. Dangerous assassin. Vulnerable and complicated woman. Wounded soul.

"No."

Jace frowned. "Do you think she'll be in contact? Or do you think she lied so we'd let her go?"

Ian shrugged. After she'd shot both Colt and Jace and been captured, he'd offered her a deal. Work for him and he'd let her go. Refuse, and she'd be turned over to the CIA—and probably imprisoned.

She'd scoffed at him, told him that she would say yes no matter what. He knew it when he'd offered. And he knew that she might not honor the agreement.

But it was all he could do. He couldn't see her imprisoned after what she'd been through. And if he could turn her, she'd be an invaluable asset.

"I don't know. She's your sister—what do you think?"

Jace closed his eyes for a second before opening them again and shaking his head. "I don't know her anymore. She was a kid when I was conscripted. And then the time in the gulag…"

Ian grimaced. He didn't like to think of what had happened to Natasha Orlova in that prison. And yet he had a very good idea. He'd done his share of time in places like that. On assignments, deep undercover, working his angles.

"All we can do is wait. She has to think, and she has to decide."

And someone had leverage over her. Leverage that

she would do anything to protect. He had an idea what it might be, but he wasn't entirely certain.

"I hope she makes the right decision," Jace said. "But I can't influence her one way or the other. For all I know, I won't ever see her again."

Ian arched an eyebrow. "She could be sitting at the next table in a restaurant and you wouldn't even know it."

Jace laughed, but it wasn't a happy sound. "Who would have thought she could become a master of disguise? I remember a little girl playing hide and seek and dressing up her dolls. And then a teenager experimenting with makeup. She wore too much and our mother made her take it all off."

"I think she's learned a thing or two since then," Ian replied.

Jace's brows drew low. "You'll tell me if she contacts you, right?"

Ian studied the other man for a long moment. "I will if I can."

Jace nodded. "Good enough." He stood. Stretched. "I'd better get home to Maddy. It's pizza and British murder mystery night."

Ian nearly laughed at how domestic Jace, one of his most lethal and complicated operators, had become. But he wouldn't. Men like him—like Ian—had to grab their slice of normalcy wherever they could find it. And hold on tight, because you never knew when it might be snatched away.

Been a long time since Ian had felt that ordinary.

"Sounds like a good time. Tell Maddy I said hello."

Jace smiled. He looked like a very happy man. Ian was glad for that. Jace deserved it more than most.

"I will, boss. Good night."

"Night."

Ian watched Jace walk out, then leaned back in his chair and studied the photo of Paloma Bruni and the Gemini tattoo. But he kept seeing Natasha's face in the interview room when he'd last seen her. The fear and anger and hatred. The despair.

He'd offered her an opportunity to get revenge on those who used her for their own ends. Those who held something precious to her.

He was still waiting for her to take it.

SHOCK COURSED through Tallie's system. Brett's mouth pressed to hers, his kiss swift and stunning. For a moment she thought she should pull away.

But that's not what happened. No, she went soft, her knees weakening until she had to put her hands on his arms to hold herself up. He was still holding her chin, but not tightly. She could break away easily.

She didn't, though. She opened her mouth beneath his, felt the tip of his tongue dip inside, and met him softly. Tentatively.

He stepped closer, letting go her chin, and

wrapped an arm around her. She didn't resist the firm tug of her body into his. She tipped her head back, her heart hammering as fire spread through her veins.

Had it really been that long since she'd kissed a man? Was she that deprived that her body reacted with eager anticipation so quickly?

She gripped hard muscles beneath his jacket. He was tall and big and she felt protected standing in his embrace.

But then his hands settled on her shoulders and he gently pushed her back, breaking the kiss between them. His green eyes seemed troubled.

"I'm sorry. That was over the line."

Tallie darted her tongue over her lips. "I, um, I'm sorry too."

"For what? I'm the one who kissed you."

"I kissed you back."

He grinned. She liked the way he looked when he smiled. It transformed him from cool and serious protector to the kind of guy she might meet at an event. Safe. Harmless. And oh so handsome.

"You did, didn't you?"

Her heart thumped. "I did."

He bent down and picked up the satchel she'd dropped, slung it over his shoulder with the black duffel. Then he took her hand in his, his warm fingers giving her courage.

"Come on, Tallie Grant. We've got a long walk across a sleepy city ahead."

"Do you think anyone will follow us?"

"Not if I can help it. And I can. I'm pretty good at this kind of thing. Just do what I tell you, like I said. I'll get you out of this. Soon you'll be back home, playing fetch with your new dog, and forgetting you ever met me."

"Oh, I don't think that's possible," she said. "Forgetting you, I mean."

He gave her hand a quick squeeze, then led her out the door and down through the halls and rooms of the palazzo until they slipped out a side door—and into a dark passageway.

Tallie's heart raced as they plunged into utter darkness. It smelled like mud and the sea and she moved a little closer to Brett. He stopped and squeezed her hand again.

"I have to get a light so I'm going to let go of your hand."

Tallie nearly whimpered, then swallowed it down and grabbed onto his jacket with her other hand. "Okay."

She told herself he wasn't going to leave her there alone, but she still felt better holding onto him. He dropped her hand and a moment later a light switched on, revealing damp brick on the walls and arching above their head. The tunnel was rounded and disappeared into blackness.

"It's a bolthole," Brett said. "It leads through the buildings nearby, concealed in the walls, and spills out into a side street far enough from the palazzo that anyone watching for movement won't see us leaving."

She tried to imagine these shadowy watchers, what they could want. The thought made her shiver and she pulled the jacket tighter. "Clever," she said.

"I guess Venice wasn't always a happy tourist mecca," he said with a quiet laugh. "Noblemen sometimes needed to get out of Dodge."

"Dodge?"

"Old Western movie reference. Never mind. Let's go. It's narrow in places, so it's best if you follow. Hang onto my jacket if it makes you more comfortable."

"I plan to. I'm not very good in dark places. Especially not after..." She had to draw in a deep breath to calm her nerves. Snatches of the past week had been popping into her mind with more frequency than she liked. She remembered long stretches of utter blackness and the feel of cloth around her face.

A hood. She could still feel the scratchy heat of it sometimes. The way her breath had filled it and made her hot and a little dizzy.

"It'll be okay. I'm not leaving you in here."

"I know."

He gave her another quick kiss, no tongue this time, and her lips tingled with the imprint of his mouth on hers. If he'd meant to distract her, he'd done a good job of it.

They emerged onto a quiet street, and then made their way through a deserted plaza, moving quickly and quietly through the city. A full moon had risen in the sky and hung over the city like a sentinel, illuminating the streets and buildings with pale light.

Tallie wished she could take her time and study the architecture, the crumbling facades and plentiful plazas with their churches. Venice was an art city, filled with Renaissance master paintings, and a part of her wanted to explore every tiny church and grand palazzo in search of them.

Another part wanted to get the hell out of there and never return. She suspected that part would quiet eventually, and she would be back again. Not alone, never that, but someday she'd return. Maybe with a lover.

Awareness of the man walking beside her crept through her then. He'd kissed her twice now, and both times had jolted her more deeply than she'd expected. She wanted to kiss him again, see how it affected her a third time.

They didn't encounter many people as they walked, but there were a few here and there. When they walked onto the Rialto bridge, Tallie wanted to stop and stare at the Grand Canal from this vantage point, but there was no time.

The shops lining the bridge were shuttered tight, but there were a few people standing and gazing at the sights. Tallie and Brett didn't pause at all, walking up to the peak of the bridge and down the other side, through the market with its empty stalls that would begin to fill soon, and deep into the city with its maze of streets.

They moved farther from the touristed areas, into the quieter residential quarter of Santa Croce—as Brett informed her when she commented on the lack of touristy stores—walking over bridges that seemed to appear out of nowhere, across canals, through archways in buildings and onto yet more cobbled side streets.

Eventually, Brett opened a gate and they slipped into a courtyard. There was a light burning in the ground floor window of a three story building. Brett tapped on the door. A moment later it jerked open and a small woman stood there, staring at them.

"Come in," she said, turning and disappearing inside.

Brett took Tallie's hand and pulled her in behind him, keeping his body between hers and the hallway they'd stepped into. Protecting her from any danger that might be there.

"You're safe here," the woman said in accented English. "My name is Giana. I've known Ian for a very long time. I'm alive because of him. He has my utmost loyalty."

Tallie frowned, wondering who this Ian character was. But she felt the easing of tension in Brett's body at the woman's words. Not completely, though. She didn't think he ever relaxed entirely. She peeked around him, but she couldn't see Giana very well. She was just out of sight.

"No offense, signora, but you would say that even if you weren't loyal to him. Especially so, I imagine."

Giana laughed, her voice smoky. "Yes, of course I would. But I owe him a debt far greater than I care to explain to you. Call him. I will wait."

"I intend to." Brett took out his phone and dialed. "Boss? I'm here with Giana. Sure."

He handed the phone to the woman and a stream of Italian issued forth. Then she laughed. *"Grazie, bello. Ciao."*

She handed the phone back to Brett.

"Thanks, boss. Talk to you at the next check in." He pocketed the phone. "You have papers for me."

"*Sì.*" Giana handed Brett a thick envelope. "Your companion is Tiffany Newport. Your wife. She is Canadian."

Tallie stiffened. She was a Canadian? Married to Brett? Why? And wasn't his name Wheeler? Or had that been a lie?

Brett opened the envelope and shuffled through the papers. Tallie heard the jingle of a key. She stepped out from behind him and thrust herself into view. Giana looked her up and down, dark eyes assessing as Tallie studied her in return. She hadn't gotten a good look when the woman had been silhouetted in the door and then blocked by Brett.

She was older, maybe in her sixties, with brown hair streaked with gray that she'd piled onto her head in a loose bun. She had deep grooves on either side of her mouth, probably from sucking on the cigarettes that lay on a nearby table.

"You are even prettier than your photo," she said. "Remarkable eyes."

"Thank you." Because what else could she say?

Brett was holding a car key, a passport, and some other papers. "The car is in the Piazzale Roma or the Tronchetto?"

"The Piazzale Roma. On the third floor. Take the elevator up, turn left when you exit, and go twenty spaces. A gray BMW X5."

"*Grazie*, Giana."

"*Prego*." She smiled at them. "Would you like a coffee before you go? Perhaps a small bite?"

Brett looked at his watch. Tallie didn't wear a watch, though she'd been wishing for one lately. She was accustomed to checking her cell phone for the time, except she'd been without it for at least a week now. It was odd not to have it. She reached for it several times a day before remembering.

"Thank you, but I think we'd better be going," he said.

"Of course." Her gaze came to rest on Tallie. "You will be fine with this man. He is like Ian. They never quit. Never. Safe journey to you both."

Brett's fingers threaded through hers, anchoring her to his side. "Thank you. For everything," he said to Giana.

"*Prego*," she replied, inclining her head. They exited her house, and then she softly shut the door.

"Brett?" Tallie said as they started down the street again.

"Yeah?"

"Where are we really going?"

"The truth?"

"Yes, please."

He glanced down at her as they walked. "I don't really know."

Chapter Nine

"Who is Ian?" Tallie asked once they were in the BMW and crossing the long bridge to the mainland. The instructions in the vehicle said to head for the Brenner Pass. Once there, change vehicles at a restaurant located in one of the rest areas. Brett knew which rest area, but he didn't yet know how the change would take place. He wasn't worried. Ian always came through.

"He's my boss."

"I guessed that back at Giana's place when you called him boss."

Brett could hear the humor in her voice. He nearly laughed, but he didn't. He was too busy glancing in the rear view and keeping on eye on their surroundings. He didn't really think Heinrich von Kassel had deployed an extraction team to swoop in and take Tallie that quickly, but he had to stay alert and think as if it were possible.

"Ian is the founder of Black Defense International. He's the one who runs the show, and he's the one who sent me to the auction in the first place."

Brett could say it because BDI had a public face, though their real operations were top secret.

"I'm profoundly glad he did."

He glanced at Tallie. She was huddled into the seat, her blonde hair as pale as milk in the darkness. "I'm glad too."

"Why do I need a fake passport if we're driving? You can cross EU borders without one. And why aren't you taking me home? I thought that's where we were going."

"I will take you home. When it's safe. I have to rely on Ian to tell me when that is. As for the passport, it's just for backup. If we need to fly and your replacement isn't ready. Or if Ian decides it's safer for you to travel under an alias until you reach home."

"How can anyone fake a passport these days?"

"It's not my area of expertise, but trust me when I tell you it happens quite often in this business. It's definitely a specialized skill."

They'd matched her passport to one of his. Brett Newport was a military equipment salesman. And apparently he was newly married.

Tallie folded her arms and gazed out the window. The first light of dawn was beginning to pinken the horizon. "I feel like I'm in a James Bond movie."

"I'm not MI6. Promise."

Her head turned. "No, but you're something secretive. CIA maybe."

"Nope. Never even set foot in the place." He'd wanted to be CIA at one point, but then Ian recruited him—and life hadn't been the same. He'd worked with the CIA on various missions, but he no longer wanted to be one of them. He had more freedom working for Ian.

"In case you can't tell, I'm trying very hard not to panic. We aren't going where you said we were going. I'm trusting you, but a part of me keeps asking why. I don't really know you. You could be taking me to something worse than where you found me. I have no way of knowing what the truth really is. I'm talking it through, trying to make sense of it all."

Brett threw her a look. He understood her fear, but it pricked him that she could still be afraid of him. "Have you ever shot a pistol?"

"Of course. I'm a Southern girl. My daddy, God rest his soul, was from Georgia. He believed in teaching his daughters to shoot."

Brett reached inside his jacket and pulled his Sig from the holster. It lay warm and heavy against his body and he felt its absence like it was a part of him. He always carried with a round in the chamber, because of the profession he was in, but he made sure the safety was on and lay the gun on the console between them. The muzzle pointed toward the dash.

"That's a Sig Sauer P320. It holds seventeen rounds. There's one in the chamber, so I'd appreciate it if you don't point it at me. But take it. Hold it. Put it in your jacket. And if you feel like I'm a threat to you at any point, defend yourself with it."

She put her hand on the weapon. Then she picked it up, dropped the magazine into her hand and racked the slide a few times to release the round in the chamber.

He eyed her, impressed that she was comfortable with a gun—and that she'd managed to pull the slide. It took strength and know how, especially for a smaller person. She tried to push the round back into the magazine, but it was full.

"You insert the mag, rack the slide, and then eject it and add another bullet?" she asked.

"That's right. An extra round might make the difference. You never know."

She did exactly what she'd just described to him. Then she lay the gun on the console again. "Thank you."

"You don't want to keep it?"

"I doubt I'm as good a shot as you. No, I don't want to keep it. And I'm sorry I keep questioning you, but this is all a bit new for me." She dragged in a breath, let it out in a rush. "I said I trust you, and I do. Thanks for quieting that part of me that wants to panic."

He didn't know why, but she got to him. Her words hit him in the chest and didn't let up. He felt responsible for her and responsible *to* her.

"I think panicking is a very normal reaction."

"Is Brett Wheeler really your name, or do you have a fake passport for that one too?"

"It's the name I was born with. I have several fake passports, all with different names and a few different nationalities, but Brett is really me. My mama said she named me for a character in a book."

"Hemingway?"

"Yep."

"His character is a woman."

"I know. Lady Brett Ashley. She loves a man she can never have. I don't know what the hell my mother thought she was saying with that name, but it's the one she gave me. She liked it and thought there wouldn't be six Bretts in the same class with me. Her name was Jennifer, so I guess she had issues with not being unique enough."

Tallie sighed. "Honestly, I wish I'd had a more normal name. There were no other Tallulahs in my class. I wanted to be an Emma or a Hope, like other girls."

"Are you named after anyone?"

"My great-grandmother. And the Tallulah River in Georgia. It's a family thing, apparently."

"It's a nice name."

"I think so now—I did not in sixth grade. Or at any point during high school, really. Everyone called me Tallie by then, but I still got teased when my full name came up. Tallulah Boolah. Moolah Lula. Little Lulu. Looney Lu." She shook her head. "Kids."

"Hey, anyone who survives high school deserves a medal in my opinion."

"No kidding. What's your middle name, Brett Wheeler?"

"Stone." He laughed at her little gasp. "No, it really is. Mama was determined her child was going to be special, I guess. I don't think she was high."

He said that jokingly, but he'd definitely seen his mother high. Many times. She'd sworn she wasn't on drugs when she had him. That she hadn't started yet. He guessed it was the truth since he'd never had any learning disabilities or other issues that typically came with drug-addicted babies.

"Brett Stone Wheeler. Wow, that's quite a mouthful. But no worse than Tallulah Margaret Grant."

He'd known her name because Ian had given him information on her, but he liked hearing her say it. She was comparing names with him, laughing. It was far better than being wary of him.

"I like Tallulah Margaret. Definitely memorable." Which wasn't necessarily a good thing since Paloma Bruni and her minions would be able to track Tallie down back in Virginia if they really wanted to. He didn't know why they'd want to.

But Heinrich von Kassel might. If it was really her eyes and not the fact they'd presented her as underage that interested him. If that was the case, Von Kassel would turn up again like a bad penny—assuming he could get her real identity from Paloma's people.

Brett picked up the Sig and holstered it. He had other weapons, but they were in his duffel. If he needed to get to something quickly, the Sig was his go-to. He probably shouldn't have offered it to her, but he'd needed some sort of gesture that would comfort her. And he'd figured by the time they were ready to stop somewhere, she'd have relaxed enough to give it back.

"Thank you, Brett."

"I mean it. It's a nice name."

She reached out and touched his hand where it rested on the console. It was a light touch, fleeting, but he felt it all the way to his balls. The electricity of it. Did she?

"I appreciate that, but it's not what I was thanking you for."

"Oh yeah? What then?"

"For understanding. For trying your best to make me feel like I have some control. It means a lot to me."

"I don't want you to be scared of me, Tallie. I'm not the bad guy."

"I'm learning to believe it." She yawned, a jaw-cracking yawn that seemed to surprise her. "Holy cow, how can I be tired after all the sleeping I did the past few days?"

"You're still recovering. And we walked a long way in fresh air. Go to sleep. It's going to be a few hours before we reach the checkpoint."

He thought she might question him further, but all

she did was smile. Then she turned toward the window, leaned the seat back, and fell asleep.

WHEN TALLIE WOKE, she thought it was still early and the sun hadn't fully risen. But it wasn't early. It was just very gray. The clouds, fat with snow, hung low and threatened to dump a lot more than the few flakes that currently swirled across the road in front of them.

On either side of the road, mountains rose up and disappeared into the cloud cover. Traffic was steady.

She glanced over at Brett. He was staring straight ahead at the road. The radio was on, classic rock issuing softly from the speakers since he hadn't turned it up very loud.

His profile made her heart squeeze. He was handsome, and she was conflicted about her feelings of attraction. His dark hair was a little long, a little curly. His features were rugged with a day's growth of beard, but still so appealing.

Not like her ex who'd looked scruffy when he didn't shave. Scruffy and like he might be planning to rob a convenience store. Not that Calvin would ever do such a thing. He was a respected attorney looking to make partner.

For a moment, Tallie felt a pang that she hadn't tried harder with Calvin. But the feeling quickly went away, especially as she contemplated the man behind the wheel.

He made her tingle. Without touching her, he made her tingle. That was some feat right there. Even when she let that little voice deep down make her panic because she didn't really know him, he still managed to make her aware of him on a level that she shouldn't allow.

As if she had a say in it.

"Where are we?" she finally asked, shifting in her seat to let him know she was awake.

He shot her a glance. "Still in Italy. South Tyrol. We'll be to the Brenner Pass in another hour."

"That explains the mountains then," she said lightly. "The Dolomites."

"Yes."

"It's pretty. I've never driven this way before. I'm usually in France, though I went to Lake Como once."

"What did you do there?"

"My sister wanted to go after a buying trip to France. We spent four days, eating and shopping and having a great time. It was our last trip together before she died. Car accident," she added, because most people asked.

"I'm sorry."

"Thanks."

Sadness wrapped cold fingers around her heart. Josie had been the outgoing one, the one who'd seemed to know exactly what she wanted out of life.

Tallie was still stumbling along and trying to figure it out.

She gazed at the rolling countryside dusted in snow, the soaring mountains. It was so pretty that she could almost pretend that's why she was here. Just to see it.

"Do you need to stop or can it wait until we get to the pass?" he asked.

"I think I can wait. Do you know where we're going?"

"Not yet. We're changing cars at a rest stop. I'll know more then."

They talked a little more, about the scenery and how far they'd traveled, and then they lapsed into silence again. Tallie stared at the countryside, thinking how beautiful and peaceful it looked.

But inside she was a mess of nerves. Not because of Brett—or not entirely because of him—but because she was thinking about how complicated everything had become, and what that had to mean for her when she got home again.

Why all the subterfuge? Why the caution? And how was she supposed to be safe in her own home after this? Though she hadn't been abducted from her house, she was beginning to worry that she really could be. Someone could break in and throw a hood over her head, bundle her off to God knew where, and the whole nightmare would start again.

It was frightening how vulnerable a person could

be, how thin the layer of civility that protected everyone from chaos and anarchy.

When they pulled into the rest area, it was packed with vehicles. There was a gas station, a store, and a restaurant. Brett found parking and then turned to her.

"Take your bag. We won't be returning to this car."

"Okay."

"Remember, I'm Brett Newport. You're my wife Tiffany Newport. We're on our honeymoon."

"Got it." They'd talked about it earlier and she'd been reminding herself what name she was going by. Tiffany. Had she ever wanted to be a Tiffany? Probably so. It was more normal than Tallulah.

The air was much colder at this altitude, and snow swirled across the parking lot. The accumulation wasn't bad yet, but if it kept up it could be. Thankfully it was only midday, and they would probably get quite a bit farther before dark.

Brett held out his hand for her. Tallie slipped her fingers into his, appreciating the squeeze he gave her. He led her toward the restaurant. They stepped inside and Brett put his arm around her, drawing her close as the hostess came over. Her gaze slipped appreciatively over Brett, then cooled as it studied Tallie.

"*Zwei?*" she asked. When German didn't elicit a response, she switched to Italian. "*Due?*"

Tallie understood that she was saying the number

two in both languages, but she didn't respond. She wasn't supposed to.

"Um, do you speak English?" Brett asked. His Southern drawl was gone, replaced by what she thought of as a Midwestern accent.

"But of course," the woman said. "Two?"

"Yes, please. Could we sit near the window? My wife has never been to Europe before."

The hostess smiled. "Certainly, sir." She led the way to a table with a lovely view of the mountain rising into the sky above them. "What would you like to drink?" she asked once they were seated. Brett made Tallie scoot over in the booth and sat beside her. Like newlyweds who couldn't keep their hands off each other.

She felt herself blushing as she lifted her face to the hostess. "Water, please."

"Still or sparkling?"

"Sparkling is fine."

"I'll have water," Brett said. "No bubbles."

The hostess walked away, her blonde ponytail swinging. Brett put his arm around Tallie and bent to speak into her ear. His breath tickled, sending a shiver of awareness snaking down her spine.

"So far, so good. Be sure to eat well. It might be awhile before we stop again—other than necessary breaks."

"I'm planning to order the biggest steak they've got." Tallie opened her menu and studied it. It was in German, Italian, and English. Her stomach rumbled at the description of pork schnitzel in a cream sauce with mushrooms. "Strike that. The biggest schnitzel. I hope it's the size of my head."

Brett laughed. He didn't take his arm from around her shoulders as he flipped open his menu on the table and glanced over it. "They have rumpsteak. You sure you don't want that?"

"Positive. Who can resist breaded pork with cream sauce?"

"Not you, I'm guessing."

"Exactly."

The hostess, who was now their waitress, returned with drinks. Then she took their order and disappeared again. Tallie watched for trouble—not that she'd know what trouble looked like unless it was painfully obvious—but none came.

It wasn't until they were finished with the meal and waiting for dessert to arrive that a woman slid into the seat across from them. Tallie assumed it was the person giving them the keys to their next car—until she felt Brett stiffen. He reached inside his jacket, but the woman shook her head.

"Not a good idea. Not a good idea at all."

It took Tallie a long moment to realize that one of the woman's hands was under the table. The other reached for Tallie's hot chocolate. Her sleeve slipped up, revealing a colorful tattoo. Something with scales, maybe.

"Natasha," Brett growled. "What do you want?"

Chapter Ten

Natasha Orlova, aka Calypso, sat across the table and contemplated them both with deep blue eyes. Contacts, probably. Her hair was black, not the blond of the last time Brett had seen her. That was months ago, inside BDI's headquarters. She'd shot Colt and Jace that night, though she hadn't killed them.

He didn't have to look under the table to know she held a pistol pointed at his balls. She picked up Tallie's chocolate and took a delicate sip.

"Perhaps I've come to collect something," she said. "Perhaps I am on a job."

Her gaze slid over Tallie, and Brett forced himself to take a deep, steadying breath. Had Heinrich von Kassel hired her to find Tallie for him? And how the fuck was Brett going to stop her if so? Calypso was legendary—and utterly cold-blooded. She'd shot her own brother. She'd been planning to hand him over to some unnamed person for a reward. She'd have done it if the Bandits hadn't arrived to stop her.

Of all the things Ian had ever done, letting Calypso walk free was the one Brett disagreed with most.

Beside him, Tallie shifted. She moved a little bit closer to him, instinctively realizing that Calypso was trouble.

"I won't make it easy for you," he told her. The waitress returned with their dessert, her eyebrows going up at the sight of a third person at their table.

"Can I get you something?" she asked Natasha.

"Yes, please. I am afraid I stole this lovely lady's hot chocolate. Perhaps another for her?"

"Of course."

The waitress walked away and Brett waited, thinking how he could turn this situation to his advantage. But Natasha put her other hand on the table then and he realized she wasn't pointing a weapon at him. Not that she hadn't placed it on the seat beside her and wouldn't reach for it if he went for his.

"You are thinking there are too many people in here for a showdown," she said. "And you are correct. I am not unarmed, but I'm also not pointing it at you. I never was."

"What do you want?" he asked her tightly, relief unfurling inside him.

Her gaze went to Tallie again. "Is he always this rude?"

Tallie shrugged. "I don't know. I think you probably bring out the worst in him."

Natasha smiled. There was a tiny gap in her front teeth. "I bring out the worst in a lot of people." She held out her hand and Tallie took it before Brett could stop her. "I'm Natasha."

"Ta—Tiffany," Tallie said.

Natasha's eyes sparkled. "Yes, of course. As for what I want," she said, dropping Tallie's hand and gazing at him again. "I want what I was promised. Tell him for me."

He knew she meant Ian. He also knew she meant she wanted revenge. But was she really trustworthy? Or was this a ruse? What did she actually want?

"How can he find you?"

She shrugged. "He cannot. I'll find him. Tell him."

"I'll tell him. But why come to me? And how did you know where to find me?"

"I know many things. You will want to be careful on your journey, Mr. Newport. People are looking for you. There is a bounty, and many who want it."

"And you don't?"

"Oh, I do. But I want what Ian promised me even more. Consider this a gift. I won't offer you another."

"Where did you learn that name?"

"Newport?" She shrugged. "I have my sources. I would change to another name soon if I were you."

Brett clenched his teeth. *Fuck.*

She slid from the booth and stood above them.

She was a frightening woman, a killer, but she seemed sad somehow.

"Any message for Jace?"

If anything, she looked sadder. But then her features hardened. "None at all."

She strode away and Brett swore. Any other time and he'd follow her, see where she went. But he couldn't leave Tallie alone.

"Who was that?" Tallie asked, looking in the direction Natasha had gone.

"Best if you forget you ever met her," Brett said, pulling his phone from his pocket and typing out a text message to Ian.

Tallie shook her head. "I doubt that's possible. She said there was a bounty for you. What did she mean?"

"It's nothing new. Don't worry about it." He didn't intend to tell her what Natasha really meant. The bounty was for her, not him.

"Easy for you to say. Everything worries me right now."

He put his hand over hers and squeezed it. "I know. This isn't the kind of life you're accustomed to. But until I'm worried about something, there's nothing to fear."

"You were worried about her. For a little while."

He nodded. "She's dangerous. The last time I saw her, she shot two of my friends."

Her mouth fell open. "Oh my God."

"It's okay. They're fine. And she's gone. She wants

me to pass a message. If she'd wanted to hurt me, she'd have done it."

The waitress returned with a fresh hot chocolate. She set it on the table. "The man sitting over there has paid for your meal. He says you are a charming couple and clearly in love."

Brett turned to look where she indicated. He didn't recognize the man, but the message was correct. "Please ask him to join us. We'd love to buy him a coffee, wouldn't we, honey?"

"Yes, of course," Tallie said automatically, though she managed to look worried instead of happy.

Brett put a hand on her knee. She jumped, but settled quickly. "Hey," he said softly as the waitress went over to the man.

Tallie looked up at him, her expression filled with doubt. The urge to kiss her was strong. He'd planned to resist, but they were supposed to be married so why the hell not?

He dipped his head and swept his tongue into her mouth, tasting chocolate. She sighed, and his dick lifted its sleepy head. Reluctantly, he pulled away, but not before he brushed his fingers against her soft cheek.

"That guy is my contact," he whispered. "He has our instructions for the next leg of the journey."

"Are you sure he's not planning to threaten you too?"

Brett smiled. "Yeah, I'm sure. Smile, Tiff. We

need to look happy. We'll be out of here in twenty minutes."

IT WAS GROWING dark by the time they pulled up to a chalet-style house somewhere in Bavaria. The house was beautiful. The bottom half was white, with wooden shutters on all the windows, while the top half was dark timber. There were shutters on the windows, and a wooden balcony running across the front. The roof was peaked, and ornate wood carvings that resembled fancy icicles hung from the roof at regular intervals.

The house perched on the side of a mountain above a village. Tallie stepped out onto the snowy drive and gazed at the warm yellow lights below.

Jagged mountain peaks surrounded them, though it was so close to dark that she couldn't really make out the extent of the mountains.

Tallie shivered. The jacket she wore wasn't quite up to the higher altitudes and colder temperatures of Bavaria. Brett stood on the driver's side of the car, staring up at the house. He turned in time to see her shiver.

"Shit, let's get inside," he told her. "I'll come back for the bags."

She shut her door and followed him over to the wooden entry. He inserted the key. It'd been inside an envelope in the car when they'd picked it up in the

Brenner Pass. The lock snicked softly and the door swung inward.

He held out a hand to stop her from crossing the threshold, reaching inside his jacket to draw his weapon. "Stay behind me."

She followed him inside. It didn't take him long to make sure no one was waiting for them. Tallie was still standing by the door when he returned and shoved his weapon into the holster.

"It's safe. Why don't you check and see what they've left us to eat."

He went outside to retrieve their bags and Tallie walked into the kitchen. There was a large picture window overlooking the snowy landscape, and she was momentarily caught by it. What would it look like in the morning when she could really see the view?

Tallie opened the refrigerator and found it stuffed with food. There was also a microwave, a big stove, and a cabinet with pans and dishes. An envelope was propped against a bottle of wine.

PLEASE ENJOY, dear guests.

BRETT CAME INTO THE KITCHEN. She held out the envelope. He walked over and took it from her fingers.

"I'll start a fire in a few minutes," he said. "There's plenty of wood and I've turned up the radiators on the lower floor."

Tallie was still wearing her jacket. It was cold inside the house, but not freezing. "There's a stocked refrigerator and pantry. We could have soup and sandwiches. I'm not sure what else yet."

"We'll figure it out." He opened the envelope and removed the folded sheet of paper. His eyes darted across it before he raised them to her. "There's a winter wardrobe in the closet upstairs. Second bedroom on the left. You should find some things to keep you warm, along with appropriate footwear."

"Oh goody. I thought I'd have to spend all my time sitting near the fireplace while we're here." Tallie frowned. "Do you know how long it's going to be yet? Did they tell you in that letter?"

"No. We just have to sit tight until I get further instructions."

Tallie blew out a frustrated sigh. "I want to talk to my mother. Hell, I want my phone back so I can answer my emails and text my friends."

He dropped the letter and put his hands on her shoulders. "I know, Tallie. I get it. But until we know it's safe for you, you can't be in contact with anyone. That's just the way it is. Think of it like witness protection, if that helps. You've seen enough TV shows or movies where the witness has to leave their old life behind and start a new one? That's you right now, except it's not permanent. You get to go back, but not until we're sure you're going to be safe. Surely you can put up with the restrictions until then."

He made her feel like a cranky teenager. Worse,

he made her feel ungrateful. Tallie closed her eyes and dropped her chin. "Yes, of course."

He rubbed her arms lightly. "You must be really close to your mother."

Tallie snorted before she could stop herself. Brett's hands stilled for a second.

"Sorry," she said. "We aren't close, but we love each other. And we're all we have left now that Daddy and Josie are gone." That wasn't strictly true, she supposed. "She has a boyfriend, but it's not serious—or at least not for her. They've been seeing each other on and off for the past three years. I doubt she'll ever remarry, though Bill would certainly like her to."

Brett didn't miss a beat. "Would you?"

"Actually, yes, I would like her to marry Bill. Josie wanted it too. He's a good guy. He might even get Mom to take some time for herself and stop throwing everything she has into the business."

"Give you a chance to run it?"

Tallie arched an eyebrow. "Oh, I don't think I'll ever run Mary Claire Grant Interiors. I'm not good enough—but that's okay. Mom *is* the business. And her reputation is stellar. If she spends a month or three in France every year with her new husband, she'd probably get more business, not less."

He didn't comment on her self-criticism. Perhaps because he didn't know what to say. Or maybe it sounded whiny and he wasn't interested. Tallie had an urge to apologize, but she didn't.

"She sounds formidable," Brett said.

"She is."

He dropped his hands from her shoulders and stepped away. She tried not to feel disappointed. She liked when he touched her. Liked the warmth and the electric sizzle that buzzed beneath her skin when he did. He made life feel normal in those few moments. She craved that right now.

"Why don't you go upstairs and make sure those radiators are on high enough? You can change into something warmer if you want. I'll start a fire, and then we'll figure out what to do about dinner."

He started piling wood into the fireplace, his back to her. Tallie watched him, her stomach twisting into knots. She wanted to ask him to hold her, to make the demons disappear, at least for a little while.

But she didn't. She couldn't see any way to do that and make it sound like it wasn't a proposition.

BRETT WAITED until Tallie was upstairs and then he took out his phone and dialed. Ian answered on the first ring.

"Sonny boy, how's the snow?" Ian sounded jovial. Probably a good thing for everyone because it meant there was nothing seriously wrong in the Bandit world at the moment. And a good thing for him because Ian wasn't ready to kill him.

"White. Snowy."

"How'd your Texas ass get up to that chalet anyway?"

"Very carefully," Brett said. He might be from Texas originally, but he'd learned to drive in snow years ago. First time he'd found himself plopped down in the middle of Siberia with an ancient Lada and needed to get the hell out of there, he'd figured it out. His mission partner—who'd been from Alaska—had ended up dead. Brett hadn't wanted to end up the same. "Did you pick Bavaria on purpose because you thought it'd be funny to send me into a blizzard?"

Ian snorted. "It's not a blizzard up there. It's snow. And it's mid November, so what do you expect? Sunshine and balmy breezes?"

"If you'd sent us to Greece, sure. Why couldn't it be Greece?"

"Not this time. Sorry." Ian paused. "Calypso found you, huh?"

"She did. Scared the ever-loving fuck out of me too. How the hell did she manage it? It's the fucking Brenner Pass on a random damned day."

Ian sighed. "No idea. She's a law of her own, I think. She doesn't share everything she knows with those who hire her. But I tell you what, I'd sure like to find out how she knew where you'd be."

He would too. It was almost psychic. Except he didn't believe in that shit, so it couldn't be that. Which meant the next most obvious thing was someone at BDI. Someone with loose lips. But that didn't seem possible either considering how rigorous Ian's vetting procedures were.

"You think there's a weak link in the chain?"

Ian didn't miss his meaning. "Anything's possible. If there is, I'll find it. And obliterate it."

Ian Black wouldn't put up with a traitor in his midst. Of that Brett was certain. "Do you think Von Kassel hired her?"

"No, I don't. I think if he couldn't afford to drop a million on Tallie Grant, he couldn't hire someone of Calypso's caliber to steal her away. That's somebody else's doing. The Syndicate, probably. They have spies everywhere."

"I'm guessing Carter Walker's cover is blown by now."

"We should probably assume so."

Brett closed his eyes. All that work. "Fuck. Sorry, boss."

"Yeah, I know. I'd have probably done the same thing in your shoes. Doesn't matter anyway because this is our new reality. We'll move forward and deal with it."

Brett didn't know how Ian managed to be so stoic sometimes. But he did. He was the chillest dude Brett knew.

"What are we going to do about Brett Newport?"

"Mr. Newport's dealings in military equipment aren't a secret, so she could have picked the name up somewhere and then taken a wild guess. Still, it wouldn't do to have anyone finding him and his new wife in Bavaria. I'll have new documents to you in two days. The house is safe enough for now since we didn't use that name to secure it. "

"Roger that, boss."

"How did she seem to you?" Ian asked.

Brett knew he wasn't talking about Tallie. He thought about Natasha's eyes. The sadness in them. The suppressed fury.

"Angry. Sad. But restrained. She had the advantage on me and she knew about the bounty. She could have taken me out and collected it. But she didn't. She wanted me to pass a message to you, which I've done."

"Yeah." Ian sounded as if he wasn't entirely happy about the message. Or maybe it was the way she'd sent it.

Brett knew what Ian had promised her. He only hoped Ian could deliver—because if he didn't, Calypso was coming for him. She'd pick him off like a fly on the wall. Though maybe Brett was giving her too much credit. Ian would be ready, and the battle would be epic if it happened.

"She said she'd find you. How do you think that's going to happen?" Brett asked.

Ian snorted then, and Brett thought maybe he'd had it wrong about the boss being unhappy or contemplative. "It's not only a message, it's an instruction. For her to find me, I've got to head out into the field again. Think I'm ready for action anyway. I'm tired of sitting at a desk and pulling strings. It's been too long."

Brett had done some dirty jobs in some serious hellholes with Ian Black. They all had. Ian was the kind of boss who got down into the trenches with you. And considering his talent with languages—he could speak over a dozen that Brett knew of—he was extremely useful during field operations.

But within the past few months, he'd gotten the opportunity to establish a headquarters with all the latest and greatest equipment—some of it even better than the military had—and he'd needed to be in Washington to do it.

"There are a million and one places you could go. How will she figure it out?"

Ian's voice was filled with laughter. "She found you in the Brenner Pass on a random day in November. I think she'll find me."

Yeah, she probably would.

He heard Tallie moving around upstairs. "Gotta go and start a fire, boss. It's cold here and my companion has about zero body fat to keep her warm. Any further instructions?"

"Nothing yet. Hold tight while I wait for intel on the situation and get your new documents."

"Roger."

"And Brett?"

"Yeah?"

"Be careful."

"Always am, boss."

The laughter was back in Ian's voice. "I'm not talking about the mission, kid. Last operator to hole up with a woman ended up domesticated."

He was talking about Jace Kaiser and Maddy Cole. Brett thought of kissing Tallie Grant, her sweet response to him when his mouth had settled over hers. How he'd wanted so much more.

But that was merely physical. He could handle physical.

"Not a danger, boss. Trust me."

Ian laughed again. "Heard that before."

"Yeah, but I mean it."

Brett could still hear Ian's laughter echoing in his ears long after the call ended.

Chapter Eleven

Tallie found a thick sweater and leggings, among other things, in the closet. There was a ski jacket, snow boots, and more leggings and shirts of varying thickness. There was enough stuff in the closet to last her for two weeks, which was both a little depressing and a little thrilling.

Thrilling because she'd be staying with Brett.

"Not a good enough reason," she mumbled to herself as she changed into the warmer clothing. The room she'd been given was small, but cozy. The walls were half-timbered, white, and there wasn't much in the way of decor other than the wooden beams. An old oil painting of a mountain and a chalet similar to this one. Maybe it *was* this one, she decided.

The bed was small, with a wood headboard and footboard, both painted with colorful Bavarian scenes. The duvet was thick and fluffy and solid white, and there was a chest of drawers beneath the dormer window with a ceramic bowl and pitcher.

The radiator creaked as steam filled it. Tallie touched it, satisfied it was working, and then headed downstairs. Brett had a fire going, though it wasn't roaring yet. He wasn't in the living room, though. The snap of a cabinet door told her he was in the kitchen.

He looked up as she walked in, his eyes dropping over her. "Warm enough now?"

"Getting there. What's for dinner?"

"I just started looking. You said something about soup and sandwiches."

Tallie went over to the pantry. "There's canned soup in here, and bread. I saw some cheese in the fridge, so we could have grilled cheese."

"Sounds good."

She handed him the bread. "What kind of soup do you want?"

He peered over her shoulder to look into the pantry. He had to move closer to see, and she could feel his presence behind her, prickling the fine hairs on her neck. She breathed him in, smelling wood and smoke.

"The goulash looks good," he said, his voice a rumble in her ear.

So close. If she turned, she could slip her arms around him and lay her head on his chest.

Not that she had any intention of doing so.

"Looks good to me too." She grabbed the can and Brett stepped away as she turned around. She went looking for a pan while he rummaged in the refrigerator for the cheese and butter.

Twenty minutes later, they were seated on the floor in front of the fire, eating grilled cheese sandwiches and soup from big mugs that they'd placed on the small coffee table. The rug they sat on was thick, and the fire warm. Tallie felt like she was finally thawing out.

It was getting colder back home, but it was nothing like the Alps. Williamsburg could get very cold, and they even had snow some years. But not typically this early in the season. It was nearly three weeks until Thanksgiving, and temperatures back home were brisk but not unbearable.

Thoughts of Thanksgiving made her anxious as she considered how this one was going to be different. And not just because she might not make it home in time. Last year, Josie had still been alive. The accident happened a week after Thanksgiving when she'd been driving home from a client's house late one night and got hit by a distracted driver. A woman texting a friend when she should have been watching the road.

"Hey," Brett said, and Tallie's gaze snapped to his.

"Yes?"

"You look upset."

Tallie took a sip of the wine he'd poured for her. "I was thinking about my sister." She cleared her throat because it sounded scratchy. "The anniversary of her death is coming. A week after Thanksgiving."

"Aw, hell. I'm sorry."

"Thanks. This is the first Thanksgiving without her. I was hoping to be home for it—though I imagine it's going to be hell anyway. If Mother had a favorite daughter, Josie was it." Tallie slapped her hand over her mouth. "Oh my God. I can't believe I said that. Josie is dead, and it's not about me at all."

Brett sat with one knee bent and his arm draped over it, wine glass in hand. He didn't look horrified by her outburst.

"It is about you. Because it's your experience, not anyone else's. You're allowed to feel what you feel. It's not a betrayal to her memory, you know."

Tears pricked her eyes. "Are you sure about that? Because it feels very selfish to resent all the ways in which she was better than I was. It wasn't her fault."

"You're human. We resent people who seem to be able to do the things we want to do so much easier than we can."

"I didn't resent Josie," she said, swiping beneath her eyes. Feeling like a jerk. "I really didn't. I just resented that Mom always seemed to approve of everything she did while nitpicking what I did. And she really was that good when it came to design in particular. But I just wanted Mom to approve of something I did, just once, the same way she did with Josie."

"What about your dad? What did he think?"

Tallie couldn't help but smile. "Oh, Daddy pretty much showered us with equal attention and love. He praised the ugliest craft projects we made when we were kids as if they were Van Goghs. Josie's were better, but Daddy didn't say that. Probably because Mom often did."

She took another drink of wine. "You know, I don't think for one minute that she was purposely making me feel badly. I think she always thought that I couldn't improve if she didn't tell me the truth. In her mind, she was making me try harder. But I just don't have that natural talent like she does. Or like Josie did."

Brett was eyeing her speculatively. "You know what they say about hard work and talent, don't you?"

She shook her head.

"Hard work will beat talent if talent doesn't work hard. All you need is drive, Tallie. You can do anything with enough drive."

"Truthfully, I'm not sure the drive is there. Not when it comes to working with my mother."

"Do you like interior design?"

She thought of the rooms in her home, how much she loved what she'd done to them. "I really do. I like helping clients see how their homes can be better. I especially like helping people on smaller budgets. It's a challenge, and I like a challenge so much more than a blank checkbook."

"Then do that. Why not?"

Tallie thought about it. The wine was going to her head, fuzzing her thoughts. Making her say things she wouldn't let escape if she were paying more attention. But what did it matter? Brett Wheeler wasn't going to be in her life for much longer—a thought that made her kinda sad.

"Tallie?" he prompted when she didn't say anything.

She pulled her thoughts together from where they'd strayed. "That's not the way Mom likes to work, and we don't have enough of those sorts of clients anyway."

He tilted his head as he studied her. "You ever think about going out on your own? Opening your own design studio where you could do the interiors you want to do?"

She had thought of it. The idea always made little happy bubbles burst inside her like champagne bubbles. But then she came back down to earth.

"I can't. My mother needs me. When Josie was alive, it might have been possible. But now? No, the workload is too much, and there's nobody else. I mean there are other designers in the firm, but I'm her daughter. She counts on me."

"You have to do what you have to do. But you're the one who said you weren't fulfilled working with your mother. I'm just asking the questions."

"I know." She twirled the wine glass in her hand, studying the play of firelight against the liquid. "I ask myself the same questions every few months. But since Josie died… I guess I decided to stay put and help my mother for the time being. Another year or two at least."

"Just be sure you do something you want to do every once in a while. Something you don't have to explain or apologize for."

"Okay, Dr. Brett. Whatever you say."

He laughed. "Fine, I deserved that. But doing what I do—well, I've learned that nothing is guaranteed. We only have right now."

Tallie stiffened. "I know that. I really do. One minute my sister was alive and the next she wasn't. But that doesn't mean I can throw away my responsibilities and break my promises."

"I've upset you. I apologize."

She pulled in a deep breath and set the wine glass on the table. "No, look, I'm sorry. You didn't sign on to be my therapist. You've got your hands full just trying to keep us safe. I shouldn't be telling you this stuff anyway."

He reached for her hand. She let him wrap his fingers around hers. She liked the feel of their skin touching. It was comforting. And exciting. Those champagne bubbles were popping in her veins again, and all because he held her hand.

"We're just talking, babe. Sitting by a fire, drinking wine, and talking. You don't have to apologize for answering my questions, or disagreeing with anything I've said."

She gazed into his green eyes. They were darker

around the outside, lighter in the middle. Pretty eyes. Knowing eyes.

Eyes that had seen too much.

Her heart squeezed.

He'd said to do something she wanted to do. Something just for her. Before she could stop herself—before her brain could catch up to her reflexes—she leaned forward and kissed him.

COLT CLIMBED onboard the flight in Rome and sank down into his first class seat, ready to sleep for a few hours and maybe watch a couple of movies.

It'd been a long trip, first the drive from Venice and then the meeting with the informant Ian had sent him to see. He'd thought he'd be returning to Venice, but Brett and Tallie were no longer there and Ian told him to head back to HQ.

Colt yawned and scratched the stubble on his chin as the flight attendant took drink orders. He downed a vodka and then catnapped until the plane was airborne and the flight attendant came around again.

He ordered another vodka, then logged onto the inflight wifi in case Ian or Brett or one of the other guys needed to be in touch. Then he kicked back and fell asleep.

His phone woke him sometime later, the buzzing indicating he had a message. He rubbed his hand across his eyes and lifted the phone to check.

And then he shook his head in case he was imagining things. Angelica Turner—Angie of the red hair and soft fingers that had stroked his cheek when he'd been in the hospital recovering from a gunshot wound —was texting him.

She hadn't spoken directly to him in months. He didn't know why, but she'd stopped talking to him once it was clear he wasn't going to die from the wound Calypso had given him. Until then, she'd sat with him, sniffling when she thought he was asleep.

Colt thought of how he'd gone with his buddies to see Tom Walls, the man who'd assaulted Angie on her job, and his gut twisted. They hadn't threatened that asshole nearly enough for his liking.

He turned his attention back to the texts, wondering what she might want after all these months when she'd barely been civil to him.

Angie: *Hi. How are you?*

Colt thought about ignoring the text, but he wasn't capable of it. *Fine. You sure you're texting the right person?*

Angie: *Um, this is Colt, right?*

Right.

Angie: *Then yes, I'm sure. Is it okay?*

He gazed at the back of the seat in front of him. Beside him, a woman watched a romantic comedy on the entertainment system.

Yes, of course. Is everything okay with you?

He watched the three little dots for a long time.

Angie: *Fine. I just… I need to apologize to you.*

Apologize? For what?

The three dots kept appearing and disappearing. Was she erasing the words and starting over? Probably. Finally, an answer popped up on the screen.

Angie: *It's my fault she shot you.*

Colt frowned. *How is it your fault? I was doing a job and it went wrong. It happens.*

Angie: *It happens? You mean you just accept the idea you could be shot and get on with your day like it's a normal occurrence?*

Colt: *Well, yeah. It's not your fault I got shot, Angie. That woman is a dangerous criminal and she took advantage of you to get what she wanted.*

He didn't say the word Calypso, or the name Natasha Orlova. Angie Turner didn't need to know those things. It was safer if she didn't. Bad enough that Maddy knew, but then again she was with Jace now so she kinda had to.

He also didn't say them because he was on a plane's wifi and that was hardly secure.

Angie: *I nearly got my best friend killed. And the man she loves. And you. I was useless during that whole thing. Maddy was strong, but all I did was cry.*

Colt sighed as he pushed a hand over his head. *You did what anyone would do who wasn't used to that stuff. There's nothing to apologize for.*

Was this why she'd avoided him for so long? Because she felt guilty?

Angie: *You're just trying to make me feel better.*

Colt: *Maybe so, but I also mean it. You aren't a cop or a* *soldier. It wasn't your job to do anything that day except try to stay alive.*

Angie: *I appreciate you saying that. I don't know why I'm even bothering you…*

Colt: *You aren't bothering me. I'm on a plane and I'm bored. Your message is the most exciting thing to happen since this tub left the ground.*

She sent a laughing emoji. *Well, that's kind of good, right? You don't really want excitement in the air.*

Colt: *No, not especially.*

Angie: *Where are you going? Anywhere fun?*

Colt: *Returning from a work assignment. On the way home now, but I've been in Italy.*

Not the only place he'd been, but he wasn't going to tell her everything.

Angie: *I love Italy! What part?*

Rome, he told her, leaving Venice out of the picture.

Angie: *Ah, the food. The ruins. So beautiful.*

Colt: *Sure is.*

He was thinking that she was too, but that was another thing he wasn't going to tell her. Not yet anyway. He'd thought she didn't like him, but maybe it wasn't that at all. Maybe she just felt guilty.

And then there was Tom Walls. Colt still didn't know if she was telling the truth about what that bastard had really done to her. She'd insisted he hadn't raped her, but what if he had? That would be enough to make her afraid of any man, wouldn't it?

Angie: *Well, I won't keep you. I just wanted to say I was* *sorry about that night. I've felt awful for a long time, and I finally got the nerve to say something about it. I should have done it a long time ago.*

Colt: *You should have so I could have told you it wasn't your fault. All this time you've been blaming yourself. It's not right.*

Angie: *You're sweet, Colt.*

Just what he wanted to be. Sweet. He drew in a breath and let it out again slowly. Enforcing calm. *So are you,* he typed.

Sweet enough to eat, he thought.

Angie: *Thank you. I'm sure I'll see you around at Maddy and Jace's sometime.*

Colt: *I'm sure you will. How about you don't avoid me when you do? I won't bite.*

Angie: *Okay, I won't avoid you. Promise. I've got a client coming in, so I have to go now. It was good to 'talk' to you.*

Colt: *You too.*

Colt put the phone down and thought back to the last time he'd seen Angelica Turner. He'd been at a restaurant with Jace and Maddy when she'd walked in wearing a blue wrap dress that hugged her curves and made heads turn. He'd had an insane urge to get up and go to her, claim her in front of all those watching eyes.

But of course he hadn't. She wasn't his. Never would be, even though she was finally talking to him again. Angie wasn't cut out for this life. And he'd never want her put into a situation where she had to be afraid like the night Calypso had taken her.

Nope, Angie, as beautiful as she was, had to stay in her safe little world. And far away from his.

Chapter Twelve

Tallie's heart pounded as she leaned into Brett and pressed her mouth against his. Part of her brain demanded to know what the hell she was doing. The other part told her this was a fabulous idea and keep on going. That was the part currently enjoying the fireworks exploding inside her and wanting more of the same.

Brett's mouth opened beneath hers and their tongues met. A rush of warmth flooded her at that simple action. He tasted like the wine they'd been drinking.

Wine.

That's why she was doing this. Why she felt brave enough.

The knowledge wasn't enough to stop her, though.

She leaned in a little more, brought her hands up to his face. His jaw was still stubbly. She liked the feel of it beneath her fingertips, the rough scrape against her chin. What would it feel like scraping against the soft skin of her thighs?

Tallie moaned a little at the thought. It'd been so long. So damned long since she'd had anything but her own fingers between her legs.

Sharon told her to buy a vibrator, but she hadn't done it. Probably should have but she couldn't envision going into one of those stores. Or, worse, ordering online and then getting lots of naughty catalogs to her house.

Brett's fingers threaded into her hair, cupped the back of her head as he tilted her toward him. Every touch of his body against hers made butterflies swirl inside. She just wanted *more.*

Another moment and he dragged her across his lap, laying her back in his arms, his mouth doing things that made liquid fire spill through her limbs, turning them languid and pliant. She could hardly lift her arms to put them around his neck. Hardly hold her head up. It was like being drugged, but not with actual drugs. She knew what that felt like too, unfortunately.

Brett's big palm skimmed her hip, up her side, beneath her breast while his other arm braced her body, his fingers skimming her cheek, her ear.

Every touch was like fire. Every touch made her lose a little bit more of her inhibition. She could feel him beneath her. Growing hard, his erection pressing into her bottom. Making her want.

She reached for the hem of his henley and started

to tug it upward. And then her hands were on smooth, hot skin, and her heart hammered like mad and her body felt like molten fire. She needed more.

Brett groaned, his throat vibrating with it as she slipped her fingers into his fly. She wanted to touch him. Wanted to see if he was as hard as he felt.

She was almost there when he broke the kiss with another groan and sat back.

Tallie found herself lying in his arms, looking up at him as if someone had just woken her from a dream.

"Tallie." He swallowed. "You have no idea how badly I want to go there with you. But I can't."

She blinked at him, fresh embarrassment beginning to drip into her veins. Carefully, she disentangled herself. Crawled off his lap and reached for her wine glass because she needed something to do.

"I'm sorry," she said stiffly. "I'm afraid I'm not thinking straight right now."

He blew out a breath. Grabbed his own glass and drained it. "That's what I was afraid of."

She dared to look at him. A lock of dark hair fell over his forehead. She wanted to reach up and brush it back, but she didn't. They stared at each other for a long moment.

"You said to do something for myself," she offered, as if explaining.

He grinned suddenly and she felt a kind of relief that he wasn't mad. "I did, didn't I? And you should.

Definitely. But how about getting a full night's sleep and maybe not drinking any wine first?"

"You think I kissed you because of the wine?"

"Didn't you?"

She nibbled her lip. "It helped, I admit. But I wouldn't have done it if I weren't attracted to you. No wine is that magical."

"Good to know. But Tallie?"

"Yes?"

"I didn't tell you to do something for yourself in order to make you sleep with me."

She felt herself coloring. "I know that. It just seemed like the thing to do in the moment."

He nodded. "It's okay. If it still seems like the thing to do tomorrow, let me know. But you need to realize that if what you want is sex, I'll give you all you can handle. But that's all I'll give you. So be sure, Tallie. Be very sure. We're only pretending to be a married couple. This isn't the beginning of a relationship."

Tallie pushed to her feet as embarrassment made her too damned hot to sit by the fire anymore. She glared down at him with all the haughtiness she'd ever learned at the feet of her mother. Her heart throbbed and her eyes stung and she wanted to lash out at someone.

Him.

"Who said anything about a relationship? You look like you'd be a good time. That's all."

His gaze burned into her. "Yeah, that's me. A good time."

They stared at each other. She didn't know why she suddenly felt as if she'd said something wrong. He was the one who'd told her not to get confused and think he wanted a relationship. So why did he seem as if she'd just slapped him?

"I'm going to go up now. Thank you for getting us here safely, and for building a fire. And making grilled cheese. I'm going to owe you big time when this is over."

"You don't owe me," he said, his gaze still hot.

Tallie was out of her element here. The undercurrents were fierce. She didn't know what to say. So she said whatever popped in her head, no matter how idiotic.

"If you ever want your house decorated or something—well, I'd be happy to do it."

Her face was on fire. *Stupid thing to say.* Decorating? For him? An international man of mystery who carried a big Sig and went undercover in criminal organizations? He probably cared about interior design as much as he cared about, oh, celebrity gossip. Which meant not much at all.

"I'll remember that," he said coolly.

"Great. Well, okay. Good night."

"Good night, Tallie."

She turned on her heel and practically ran for the stairs.

BRETT CLEARED up the dishes and then opened the door and walked outside. Without his jacket.

He needed to cool the fire in his blood before he went back inside, and standing in the cold was a good way to do it.

The house he'd brought them to was perched above a village that glowed with golden lights below. There were other houses nearby, and he could hear the barking of a dog as well as the tinkling of a cowbell somewhere in the distance. It was peaceful. Beautiful.

The snow wasn't thick this early in the season, though it would certainly be thicker on the slopes of the mountains above. There would be skiers up there tomorrow. He wished he had time to hit the slopes himself, but it wasn't likely.

He wasn't a great skier, but he'd learned well enough and he was qualified for mountain ops if necessary. He liked to stay in practice whenever he could.

His breath frosted in the air above him. He turned to look at the house. Warm light spilled from the downstairs windows. Tallie's room was at the back of the house, so no light showed from upstairs.

Whoever had readied the house had chosen the room for her when they'd placed the clothes in the closet, but it was the correct room. Small, with one dormer for access, and at the rear of the house. Of course it had been a BDI operative who'd done it. Ian left nothing to chance.

Brett blew out a breath and shoved his hands into his pants pockets. Tallie was up there now, getting ready for bed. Removing her sweater and bra, perhaps putting on a T-shirt to sleep in. Her breasts would be free beneath the shirt, her nipples rubbing the fabric.

He could have had his hands on her breasts. His tongue. Hell, he could be balls deep inside her right this minute if he hadn't gotten all noble about her decision-making ability.

Brett shook his head and stifled a groan. She'd tasted so sweet. He'd wanted more. But it had only been a few days since her ordeal, and she'd been drinking. What if she woke up in the morning and regretted it?

He'd had the impression she was doing something to prove to herself she could, not because she really wanted to do it. That wasn't a reason, in his book. He refused to take advantage of a weak moment, no matter how much his body responded to her.

What the hell had he been thinking to tell her if she wanted sex tomorrow, he'd give her all the sex she could handle? He didn't typically sleep with the women he was protecting. It was a bad idea for many reasons, not the least of which was that sex clouded judgement. He didn't need his judgement clouded. He needed a clear head and he needed to focus on the assignment.

Heinrich von Kassel was still out there. Paloma Bruni and her kind were still out there. Tallie Grant might be in the clear, but she might not be. They simply didn't know yet.

He thought of what she'd said to him about looking like a good time. He'd let that get to him more than he should. She'd been lashing out, he knew that—but it was an uncomfortable echo of something Julia had said to him when he'd told her he was filing for divorce. He'd asked her why the fuck she'd chosen him in the first place since she obviously didn't care for anyone but herself. She'd shrugged and said that she'd thought he was the kind of guy who could show a girl a good time in bed.

His entire fucked up marriage summed up in one blithe phrase. And now Tallie had said it to him tonight, and he'd been more pissed than he should have been.

After one last look at the village, Brett walked back inside and locked the door behind him. Then he banked the fire and threw himself onto the couch, grabbing the remote and turning on the television. He spoke tolerable German, but he surfed around until he found an international news station in English and settled back to watch what was happening in the world.

Occasionally, he heard Tallie moving around upstairs, but he didn't think she was really all that tired anyway. She'd slept part of the afternoon away in the car, not to mention all the sleeping she'd been doing while on the drugs, so he figured she was more awake than she'd wanted to admit.

He hadn't slept nearly as much as she had and the long day started to get to him, making his eyelids droop. He finally lay back on the couch and let it happen, dropping off into the kind of sleep from which he'd wake quickly if anything happened.

He'd always been a light sleeper. Something he'd probably learned as a little boy waiting for his mother to come home. He'd lain awake at night, trying to sleep, but unable until she'd come crashing inside at some ungodly hour, either with or without a man in tow.

Until the night when she'd brought home a man who'd strangled her after he'd had sex with her. Brett would never forget that night. Still saw it in his dreams sometimes. Still felt as helpless as that little boy who'd been freezing his ass off and hoping his mother would wake up even when he'd known she wouldn't.

Brett startled awake, sweat breaking out over his body. He lay still and dragged in air, wondering what the hell had triggered that memory. That dream. Because he had been dreaming. About that night.

About the man who'd killed his mother and then left without closing the door. He hadn't known Brett was there. What would he have done if he had?

Killed him too, naturally. Brett sat up, scraping a hand through his hair, and swore. He'd definitely been dreaming about that night. It wasn't real. Not now. It was long in the past, and nobody was going to strangle him in his sleep.

"I'm sorry," a soft voice said. "Did I wake you?"

Instinct told him to reach for his weapon. Common sense told him he was in a house in Bavaria and the voice belonged to Tallie.

"It's okay," he said, his voice rusty. "I need to find my bed. This couch isn't going to cut it."

"Oh. Of course."

It occurred to him that it was strange she'd be there, standing halfway between the stairs and the couch, her body clad in what looked like flannel pajamas—there went his fantasies of thin T-shirts and nipples poking through the fabric. But it wasn't strange in the sense he needed to draw down and prepare to fight.

"Is everything okay, Tallie?"

"Well, actually—no. The radiator in my room seems to have stopped working. It's getting cold. I was coming down here to sleep on the couch."

"You can take my bed," he said automatically. "I'll stay here."

"But you just said you weren't comfortable."

"Not on the couch. I'll sack out on the floor. It'll be fine."

Tallie came closer, the glow of the fire illuminating her pale skin. And those pajamas. He saw now that they were Christmas elf pajamas. Somebody in BDI had a sense of humor. It wasn't that damned close to Christmas. Though on the other hand, it was close enough and the pajamas were probably plentiful in stores.

Tallie must have noticed him staring because she dropped her gaze. Then she looked at him with a sheepish smile. "They're warm, even if a bit ridiculous."

"They look warm. I wonder if I have any upstairs?" He said it to make her laugh. It worked.

"Did someone think we were planning a pajama party or what?"

Brett shrugged. Damn he was tired. Still. "You never know, I guess."

"You can't stay here, Brett. Take your bed. I'm shorter than you are and I can sleep on the couch. No problem."

"It would be a problem. I can't protect you if I'm upstairs and you're down here near the door. Why do you think I have the room closest to the stairs and you have the one farthest?"

"I didn't think of that."

"It's not your job. But it is mine." He levered up off the couch. "I'll have a look at the radiator. Maybe it's stuck or something. If not, you'll take my bed and I'll sleep here."

She followed him upstairs. He went into her room and over to the radiator that sat beneath the window. It wasn't as hot as it should be. In fact, it was growing cold. He twisted the dial, but it was all the way open. Sometimes the valves got stuck, but that was usually when the radiators had been off for a long time. He didn't think these had been because it wasn't the first cold day in Bavaria this fall.

"It's cooling off," she said.

"It is. And I'm not a radiator repairman, so let's leave it alone for tonight. You take my room. It's a single night."

"I'll stay downstairs with you."

He gaped at her. "Why?"

She dropped her gaze. "Honestly? I don't want to be alone. Whenever I close my eyes, I hear things and see things—and I hate it."

He stared at her. How could he argue with that? He understood where her fear of being alone came from.

"You slept alone in the palazzo."

"I know. But the room was big, the ceiling tall. I didn't feel quite as confined. Here… I feel claustrophobic. I can't help it."

She looked around and Brett followed her gaze. The room was small with walls that seemed to close in. With the lights out, it would be worse. Maybe if they'd been in the village, the street lights would help. But it was very dark up above the village.

Brett sighed. "All right. Let me see if I have any Christmas elves to wear and we'll go downstairs. You can have the couch. I'll take the floor."

"You can use your duvet as a mattress. It's very fluffy." She grabbed hers off the bed and dragged it with her. She stood outside his bedroom door while he went inside and turned on the light.

His room was spacious. There was a door that opened onto the balcony, and plentiful windows, though the blinds were down right now. The bed was a queen. He thought about suggesting they share it, but discarded the idea. Better to be on the floor while she was on the couch. Fewer opportunities to make stupid mistakes.

Brett found sleep pants in the drawer. And damned if they didn't have Christmas elves on them. He pulled them out with a disbelieving snort. Who the hell had readied this house? Whoever it was, he felt like they were playing a heck of a joke on him.

He turned to Tallie and held up the pants. She laughed.

"Oh my God. That's so cute. It's like we're newly married and ridiculously nerdy or something."

Brett shoved the drawer closed with a grumble. "Ridiculous is the correct word. Go ahead and go down and I'll change and grab the duvet."

"Okay. Meet you by the fireplace." She disappeared, but then popped her head back into the opening. "Should we fix cocoa and sing carols or what?"

She was too cute with her short blonde curls bouncing and the sparkle in her eyes. He had a sudden vision of sitting beside a fire with her, drinking a hot beverage while a Christmas tree sparkled nearby and snow fell outside the windows.

It was such a cozy, homey scene—and it hurt deep down inside where a little boy who'd never had a decent Christmas in his life ached for the storybook

Christmases like they had in movies. His mother could never afford Christmas gifts, much less a tree and lights. When he'd gone into foster care, he'd had such a shit run of foster homes that by the time he got into a decent one, he'd been too old to believe in perfect storybook Christmases. Santa and carols and cocoa were no longer anything he'd thought he needed.

Tallie's smile turned to a frown. "I was just kidding, Brett. Don't look so worried that I'm going to make you sing with me."

He cleared his throat and shot her a grin that he didn't quite feel. "Spike the cocoa and skip the carols and you've got a deal."

She rolled her eyes. "You can spike yours. I'm not ruining perfectly good chocolate that way."

She traipsed down the hall, the duvet dragging behind her. He listened to the sound of her steps as she went down the stairs. His heart still throbbed and his chest ached. What the fuck?

With a growl, he tugged off his shoes and jeans and changed into the sleep pants. Then he grabbed his holster and extra mags and went downstairs to join the cute blonde who made him ache for reasons that didn't surprise him—and a few that did.

Chapter Thirteen

Tallie fixed hot chocolate because she wanted a hot beverage and she didn't want caffeine. She'd had trouble falling asleep because every time she closed her eyes, she felt like the walls were closing in. She'd left the lamp on, hoping that would help, but it didn't.

And then the room started to grow cold. It had taken her a while to realize the radiator wasn't heating. By the time she'd figured it out, she was more than ready to leave the confines of her room.

She huddled on the couch, her legs stretched out, and sipped the cocoa. Brett lay on the floor, one arm behind his head, his eyes closed. She didn't think he was asleep though. His breathing wasn't deep enough.

No, he was probably avoiding talking to her. She wasn't sure why. It wasn't over the cocoa and carols. That was such a non-issue. Maybe it was because she'd kissed him and he'd pushed her away.

Or maybe it was what she'd said about him seeming like a good time.

"Brett?" she whispered.

"Yeah?" His answer was immediate, so she knew he wasn't sleeping.

"I'm sorry if anything I've said at any point today has upset you."

He cracked an eye open and fixed it on her. "What?"

"If I've annoyed you or insulted you or something. I'm sorry."

Half his face was in shadow. She couldn't quite tell what kind of expression he had at the moment.

"You haven't upset me, Tallie." He said it quietly, seriously.

"I hope not. It wasn't my intention."

"You haven't."

"Okay. If you're sure."

"I'm sure."

She hesitated. "Do you want some cocoa? There's more. And I saw a bottle of brandy in the kitchen, so you could spike it if you really wanted to."

"I think I'm fine. But thanks for offering."

Tallie stared at the flames. Brett had stoked the fire up again and the logs were glowing. The dark bulk of his gun and holster lay beside him, away from the fire. She'd handled the weapon today, though it'd been a long time since she'd shot a pistol, and she could still feel the weight of it in her hand.

"Do you think we're safe here?" she asked him, thinking about the seriousness of that weapon.

"Safe enough," he told her. "For now."

"That woman. Natasha. Do you think she knows where we are?"

He blew out a breath. "No, I don't. But I think if anyone could find out, it'd be her. She's not after us though. She wants something else."

"Something Ian promised her."

He was staring at her again. "It'd be best if you forgot everything you heard her say. In fact, forget her face and her name. Forget she exists. She's dangerous, Tallie. You don't want anything to do with her."

Tallie thought of the woman who'd sat across from them in the restaurant. She'd been pretty with her dark hair and deep blue eyes. And so alone. "She seemed sad to me. And scary. I won't deny that."

"I'm not talking about her so find a new topic. Or go to sleep."

"I'm trying. That's what the cocoa is for. My dad used to fix it for me and Josie when we couldn't sleep."

"That's counterintuitive. Hot chocolate is full of sugar, which tends to amp kids up."

"I know. I don't think he gave us much, or he made it with low-cal sweetener or something. But he'd make the cocoa and tell us stories. It was something my mother never did—but she was building her business, even then."

He stared up at the ceiling. "What did your dad do?"

"He was a carpenter, but he worked at home building stuff for Mom, so he was the one who spent the most time with us. We'd go to his shop in the back yard and play with wood shavings and stuff. To this day, I love the smell of shavings."

"Sounds like you had a nice childhood." He sounded a little wistful, maybe.

"I did for the most part. Mom has always been very driven to succeed, so there were times when she chose the business over us. But she did it for us so we'd have a good life. I know that now."

"You would have liked more time with her."

Tallie frowned. "Yes. I think we all would have. Dad most of all, probably."

She often wondered if it was the empty nest after she and Josie had left home, and the fact her mother still worked as hard as ever, that had led to her father's suicide. Maybe he'd expected a different life by then. Or maybe he'd just lost his way when he no longer had children at home to care for.

Logically, she knew he'd suffered from depression and that was what caused it in the end. But she still wondered if the changes in his life had finally driven him to it. She would probably always feel some guilt about that.

About growing up and leaving him.

"It's tough to lose a parent so young," Brett said.

"You think they're going to be there for you for a long time to come."

She remembered what he'd told her about his mother. He'd said she was gone, but he hadn't said when she'd died. "How old were you?"

"Eight."

Her heart squeezed tight. "I'm so sorry. That had to be hard for you and your dad both."

"I didn't have a dad."

He said it matter-of-factly, but she still felt like the biggest jerk on the planet. She'd made a stupid assumption based on her own life. He'd told her his mother sold her body for money, so what had made her think there was a father in the picture?

"I'm sorry. I shouldn't have assumed. I don't know why I did—"

"It's fine, Tallie. It's a natural assumption. But I never knew my father, and my mother was a drug addict as well as a sex worker. When she died, I went into foster care."

She imagined him as a little boy, his mother gone, being shuffled into a new home with new people who didn't know him. She had absolutely no experience with what he'd been through.

"I shouldn't be talking about myself so much," she said. She was feeling the stress of the past few days and it made her chatty. Not to mention the tension between them that had her as jumpy as a cat.

"I like hearing about your life. Talk all you want."

She didn't know if he was just being polite or if he

meant it. Regardless, she felt awkward. "It's your turn. Tell me about you. How did you get into this profession—whatever this profession is?"

"It's not exciting. I joined the Army as soon as I was old enough. Did my time, and then Ian found me. Here I am."

"Seriously, that's all you're giving me? Your life in two or three sentences?"

"It's just not that interesting. I joined the Army because I had no chance of going to college without the tuition assistance a stint in the military would give me. I also wanted out of the system, and I never wanted to go back to Houston. The Army was my ticket."

So he was from Houston originally. She hadn't known that. "Did you go to college?"

"Night classes and online classes. But yeah, I got my degree, though it took me a lot of years to do it. I did four years in the Army, got my Ranger tab, and thought I was going to re-up. But I met Ian when we were deployed to Iraq, and I knew I wanted to work for him. So that's what happened."

Tallie figured it was more complicated than that, but it was a lot more than he'd said before. Ridiculously, it made her happy that he'd said as much as he had. As if they were really getting to know each other.

"Sounds like you've worked hard to accomplish your goals."

"I did what I had to do. My mother let life beat

her up and spit her out. I wasn't going to do the same."

Tallie'd had everything she'd wanted from an early age. Except for her mother's time and attention. But that wasn't anything compared to what he'd gone through. "I think that's admirable."

"I don't know that it's admirable so much as necessary. It was either that or become a drug addict like she was. I could have turned tricks, too."

Tallie must have made a shocked noise because he gave her a look. "You didn't think of that? Boys can be sex workers, too. Teen boys especially. I knew a few, but I thankfully avoided that fate."

Her throat was tight. "I had no idea. I mean I guess I *should* know. I'm not uneducated or sheltered and I know the world is an evil place for some people. But I guess I never really thought of teen boys turning to prostitution. It makes sense, I know it does—and I feel terrible that I've never considered it before."

"You're from a different world. And it's not as talked about as it should be. People don't get mad enough about trafficking—sex or slavery—because it doesn't affect them. The ones it does affect are typically powerless. They're already marginalized in some way." He blew out a breath. "And yet people who aren't marginalized—people like you—also get pulled into that world sometimes. That should scare the hell out of everyone. It should make people want to *do something.*"

"But what can they do? What can *I* do?" Because

she didn't want to sit idly by and do nothing, or pretend it didn't exist. Now that she was intimately aware, she wanted to help stop it however she could.

"It might not seem like much, but try to be aware of where the things you buy come from. There are companies and countries that are known to use forced labor. Don't buy stuff that comes from them. Donate money to organizations that fight trafficking. Get involved on some level, a level you're comfortable with, and don't forget that it happens every day to someone."

Tallie's heart hurt at the thought of people being forced into labor or sex work. "Or pick up a gun and fight the way you do."

His smile was gentle. "That only works for trained operatives like me. And I don't kill traffickers, as much as I might like to. I work to dismantle their organizations at the root. It's not all I do, but it's something I'm dedicated to."

"I hope you get those bastards who kidnapped me," she said fiercely.

"It's the plan." He frowned at her. "You know, all the cocoa in the world isn't going to help you fall asleep if we don't talk about something nicer."

"I know—but I'm not the one who brought it up. You did."

He looked sheepish. "Sorry, occupational hazard. Why don't you tell me where you went to college and what you majored in?"

"How do you know I went to college? I could have

gone to work for my mother straight out of high school."

"You could have, but I doubt it. You're from a college town. Did you go to William & Mary?"

"I did. I majored in business at Mom's insistence. And French, of course."

"And you learned interior design from her."

"That's right. She trained at SCAD in Savannah. You don't get much better than that for an interior designer. Josie and I both went to Willam & Mary, but Mom taught us design from the cradle."

They talked for another hour about various things before Tallie was ready for sleep. She washed her mug, dried it, and shuffled back to the couch. The fire glowed and the room was warm. Brett lay between her and the door, hands behind his head, eyes closed. She stared down at him for a second, her heart throbbing as she studied the lines of his features. He was a grown man, a big man, but she could see the little boy if she looked hard enough.

The little boy who'd lost his mother at age eight and gone into foster care. She ached for the frightened child he must have been.

Tallie stretched out on the couch, beneath her thick duvet, and closed her eyes. But sleep was a long time coming.

IT HAD SNOWED OVERNIGHT and the driveway

was covered. Not that Brett thought they were leaving today, but he was going to have to shovel it just in case.

He'd just woke up, and now he stood and stared at the bright white blanket that coated the landscape as far as the eye could see. The sky was gray with more snow clouds, but the mountain peaks were visible. It was, without a doubt, breathtakingly beautiful.

"Want some coffee?"

Speaking of breathtakingly beautiful.

Brett turned to the smiling blonde who'd come in from the kitchen. She wasn't wearing the elf pajamas anymore, and he started at the evidence she'd gotten up and gotten dressed without him knowing it. He usually could hear a pin drop.

But not last night, apparently. When they'd finally stopped talking and he'd closed his eyes, sleep ambushed him. It had also held him down for hours before loosening its grip.

"That would be great. Thanks."

He followed her into the kitchen where she found a mug and poured in fresh coffee before sliding it to him along with a sugar bowl and a jug of cream.

"Isn't it amazing?" she asked with a happy expression, her gaze on the landscape beyond the windows. The village spread out below them, covered in white, and the mountain peaks were even more breathtaking from these windows. "I just want to go outside and yodel or something."

Brett managed to swallow the mouthful of coffee

he'd drank before he snorted it through his nose. "You want to yodel?" he asked her with laughter in his voice.

She blinked up at him, her extraordinary eyes clear this morning. One golden hazel, one blue. He stared because he couldn't help it. She shrugged, seemingly unaware of the reason for his staring.

"Well not really, but I sure did love the heck out of *The Sound of Music* growing up."

"They don't yodel, do they?"

"Well, Julie Andrews does. Just a little bit."

"Ah."

"You've never seen it?"

"Once maybe. I don't remember any yodeling."

"We could also go outside and scream *reeeecola*. See if it bounces back to us."

This time he did laugh. "Aren't those supposed to be Swiss cough drops?"

She rolled her eyes. "Whatever, spoil sport. It's the Alps—and these are Alps!"

"They sure are. I take it you've never been here either?"

She shook her head, blond curls bouncing. "Nope. I've been all over France searching for antiques. I've spent time in London. Aside from my latest foray into Italy, I've been there once on purpose. Germany wasn't on my radar. But you know, I do rather love the painted Bavarian furniture. I may have to purchase some of it for the shop the next time I travel for business." She paused. "Okay, not for the shop. Mom would probably have a fit. I'll buy some for me. I could see how one or two pieces in a house could really be showstoppers."

He loved seeing her excited about something. Happy. It was as if the gloom of last night was gone now that it was daylight.

Maybe it was. The dark hours had a way of making fear seem larger than life sometimes.

"I think you should buy it if you like it. If you do, others will too."

"You think so?"

"Yep. Isn't that how it works? We don't all like the same things."

"True."

He pulled out a chair at the bar by the window and sat. She poured another cup of coffee for herself and got busy taking eggs and cheese from the fridge.

"Omelet?" she asked.

"Sounds good to me."

"Me too. I don't think that's what they eat here, but we're Americans, right?"

"All day long." He took another swallow of coffee. She made good coffee. Not everyone did. He didn't like it too strong or too weak. "The coffee's good. Thanks."

"You're welcome."

She shot him another of those sunny smiles and he felt like he'd stood in a ray of sunshine. And sugar. Couldn't forget the sweetness.

"What's got you in such a good mood today?" he asked.

She blinked. And then she waved her hand at the windows. "Hello? Did you see those mountains? Incredible."

He sat back, grinning. She was cute. And her mood was at least a little bit infectious. "I saw them."

She stopped what she was doing for an instant and just stared out the window. "You forget how incredible this world is until you're faced with something so majestic that it takes your breath away." She turned to him. "I refuse to allow people to take away my joy. I had a lucky escape, thanks to you and your friends, and I'm going to be happy. Right now, right this minute, I *am*. So I'm going to enjoy it."

"That's great, Tallie. Don't let this experience change who you are."

"That's the plan."

He didn't want to rain on her parade, but he couldn't pretend it was all sunshine and rainbows either. "Just be sure, if you feel anxious when you get home, to talk to a professional, okay?"

"Got it, Dr. Brett," she said, aiming a fork at him and winking before turning back to the bowl she'd cracked the eggs into. "Are we going to be able to go outside at all? Into the village, maybe?"

"Only if you put in contacts."

She made a face. "I saw those in the drawer."

"It's for your protection. Your eyes are attention-getting."

"I know. I'll put them in. I'll put on a pink tutu if you think that'll help, so long as I get to go for a walk outside today. Whatever it takes."

"I think we can skip the tutu."

"Good, because I hate tutus. Eight years of dance class, from ages four to twelve. I never want to see another recital in my life."

"Huh, I thought little girls loved ballet."

"Only some of them do. Some of us would have preferred a pony, except our mothers thought ponies were dangerous and smelly."

"Aren't they?"

She put a large dollop of butter in the pan after she turned on the gas. "That's beside the point. And I don't think they're all dangerous. They just have attitude because they're pint-sized and cute and probably get their little noses kissed a lot."

"You're pint-sized and cute. Do you have attitude?"

She stopped what she was doing and looked at him with an open mouth. Then she laughed. It was a good laugh. A belly laugh. "Nobody has ever said that to me before—but yes, I have plenty of attitude. I hated being short growing up. I still hate it, but at least I can wear high heels to make myself seem taller."

She poured the eggs in the pan and made a fluffy omelet filled with cheese. She slid it onto the plate she'd taken from the bar in front of him and handed it back. Then she started another one while he waited patiently for her to finish it.

"Start eating, Brett. It'll get cold."

"You sure?" He wanted to eat now, but he'd learned in one particularly strict foster home to wait until everyone at the table had their meal.

"Positive. Eat it."

He did as she said, savoring the deliciousness of the omelet, and finished every bite before she sat down with hers. She gaped at his plate.

"Do you want another one?"

He thought about it. "Nah. I'm full." He was full, but he considered eating another one anyway. Just because she was making it.

He watched her moving in front of the stove, cooking and humming a tune, and something inside him shifted. He could get used to this kind of thing. Typically whenever he spent the night with a woman, he got the hell out first thing in the morning.

He hadn't even slept with Tallie, but already he was thinking of what it would be like to sit in a kitchen with her every morning and watch her fix breakfast while humming and laughing and talking about tutus and ponies.

Brett swallowed the rest of the coffee, scraped the chair back, and stood. Tallie smiled at him, and his heart actually skipped a single beat.

Coincidence. Hearts skipped beats. It happened to everyone. It wasn't mystical or predictive or anything.

"I need to shovel the drive and walkway," he told her. "Before it snows again."

He didn't know if it would snow again, but it was as good a reason for urgency as any. There was also the radiator to fix, but he'd worry about that later. If they had to spend another night in the living room, so what? They weren't going to be here more than another day or two anyway—and a warm radiator wasn't going to make it any easier on Tallie to sleep in that small room.

She set her plate down on the counter. "I can help if you want to wait five minutes."

"That's okay. Won't take me long. You stay in here and keep warm. Put those contacts in," he added. That was a reason she'd probably easily accept. He hoped so anyway.

Brett tugged on a jacket and boots before stepping outside into the bracing air. Then he went in search of the shovel, determined to clear every last inch of driveway and sidewalk before he had to face Tallie again.

He hoped it took a long time—because he was going to need every minute to kill those thoughts about how nice it would be to start his days with Tallie fixing breakfast for him.

The last time he'd had thoughts about spending time with a woman, he'd ended up married to a psychotic bitch. Biggest mistake of his life. And not one he ever intended to make again.

Chapter Fourteen

Tallie put in the contacts—brown ones, which wasn't her usual style though it definitely made her look different—and wrapped up in warm clothing. Brett was still shoveling the walkway when she stepped outside. The cold air hit her in the face and she breathed it in happily.

It was fresh and clean and crisp. Just what she needed at the moment. She stood and spun in a slow circle, taking in the white blanket of pristine snow and the mountains all around. The house was set against the hillside, looking cozy and warm.

In the village, a church with an onion dome dominated the skyline. There was a bell that rang out the hours, and she knew the church would be open for anyone who wanted to walk inside and say their prayers. Maybe she would.

Brett looked up from shoveling. His cheeks were red and his eyes sparkled in the cold. Tallie gazed at all he'd done to clear the walkway and drive. And he was barely breathing hard.

"You're ready for that walk, I take it?"

"Yes. But what about the radiator?"

He came over and propped the shovel against the house, then made sure the front door was locked. "I'll take a look when we get back. If I can't get it working, I'll call someone."

They headed down the drive to the sidewalk that ran into the village. It took a good twenty minutes before they reached the outskirts of town. It wasn't big, but it was laid out like most German towns. Houses clustered around a center that featured shops, squares, restaurants, and the church.

Brett took her hand when they passed beside the sign proclaiming the town name. Tallie startled, but he squeezed softly.

"We're newlyweds. Brad and Terri Taylor from Cincinnati, Ohio."

"Since when did we change names?"

"Since Natasha knew who we were in the Brenner Pass."

"You didn't tell me before."

"We were alone. There was no need. Besides, Ian just texted me the names this morning. We'll get new documents tomorrow."

Tallie's pulse shot a little higher. She was really starting to hate this cloak and dagger stuff. "When do we get to go home, *Brad?*"

"Soon, I hope."

"You've been saying that."

"It's only been a few days since I found you in Venice. Patience, *Terri.*"

"I'm trying," Tallie grumbled. "I feel like my life is on hold. I'm completely out of touch with everything and everyone."

It hit her then how much more relaxed she felt when she wasn't checking her phone every hour. No email, no Facebook, no news. Those things had given her a low-level anxiety that she hadn't even realized she'd had.

Not that she was completely relaxed now, given the situation she was in, but the added stress of being overly connected to a world she couldn't control was missing. Maybe, when she got her phone back, she needed to unplug a bit more often. Not completely, because she needed it to connect with friends and clients, but perhaps some periods of enforced distance weren't a bad idea.

"It won't last forever," he told her.

"Feels like it at the moment."

But how bad was it, really? She was walking into a quaint Bavarian village on a picture perfect snowy day, holding hands with the sexiest man she'd ever held hands with. The mountains were magnificent, the air clean, and the day filled with possibilities. Hadn't she vowed to enjoy every moment and not let what had happened to her affect every waking second?

Brett stopped and tugged her to face him, slipped

his arms around her, and danced them through the town square they'd just emerged into. Tallie was shocked at first, and then she laughed, throwing her head back as she clung to him.

"See, Terri? Not so bad to be off the grid," he said in her ear, his hot breath tickling its way down her spine in a series of shivers that had nothing to do with the cold.

"Okay, Bradley. Show me a good time today."

He twirled her around and then dipped her, strong arms holding her securely. "I intend to, sugar."

For a moment, she thought he might kiss her. His face was close, his eyes searching hers, but then he straightened and pulled her upright, setting her a couple of steps away with firm hands on her waist. He grinned as her heart pattered and her pulse skipped. As heat throbbed in her core and her nipples tightened.

"You're as delicate as a snowflake," he told her, hands still holding her firmly in place. "But that's not the whole truth, is it?"

"What do you mean?" she asked a touch breathlessly.

"I mean you have a core of steel inside, but you're also optimistic about life and determined to see the best in everything. And maybe everyone."

Her chest ached just a little bit at his words. It was as if he'd peeled back a protective layer and stared into her soul. "How could you possibly know that in so short a time?"

"It wasn't that long ago when I watched you staring at the mountains and proclaiming life was beautiful. That's the optimist in you. The strength comes in the ability to be that optimistic so soon after a terrifying experience."

"How else should I be? I don't want to spend my life cowering in a corner. Though deep down, that's exactly what I want to be doing. I'm scared but I'm not going to let it rule me."

He lifted a hand and brushed a lock of hair off her cheek. "See? Strong as steel. Not everybody can do that."

"You can."

"Yeah, I can. I had to learn it early or I wouldn't have amounted to much."

He let her go and she stood for a second feeling strangely empty. But then he held out his hand and she slipped hers inside, thrilling at the warmth and firmness of his touch through the gloves they both wore.

"Come on. Let's go into some shops and then have lunch at the restaurant. You up for that?"

"Sounds like my idea of a fun day."

"I thought it might."

They walked across the square and Tallie gazed up at his profile, feeling oddly content. "What's your idea of a fun day?"

He was quiet for a minute. Thinking.

"Doing this with you."

BRETT WAS on his guard as they walked through the village, but nothing out of the ordinary happened. It was a small village, picturesque—which meant tourists. Brett studied the people they passed. No one stood out. He looked especially hard at the women, in case Natasha Orlova was masquerading as one of them, but she didn't seem to be there.

Tallie happily browsed in shops, stomping snow from her boots before they went inside, then looking at everything until she was ready to move on to the next. They popped into a restaurant on one corner of the square that served hearty German fare and ate lunch, with wine for Tallie and a beer for him.

Brett was careful how much he consumed, just in case, but Tallie didn't seem to notice. She finished her wine and ordered a second glass. Her cheeks were flushed and she talked animatedly about the things they'd seen in the shops.

"Oh, I could really see a use for that cabinet in one of my interiors. And that fabric. Gosh it's pretty…"

She went on like that for a while. Brett nodded and made appropriate remarks, but he felt somewhat like he was in two places at once.

Part of him was playing the part of doting new husband and part was watching their surroundings for any danger. But the part of him watching for danger was also thinking about what he'd said to her earlier.

That his idea of a fun day was spending it with her. He still didn't know why he'd said it, but right now it was as true as anything.

He wanted to kiss her. And then he wanted to peel those clothes from her body and kiss the rest of her. He was starting to tell himself it wasn't that bad of an idea, that it was a great way to pass the time. That they were both adults and they wanted each other. What was wrong with that?

"Earth to Brad," Tallie said, snapping her fingers, and Brett's attention bounced back to her. She watched him with an arched eyebrow, her pretty mouth twisted in a smirk. "Daydreaming, pookiebear?"

Pookiebear?

"A little bit," he admitted, glancing at a nearby table. The people sitting there weren't looking at them at all. They were laughing and chatting in German. He'd have known they were European even without the language cue. They ate with their forks in their left hands, pushing food onto them with knives in their right.

Whenever he was pretending to be European, he did the same thing. It was a subtle difference from how Americans ate with forks in the right hand, but it's also what made them stand out in a European crowd if you were looking for them. It was the little things when you were undercover that made all the difference.

"Okay, so what about?" Tallie asked, eyebrow still arched.

He could have said anything. Could have made up any reason he wanted to. But he told her the truth. Or part of it anyway.

"You, baby. Taking you home and getting you naked."

Her mouth dropped open. A fresh wash of red bloomed over her cheeks. Then she shook her head as if to clear it before leaning forward, frowning hard. "You're kidding, right? This is Brad to Terri, right?"

He picked up his beer and took a drink. "Would it bother you if that's not all of it?"

Her gaze dropped, shading her eyes. Brown eyes. She was still pretty with her eyes covered, but he missed the blue and gold of her real gaze. "You're confusing me. I don't know what's real and what's not," she finished softly.

"Hell, neither do I," he admitted, sitting back again and studying her.

She lifted her lashes. "Maybe we just need to stick to the plan. You said last night that it was a bad idea. I think you were probably right."

He had said that, hadn't he? Not in those exact words, but he'd told her he couldn't have sex with her. Because she'd been drinking wine—like now—and that's why she'd kissed him. She hadn't been thinking straight and he hadn't wanted to take advantage of her.

Now? Hell, now he'd crawl over hot coals if she'd let him strip her naked and explore her body.

Why? Because she'd fixed him breakfast and he'd enjoyed watching her do it? Because he'd told her more about his life last night in front of the fire than he'd told most people?

Or was it because she was full of the kind of joy, despite her experience with the traffickers, that he'd forgotten existed?

"Yeah," he told her, because she seemed to be waiting for an answer. "Probably right. You ready to get back to the house? We've been gone a while and I need to get some work done."

Which was code for contacting Ian and getting a status report.

She seemed uncertain. Then she nodded. "I'm ready. It's been a great time though. Thanks for bringing me to the village and putting up with the window shopping."

"It wasn't bad. I'd do it again. Your knowledge of antiques is fascinating."

"I don't know a lot about German antiques. I could learn more."

"Doesn't matter. I don't know anything. You could have told me whatever you wanted about that stuff and I'd have believed it."

She gave him a mischievous look. "How do you know I didn't?"

He laughed. They were back on safe ground for now. He signaled the waitress and paid the bill, then they headed outside and strolled side by side down the street. But they didn't touch, not this time. Tallie shoved her hands in her coat pockets. He did the same.

The trip up the hill was silent, except for the noise of cowbells in the fields and the occasional barking dog. Brett kept a careful eye on the terrain. There were places a sniper could perch, but it'd be a hell of a trick for anyone to find them here so soon after they'd arrived.

They rounded the hill and started up the walkway to the house. When it came into view, Brett's senses prickled. Something wasn't right but he didn't know what. Still, he didn't ignore feelings like this one.

He thrust an arm in front of Tallie, stopping her forward motion. She looked up at him with wide eyes. "What's wrong?"

He pushed her behind him. Reached into his jacket for the solid weight of his Sig.

"Not sure. Follow me—and don't make any sound, no matter what."

Chapter Fifteen

TALLIE'S HEART WAS IN HER THROAT BUT SHE swallowed it down and told herself to do whatever Brett said. She crept up the sidewalk behind him, straining her ears to hear any unusual sounds. All she heard was the dog and the cowbells.

What had he seen that alerted him?

She concentrated on his back, the broadness of it, the safety. But what if someone got to him? What if they shot him and then she was exposed?

Don't go there.

She shook her head. No, she wouldn't. Brett knew what he was doing and he was going to take care of her. Of both of them.

When they got closer to the house, he took her through the bushes and placed her behind the woodpile, pushing her shoulder to make her squat down.

"Stay here," he said, his voice a low rumble. "I'm going to circle around and see if anyone is there."

"Okay."

"No matter what, Tallie, *don't* get up. Until I come back for you, don't move."

Her heart thumped. "What if you don't come back?"

She hated to ask that question, but she had to.

One corner of his mouth lifted in what she thought was approval. "Wait until dark and head for the village. Go to 325 Bahnstrasse and ring the bell. They'll call Ian."

"Okay." She grabbed his jacket when he started to rise and he turned to her with a question in his eyes. She tugged him down and pressed her mouth to his, hard and swift. "Come back, Brett. I don't trust anyone else."

He waggled his eyebrows. "I intend to, sugar. If for no other reason than to get another of those kisses."

"As many as you want."

"Well there you go. I'll definitely be back to collect on *that* promise. Now get down behind the wood and don't come out."

Tallie shrank herself into a tight little ball, knees up, arms wrapped around them. Brett reached out and tugged her hood up over her head. "Got to hide all that pretty golden hair."

He smiled at her and then melted away into the gray gloom that had settled over the mountain. Tallie concentrated on breathing and strained to hear anything over the blood pounding in her ears.

The dog had stopped barking. Even the cowbells stopped ringing. A snowflake drifted down to settle on the ground, and then another followed it. Soon, the snow was falling faster and Tallie bent her head back to look up at the sky.

It was white, the flakes erasing the gray of before. They were fat flakes and she stuck her tongue out, catching a few as they fell. She couldn't remember the last time she'd done that. And she didn't know why she was doing it now when everything was so serious. What if Brett didn't return? What if something happened to him?

And what if they captured her? She clenched her hands together where they rested around her legs. She wasn't going back to that terrible place where men bid for the right to own her body. Nobody owned her and nobody would. She'd resist until her last breath if that's what it took. She would never surrender to those people.

Tallie rocked back and forth to keep warm, listening and watching for signs of Brett. Presently, she heard snow crunching softly as someone moved toward her position. She wrapped her fingers around a piece of wood that lay propped against the stacked logs. Quietly, she got to a standing position, keeping her head and body behind cover. She gripped the log in both hands and readied herself.

The footsteps came closer. Tallie's heart hammered. A body appeared around the corner of the woodpile and she lunged at it, knowing her only chance was the element of surprise.

"Tallie, it's me!" Brett caught her as if she weighed nothing at all, restraining her easily.

Her breath razored in and out, her heart raced, and adrenaline rocketed through her veins, leaving her jumpy as hell.

"Why didn't you tell me it was you?" she yelled at him. "I could have hurt you."

He was still holding her close. He laughed, and that only made her madder. "I think I'm going to be okay."

She jerked out of his grip, still angry with him for sneaking up on her. And for laughing at her when she said she could have hurt him. How the hell did he know she couldn't? A well-placed blow to the head—or the balls—would surely take him down for a bit.

"What happened?" she demanded. "You took off out of here like you were expecting an attack."

"I always expect an attack. That way I don't get ambushed."

He reached for her hand. She jerked it away.

"I'm mad at you. You scared the hell out of me. You couldn't have called my name?"

"I should have. I didn't think you'd try to fight me."

She sniffed. "I'm not going to sit around and let things happen to me. If I'd known how to fight before, maybe those men wouldn't have taken me so easily."

She knew that wasn't entirely true. She'd gotten into a taxi, which was how they'd abducted her. Knowing how to defend herself wouldn't have helped then. It might have helped when they took her to that warehouse and drugged her though. If she only could have fought...

Brett was frowning. "I'm sorry, Tallie. I didn't think about any of that. I was coming to get you and tell you it's okay. It was a teenager who hid his pot stash in the house. He was coming back to get it. Not just coming back, but rolling a joint and having a smoke with a girl in the kitchen."

Tallie stepped out from behind the wood. Her body ached from the cold and staying still for so long. The snow was still coming down, harder now. It would accumulate quickly.

"You're sure they were teenagers?"

He grinned. "That's my girl. Suspicion is good. But yeah, that's all they were. The boy's mom cleans the house when it's not in use. He knew where she kept the key. He didn't know anyone was staying."

"I hope you put the fear of God into him."

"Oh, I'm pretty sure I did. He won't be back anytime soon. His mother is about to find out what he was up to when someone from HQ calls, so he's going to have a new problem to deal with soon."

They walked up to the house and took off their boots on the porch, then set them on a tray inside. Brett grabbed some logs from the basket by the front door and went over to place them on the grate.

Tallie took off her coat and scarf and hung them

by the door. Brett did the same, then went to start the fire. She watched him work, studying the play of muscles beneath his heather gray henley as he shifted logs around and strategically placed kindling and fire-starter beneath them.

"Brett?"

"Yeah?"

"Can you teach me how to defend myself?"

He stopped what he was doing and turned to face her. "I can show you some things, sure. But it won't be a substitute for taking some training when you get home."

"I know. It's just when I was waiting for you, I realized I didn't know even the most basic thing to do if someone tried to grab me. I don't want to be unprepared if it ever happens again."

TALLIE WAS A QUICK LEARNER. Brett taught her a couple of moves for gouging out eyes, stomping insteps, and how to break a choke hold. It wasn't a lot, but it was enough for now. He made her repeat it again and again, until it was natural for her to make the moves instead of freeze.

By the time they were done, they were both sweating. But Tallie looked determined and happy at the same time. She pushed her hair from her eyes and grinned as Brett rubbed his smarting nose. She'd knocked him good that last time.

"I'm sorry," she said. "I shouldn't have hit so hard."

"No, that's exactly what you should have done. If somebody grabs you, do it even harder. And faster. Speed is key. They won't expect it, and it'll give you time to escape."

"But what if they have a gun?"

Brett shook his head. "No, different moves for that. We'll worry about that one later."

"Okay." Her skin was shiny with sweat, but she was beaming too. "How about we go outside to cool off? I think the snow would feel pretty awesome right about now. I might even lie down and make a snow angel."

"I'm all for stepping outside. But you can lie in the snow by yourself."

She laughed as they headed out onto the front porch. The snow was still coming down, but they were protected by the overhanging balcony. It was nearly dark and the village below them glowed yellow and warm.

Tallie wrapped her arms around her body. She was wearing a sweater that hugged her curves and her feet were bare except for thick socks.

She didn't move to slip on her boots, so he figured the snow angel idea was out.

"I bet this place is amazing at Christmas."

That old twinge of emotion—disappointment, doubt, shattered dreams—stung him the way it usually did with talk of Christmas. It was an old, dull pain. He was used to it.

"I'm sure it is."

"Williamsburg is pretty amazing too. Colonial Williamsburg is something to see with all the decorations and the people in period costume. There are illuminations, caroling, and a firing of the Christmas guns."

"Sounds interesting."

"It is. You should come and see." She dropped her gaze and stepped away, almost as if she were embarrassed for saying anything.

He liked that she had, even if they probably wouldn't see each other again after he took her home. He didn't know why, but that thought made a different ache flare inside him.

"Maybe I will," he told her.

She looked up again. "You're just being nice. But that's okay."

"No, I'm not. Maybe I will. If I do, I'll make sure to call you."

She stared at him. Then she laughed.

"Why is that funny?" he asked.

"Because this is the moment where one person says to the other 'give me your number and I'll call you so you can capture mine.' But we can't do that because I don't have a phone. It's been so long that I'm past withdrawal. I may just get a flip phone when we get home. Who needs all that crap on a smartphone? It just makes me anxious anyway."

"Not a bad plan. But texting's going to be a bitch."

"Oh geez, you're right. I don't have any clue how to use numbers to find letters and words, though I guess I could learn."

She made him chuckle. "I'm pretty sure you can learn anything you set your mind to, Tallie."

Her smile was dazzling. "Thank you."

"You know," he told her, because he liked teasing her, "I seem to remember you promising me another one of those kisses when I left you behind the woodpile."

"I did. I was under duress. I'd have promised you anything as long as you said you'd come back for me."

"Anything? Well, hell, missed my opportunity there, didn't I?"

"Guess so." She looked mischievous as she grinned at him.

So pretty, this woman. Sweet and fun and smart.

He reminded himself those weren't reasons to get involved. His ex had seemed, if not sweet and fun, nice enough. She'd initially been attracted to him because he'd nearly broke some guy's wrist for grabbing her ass when she was waiting tables. He'd eventually fallen for her because she'd turned herself into exactly what she thought he wanted her to be. It all changed once they were married and her real colors came out.

Julia was petty and selfish and obsessed with her

looks and status. She was also the biggest damned mistake of his life.

Tallie snapped her fingers. "Earth to Brett. You okay there, big boy?"

"Yeah, fine. Just lamenting my misfortune."

"What misfortune?"

"The one where I failed to ask for more than a kiss."

Her mouth twisted in a cute little frown. "That is *not* what you were thinking about."

Damn, how did she seem to know him so well already?

Maybe because you told her stuff you never told Julia. Or any woman. Maybe because she really is what she seems to be.

He made a decision. "Okay, fine. I wasn't. I was thinking about how I met my ex-wife."

She threw her hands up, palms out. "Whoa, whoa, whoa. You were thinking about your ex-wife when you were talking about kissing *me?*"

"Yep. I was thinking that you're nothing like her. Trust me, that's a good thing."

She tilted her head as she studied him. "Does this usually work for you? Talking about your ex-wife to other women?"

"You tell me. I haven't tried it before."

"I'm a first, huh?"

"Definitely a first." For more reasons than she knew.

He didn't know what she'd do, but she closed the distance between them, until she was standing in front of him, head tipped back to meet his gaze. "It's a risky strategy, Brett. But honesty is much better than a lie, so you get points for that one. And you know what else?"

He shook his head.

"I'm pretty much to the point where I just don't care about anything other than right here and right now. Life is precarious, and I want to take a chance. I'm not drunk, and I'm not making any decisions under duress. Just so we're clear."

A hot feeling flared in his gut—and lower. "We're clear."

She put her hands on his abdomen, slid them up his chest to his shoulders. Then she stepped in closer. Her body was small and warm and it fit into his like it was meant to be there.

"Go ahead and kiss me, Brett. I want to see where this goes."

Chapter Sixteen

TALLIE HAD ABSOLUTELY NO IDEA WHAT SHE WAS doing. Earlier, when he'd said something to her in the village about getting her naked, she'd thought there was no way she was going to agree to it. Not after he'd turned her away last night.

She'd decided that maybe he was right after all and she hadn't been thinking clearly enough to make that choice. Besides, with all the chaotic emotion of the past week, she didn't need to add more confusion by sleeping with her protector.

No matter how appealing the idea.

But here she was, sidling up to him and basically telling him she wanted him. She knew why. It had everything to do with the minutes she'd been hiding behind the woodpile, waiting for him to return and worrying that he might not. That someone would kill him and then come for her.

You really did have to seize life by the horns sometimes. Do the thing that scared you because it might just make you feel amazing when it was over.

Brett loomed large, his breath frosting in the air above her. His green eyes glittered with heat and need. A moment later, when she thought he might push her away after all, he wrapped an arm around her waist and tugged her in close. Fitting her to him. Making her go weak with the evidence of his arousal pushing against her belly.

"Are you prepared for where this might go?" he asked, his voice heated. "Because it might go into some hot and sweaty places before we're through."

Tallie swallowed. But there was no panic, no voice telling her this was a bad idea. There was only heat and need and anticipation.

"I'm prepared, Brett. If I weren't, I wouldn't be standing here. I'm not the kind of woman who tells a guy she wants him and then changes her mind halfway through."

He arched an eyebrow. "I appreciate that very much. But if you *do* change your mind, you only have to tell me to stop. I want you to enjoy what's happening, not feel like you have to go through with it."

"Wow. What kind of man says he'll stop in the middle of sex?"

"This kind. I mean it, Tallie."

She ran a hand up his neck, toyed with the dark hair curling over his collar. "I believe you do. But trust me, if I'm standing here telling you I want this, I'm not going to change my mind."

He frowned. "You might not think so, but if something triggers a memory of when you were captured—well, you might want to."

She loved that he was concerned. That what had happened to her was important to him, not just because he was protecting her from further harm, but because he really did care about how she'd been treated.

"Okay. We'll cross that bridge when we come to it. Now please kiss me."

He started to drop his head, then stopped when he was mere inches away. Tallie opened her eyes to discover it when his mouth didn't touch hers.

"What?"

"You aren't a virgin, are you?" he asked.

She blinked. Laughed. "No, of course not. I'm twenty-six and I had a serious relationship. Why would you think that?"

But she saw it in his face and she knew. The nightie she'd worn, the juvenile makeup.

"Oh my God—they said I was a virgin, didn't they?"

He nodded. "It's part of how they got such a high price. I didn't think it was true once I knew who you really were, but I thought I'd better ask. Just in case."

"Not a virgin. And not seventeen. God, what disgusting people."

"Definitely."

Tallie shook her head. "I don't want to talk about them anymore. I don't want to talk about any of it. I just want you to kiss me."

He hesitated and she feared he might not do it. That he was thinking of reasons he shouldn't. But she was wrong. He dropped his mouth over hers, and Tallie sighed.

They'd kissed five times now, not including the brief press of lips when she'd told him to come back, and each time was a revelation. The sparks she'd felt the first time were still there. If anything, they were stronger than before.

Tallie wrapped her arms around his neck. Their tongues met, and liquid heat dripped down her spine. Yes, it had been a long time since she'd been with a man—but she didn't remember it feeling like this the last time.

Had it ever felt this exciting and new?

The air around them was cold, but the heat sizzled between them. Tallie didn't know how long they kissed, but when he pulled away, she lacked the ability to stand on her own. Thankfully, he didn't let her go.

"You ready to go inside?" he asked.

Her mouth was tender and aching, her nipples were hard little points beneath her sweater, and she'd passed wet and gone straight to soaking through her panties the moment the kiss began.

"Yes," she told him, feeling dazed and excited all at once. "I'm definitely ready."

He grinned. She thought they might walk inside together, but he didn't give her the chance. Instead, he swept an arm beneath her knees and gathered her up as if she was made of nothing but air.

Then he carried her over the threshold and kicked the door closed.

IF HE WAS A SENSIBLE MAN, he wouldn't be doing this. But Brett wasn't sensible right now. Kissing Tallie melted his brain. He wanted more of the same.

Brett carried her over to the couch. He could take her up to what was supposed to be his bed, but he wanted to do this in front of the fire. It was crackling steadily, lighting the room since he'd flipped off the light switch. He set her on her feet and reached for her sweater.

"May I?" he asked.

"Please."

He tugged the sweater up and over her head. She smiled at him. Her skin was creamy pale and her bra was white and lacy. Her nipples beaded beneath the fabric and he skimmed his thumb across one. Tallie shuddered.

"I don't have a lot to play with," she said apologetically.

Brett didn't stop rubbing his thumb across her sensitive flesh. "You have all I need," he told her. "More than enough."

She bit the inside of her lip as she gazed big-eyed at him. "You're so nice to me."

"Why wouldn't I be?"

"I don't know."

He bent and kissed her. "Any man who is critical of you for any reason to do with your body is an asshole. Understand?"

She nodded, her eyes liquid pools he could drown in.

"Let me hear you say it, Tallie."

"A man who's critical of my body is an asshole."

"Damn straight. You're beautiful."

"So are you. Please take your shirt off so I can see you too."

He ripped the henley up and over his head, dropping it on the floor.

Tallie's eyes widened. "Oh my." Her fingers skimmed over his abs, his pecs, back down to the knife scar on his side. There were old cigarette burns on his flesh as well, but they were faded now. If she noticed those, she didn't comment. "You've been in battle."

"A few."

"And you're not afraid?"

"I didn't say that. Of course I'm afraid. Like any sensible person, I'd like to preserve myself as long as possible."

"Then why do you keep doing it?"

It was a question he'd asked himself years ago. He didn't ask anymore. "Because somebody has to. Because it's the right thing to do."

Tallie bent and pressed a kiss to the knife scar. Brett hissed in a breath at the feel of her lips against his skin. It was like being branded, only he wanted more of it not less.

She straightened again and he pulled her to him, then attacked her mouth with a sensual barrage of kisses and nips. She moaned and his heart rate climbed.

He went for her jeans at the same time she went for his. Another moment and they both stood in their underwear. Hers was lacy and white, as virginal as anything she'd worn on the auction stage. She looked up at him shyly.

"It's been a long time since…" She whispered the words, but didn't finish the sentence.

He knew what she was saying. It seemed impossible that a woman as gorgeous as she was hadn't been having regular sex, but then again neither had he. Not for the past couple of months anyway. He'd grown tired of one-night stands and morning-after emptiness.

Maybe he'd feel empty after this one too, but right now he was too far along the path to care. That was a problem for later.

Brett ran his hands down her sides, around and up and over her breasts. Softly, sensuously. Her skin prickled with goosebumps.

"I'm going to be gentle with you, Tallie. And remember, if you want to stop, we'll stop."

"Okay." She bit her lower lip, and he loved the way she looked when she did.

"I mean it," he told her, just to emphasize it because he didn't think she really believed him. "If you change your mind at any point, let me know."

"I will. But I doubt I'm going to change my mind."

"I doubt I'm going to change mine either."

She blinked, surprised. She clearly hadn't considered that possibility.

He laughed. "Honey, the only thing that's stopping me, besides you, is if we get interrupted and I have to respond to it."

"Then I hope that doesn't happen."

"Me too." He traced the band of her bra around to the back. "May I?"

She nodded and he unclasped the little hooks, then pulled the fabric free. Tallie was small breasted, but they were perfect little mounds crested with pink. Her nipples stood up straight and tall, begging for his attention. He bent and licked one and Tallie gasped. Her hands went to his shoulders, clutching him. He loved her reaction so much that he licked the other one.

Tallie moaned, so he sucked her sweet little nipple between his lips and tickled it with his tongue.

"Oh, Brett."

"Feels good?"

"Feels amazing."

He dropped to his knees and hooked his fingers into her panties, dragging them down her hips until they fell at her ankles. The hair on her mound was darker than on her head and neatly trimmed. He didn't know if she'd done it, or if Paloma's people had. He wasn't going to ask either. He didn't want that coming between them, not when everything was honest and raw and new.

He pushed her back onto the couch and spread her legs, walking on his knees until he was between them. She watched him with glittering eyes and he realized she was still wearing the contacts. He had a moment where he wanted her to go remove them so he could see her real color, but there would be time for that later.

Besides, she was still beautiful even with brown eyes. And he wasn't the kind of man who obsessed about her uniqueness. Not like the Heinrich von Kassels of the world, who didn't care about who she was inside but only about what she represented.

Tallie was a treasure, but not for the reason Von Kassel believed.

Brett ran his fingers up the insides of her thighs, then slipped a finger into the wet heat of her. She was so wet that he groaned with it.

"Beautiful," he told her as he leaned over her and captured her mouth. She stretched up to him, her tongue stroking his eagerly. He could kiss her forever like this, but he had other important tasks to complete.

Brett continued stroking between her legs, softly and slowly, while he kissed his way down her body. He sucked each perfect nipple in turn and then drifted down her abdomen until he found himself at her pretty mound. He glanced up at her, met her heated gaze.

"I'm planning to lick you senseless, Tallie. You okay with that?"

She nodded and he dropped to press a kiss on the apex of her mound. Then he spread her with his thumbs and skated his tongue over her clit.

Tallie hissed in a breath, then moaned it out again. Brett loved the sound of her pleasure. It drove him to make her moan even more.

Her flesh was slick with arousal and he slipped a finger inside her, testing how easily she took him. Tallie wasn't a big woman and he didn't want to hurt her when it was time to slide his cock inside her body.

Brett flicked his tongue against her clit again and again. Her bud was hard, swollen, and she writhed on the cushions as he licked her into what he hoped was the kind of orgasm she'd never forget.

He didn't have long to wait. Just after he inserted a second finger inside her, fucking her a little faster, she stiffened beneath his tongue. Her hands came up to clutch either side of his head, her fingers tangling in his hair.

"Brett!" she gasped, her hips jerking as she rode

his tongue and fingers to an explosion he could feel as she stiffened and moaned out his name again.

He licked her faster, draining every last bit of pleasure from her that he could, until she pushed him away and tried to close her legs.

Brett let her because he knew she was sensitive right now, but he intended to make her come this way at least one more time before he moved on.

His dick ached but he wasn't about to hurry this. There was time—at least he hoped there was. If Ian called with a go order, he'd have to stop and get them out of there. He prayed that didn't happen, but the truth was that he never knew. The job was the job and sometimes it was inconvenient as hell.

Tallie lay back on the couch with her arm across her eyes. Her body twitched from time to time and Brett felt a hell of a lot of satisfaction at making her do that.

"You okay?" he asked after a few more moments. He stroked her skin, learning her by touch. She was silk and flame beneath his hands, and he wanted more.

She lifted her arm. Smiled at him. "Yes. I'm great. That was… incredible."

"You're incredible, Tallie. Thanks for trusting me to take care of you."

She frowned slightly. "You aren't quitting, are you?"

"Hell, no. I'm just getting started."

"Oh, good. It sounded like you were quitting for a second there."

As if he could.

"Nope." He leaned over, pushed her legs apart again, and hovered over her pretty little pussy. "I'm planning to lick you into another orgasm, sugar. For starters."

Chapter Seventeen

Tallie's body still zipped with sparks from the first orgasm he'd given her. When he touched his tongue to her clit again, her body responded, her back and hips arching her toward him.

It was incredibly erotic to see Brett kneeling between her legs, all his attention focused on making her feel good. On making her come.

It wasn't going to take long. He slipped a hand up her body to her breasts, pinched her nipples as he sucked on her clit and lapped at her juices.

The firelight played over her skin, over his. She'd been cold earlier and now she was so hot she thought water might steam if she touched it.

This was not how she'd envisioned the day going, and yet it was perfect. So perfect.

Brett slipped two fingers into her again, and the walls of her pussy tightened around them. The friction as he slid them in and out was amazing—but it was the friction on her clit that made her crazy.

She tried to hold on, tried to make it last, but there was no stopping the freight train of her orgasm as it slammed into her. Every nerve ending in her body tightened into a hard knot—and then exploded outward in a shower of sparks and heat.

Tallie couldn't speak. All she could do was feel. And Brett made her feel everything. He didn't stop pushing her for more, didn't stop tasting her until she cried out and pushed him away. It felt incredible—and she couldn't take another second of it.

She rolled to her side, curled her legs up onto the couch, and lay there trying to piece herself together again. She heard Brett move and guilt speared into her. He'd just given her two of the best orgasms of her life and she was ignoring him completely.

His big palm skimmed over her hip, around to her naked butt, up her back. It was soothing and sweet and her heart ached just a little bit at his touch.

Calvin had never touched her like that. Sex with him had often been a rushed affair because he had things to do afterward, or it was late and he had to get up early.

Two orgasms with Brett and she had to wonder why she'd ever put up with that. There was clearly much more to sex than she'd experienced before.

When she could move again, she unfolded herself and rolled onto her back. Brett was still on his knees. He had a look of patience and incredibly intensity rolled into one and she knew that what had happened so far—how good it had felt—was only the beginning.

It occurred to her that she was utterly naked and he still had on his underwear, a pair of boxer briefs that clung to his muscular thighs and outlined the hard bulge of his cock. She wanted to see him and she pushed herself onto an elbow to slip her fingers into his waistband. He didn't stop her from pulling his boxer briefs down. When he sprang free, she had a moment of apprehension.

He was big, but it wasn't necessarily that. It was how personal this had all become. And so soon after she'd stood on a stage and been sold into what was supposed to be sexual slavery.

Except that this man had been the one to buy her, and he wasn't doing it to make her into a slave. She knew, if she suddenly changed her mind, he'd back away and let her get dressed.

And that made him worth more in her estimation than any man she'd ever been with before now. She didn't have a lot of experience with men, but none had ever been as selfless and caring as this one.

It made her heart throb and her eyes sting.

She reached for him, for the hard length of him, and he hissed in a breath as she wrapped her hand around him. His eyes glittered hot and sharp on hers.

She stroked him, felt a dark urge seize her as he thrust into her hand, his body straining and controlled at the same time.

A series of shivers cascaded down her spine and

over her nerve endings, until goosebumps rose on her skin despite the fire's heat.

Tallie shifted toward him, intent on doing to him what he'd done to her, but he stopped her as she bent toward his cock.

"Not this time," he said, shaking his head.

Tallie blinked. "Why not?"

"Because I want it to last, not end within seconds."

She gaped at him. "I doubt I'm that good. I mean I know how to do it and all, but I'm certainly not an expert."

He pulled her gently to a sitting position so that they were at eye level. He brushed her hair from her face. Her body reacted to that simple touch, wanting more, as she leaned into his palm.

"Trust me, Tallie. You are that good. I'd explode far too quickly for my liking if you put your mouth on me. We can leave that for another time."

She grinned. "Okay, if you say so. We need a condom though."

"Well aware. There are some in the bathroom upstairs, or didn't you notice?"

"I didn't."

He pushed to his feet with a sultry smile. "I'll be right back. Don't go anywhere."

"I don't plan on leaving."

She was mesmerized by the play of light and shadow on his muscular form as he walked away. He was perfectly proportioned, his body packed with lean muscle, and she wanted to run her fingers over him endlessly.

He was back before she could question the wisdom in sleeping with this man she barely knew and might not see again after he took her home. She wanted to see him. She knew that much.

But would he want to see her? That she didn't know. It almost made her tell him to stop, because of that old saying about cows and free milk, but that was ridiculous because she wasn't a cow and she didn't want him to buy, aka marry, her anyway.

He sauntered over to her and dropped a strip of condoms on the coffee table. Tallie arched an eyebrow. Brett laughed.

"I want to be prepared."

"I'd say you will be," she replied.

He was still hard, his cock jutting out from his body impressively. He pushed her back onto the couch, hovering over her as he dropped his mouth to hers. He didn't lay on her, and she appreciated that. He kissed her sweetly, softly, then trailed his lips down her neck, over her collarbone, and then on to her nipples. He took his time with them, sucking them into hard points that stood tall and proud.

He cupped her breasts, worshipped them, and any embarrassment she felt over her lack of boobage began to fade. Brett didn't seem disappointed in the least.

Tallie reached between them and wrapped her hand around him. He groaned softly and thrust into her hand like he had earlier. For some crazy reason, that particular move made her feel powerful and sexy.

"I need to be in you," he said as he dragged his mouth from her breasts and reached for the condoms. "Are you ready for that?"

Her tummy did a slow flip. "Yes. So ready."

He ripped a condom packet from the strip and tore it open. Then he took out the round rubber disc and rolled it onto his penis. Hot eyes met hers as firelight flickered over their bodies.

"I think maybe you should be on top," he said. "Control the pace."

She loved that he thought of it. "I'd like that."

He sat on the couch and she climbed onto his lap, straddling him with her knees on either side of his thighs. He was so gorgeous that she took a minute to look at him, at the defined muscle and glittering eyes of the man who'd saved her from a fate that would have stolen control of her life away and given it into another's hands.

Tallie put her palms on his shoulders to steady herself. Between them, his sheathed dick rose up proud and ready. He held himself steady as she sank down on top of him, her heart hammering and her pulse tapping out a fast rhythm in her veins.

She went slow, getting used to him by degrees. He didn't hurry her. Every inch of him stretched her full and wide, but the sensation was amazing. When she'd sunk to the hilt, they stared at each other.

"That already feels incredible," he said, sounding like he was on the edge of control.

Tallie closed her eyes and tilted her head back. He wasn't lying. It was amazing, and they hadn't even begun to move.

Tallie shifted then. Brett gripped her hips to stop her. "Need a minute," he said. "Or this will be over far too fast."

Tallie found herself laughing, but it was a sexy laugh. A laugh made possible by the power she felt as this man admitted he wanted her so badly he was afraid of coming too quickly.

"I'm starting to wonder about you," she teased. "Have you always had trouble with premature ejaculation?"

His eyes widened. Then he growled, but it wasn't an angry growl. "Never. You're just so fucking sexy. And tight. So damned tight and wet and hot. I want to thrust hard and fast, until I explode, but I also want it to last long enough to make you come again."

Tallie smiled softly as she ran her fingers over his jaw. "You're sweet."

"I don't feel sweet. I feel like the big bad wolf about to eat you up."

Tallie leaned forward to press her mouth to his. But she stopped a whisper away. "Please, big bad wolf. Eat me up. I want you to."

BRETT WANTED CONTROL BADLY, but he'd given it to Tallie because he felt like she needed it. After what she'd been through, he wanted her to make the decisions about how fast and furious things got. He needn't have worried that she'd be too timid or afraid. She fused her mouth to his, shoved her tongue between his lips, and he drank in the hottest, sexiest kiss he'd ever experienced.

He eased his grip on her hips and she started to move, sliding up and almost all the way off of his dick before slamming back down again. Her movements were frantic, intense, and he wrapped his hand around her breasts, tweaking her nipples while she rose and fell again and again.

Soon, she dragged her mouth from his and threw her head back, riding him with abandon. He watched her with awe and lust and his balls tightened ominously as she made little noises that heated his blood.

Brett slipped a finger between them, stroked her clit with every thrust—and Tallie went wild. Her enthusiasm made him feel both protective and possessive of her.

She came in a wild rush, gasping his name and clutching his shoulders. Her pussy gripped him tight, her walls gloving him perfectly. He took a chance more on instinct than anything and flipped her onto her back, spreading her legs wide and driving into her.

She rolled her head back and forth on the cushion, her eyes closed tight, and made the kind of hot noises that told him she was in the middle of a long and beautiful orgasm.

He drew it out as long as he could, though his balls were beginning to hurt with the effort to hold back his own release—and then he let go, driving into her one last time, his orgasm slamming into him and stealing his ability to say a single coherent word. All he could do was groan and enjoy the way his body tingled from head to toe.

Beneath him, Tallie went still. They were cheek to cheek now and he wasn't sure what her stillness meant. Reluctantly, he pulled himself up to look at her.

She opened her eyes and smiled at him, and relief rolled through him. He hadn't realized that he'd been afraid of hurting her until he saw that she wasn't hurt at all.

"Wow," she said.

He snorted. "Yeah, wow."

"And to think I told you no earlier."

He traced a thumb over her lower lip. So soft. "You did, didn't you? What changed your mind?"

She nipped his finger. "Honestly? Sitting in the cold behind that woodpile and not knowing if you were coming back. Made me think about the uncertainties of life. As if I hadn't had enough of a demonstration of that in the past several days," she finished, her mouth twisting into a frown.

"I'm sorry for the uncertainty while you waited for me. And I'm definitely sorry for all that happened to you before that. But I'm damned glad you decided that saying yes was a good idea after all."

Tallie yawned then. Brett skimmed his lips along the edge of her jaw. "I need to go take care of this condom."

"Okay."

He hated withdrawing from her body, but he had to do it or risk the condom loosening and semen spilling out. He got to his feet and Tallie snuggled into the couch cushions. It wasn't the most comfortable place to sleep, but it sure worked great for hot sex.

"I'll be right back. You want anything from the kitchen? Water? Wine? Hot chocolate?" Because he knew she loved it.

"How about some water?"

"You got it, babe."

Brett went to take care of business, disposing of the condom and then looking up to see his face in the mirror. He looked pretty satisfied. Content even. He gave himself a grin and then brushed his teeth and washed his face before going to rejoin Tallie.

He got the water and returned to the living room. The fire was burning merrily, blue flame licking the side of a log as the coals glowed red hot. Tallie lay on the couch with her eyes closed. She'd pulled a blanket over her body.

"Here's your water, babe."

She didn't answer him. A soft snore escaped and

Brett couldn't help but smile. Tallie was completely worn out. He didn't know if it was the walk into the village and all the fresh air, or the smoking hot sex that had done it.

Regardless, he'd watch over her until she woke. And then he'd do the hot sex part again if she let him.

Chapter Eighteen

Brett jerked awake at the buzzing of his phone. It took him a few seconds to realize that's what it was, but once he did, he snatched it up and glanced at the screen.

Ian.

He slid the bar to answer and disentangled himself from the warm body of the woman who'd wrapped herself around him in her sleep. He didn't remember falling asleep while sitting on the couch, and he didn't remember Tallie cuddling up to him. All he remembered was a feeling of contentment and rightness that wasn't typical for him. He wanted to examine those feelings, but he didn't have the time.

"Yeah, boss?" he whispered

He shot a glance at Tallie, who hadn't woken, and walked into the kitchen. He'd pulled on his underwear earlier but he still wasn't clothed. It was chilly, but not freezing.

"How's it going, Brett?"

"Other than the kid rolling a joint in the kitchen, it's fine."

Ian snorted. "He won't be doing that again. His mother took the breach very seriously. He's headed for a rehab program for a few weeks."

"Good. He scared Tallie because I had to leave her parked behind a stack of wood. And give her instructions for what to do if I didn't come back."

Brett could still see her standing behind the wood, a log in her hands, waiting to wallop him with it. He'd taught her a few things tonight, but he hoped she'd never have to use them.

"How's she handling it now?"

Brett thought of her riding him earlier. His dick started to harden at remembered sensations. God that had been hot. He wanted to do it again as soon as possible.

"She's fine."

"Good. Word on the street is that Von Kassel has decided our girl isn't worth the expense of retrieving."

Brett's heart skipped a beat. But he dismissed it and told himself to focus. "Do you believe it?"

"Not entirely. But it might be accurate. Von Kassel's fortunes are in trouble these days. He's mortgaged the family estate and his company is in the red. Of course he still has a personal fortune, but it's not as flush as it once was. And his habits at the gaming tables are well known, which means most casinos aren't extending credit like they once did."

"Boohoo. Poor billionaire."

"He could have put up the one or two hundred grand for one of the other girls. But a million for Tallie Grant was beyond him."

"Sick bastard." They were all sick bastards in his estimation. "How's progress on locating the other girls?"

"It's going. We've liberated four so far. We'll get them all."

Brett was thinking. "If Von Kassel no longer wants Tallie, are you calling to tell me to bring her back?"

"Yes. I'll have your papers waiting at the Delta counter in the Munich airport tomorrow afternoon. There'll be two tickets to Dulles. I'll have someone meet you when you land and take her to a safe house for a day or two."

Brett heard what Ian wasn't saying. "She trusts me, boss. She's not going to want to go with anyone else."

Ian didn't say anything for a long minute and Brett knew he'd been right. Ian had been planning to hand Tallie over to another operative. "And what about you, Brett?"

"What about me?"

"You don't want her going with anyone else, do you?"

Brett frowned. He could do this without admitting to the personal element. To the fact he'd crossed a line and slept with the woman he was supposed to be rescuing and protecting. He wasn't wrong to want to stay with her until she was home safe again.

"No, I don't. I feel responsible for her, boss. I bought her from that sick auction and I had to get her to trust me. It wasn't easy, either. But she does. She's accompanied me across half of Europe and she's done everything I've asked of her. I promised I'd get her home again. And I will."

He thought Ian might be chuckling. "Fine, fine. Bring her to HQ then. We'll get it sorted."

TALLIE WOKE IN A BED. It was a soft, fluffy bed. She was warm and comfortable—and completely alone. She sat bolt upright, eyes darting over the room.

It was Brett's room, the bigger room near the stairs, and light poured in from high windows set in the wall above. She lifted the covers.

Completely naked.

Tallie smiled to herself and dropped them again. She remembered what she'd done.

What *they'd* done.

She closed her eyes as her nipples started to ache. She wanted his mouth on her again. Everywhere. She'd thought they'd do it again last night, but apparently she'd fallen asleep and hadn't woken until now.

He must have carried her up to the bed at some point. She didn't remember it. She'd crashed hard.

Probably because the orgasms wore her out. She couldn't ever remember coming like that before.

Sex was good and fun and necessary. But sex with Brett Wheeler was somehow the most wonderful thing she'd ever experienced. Maybe it was the circumstances, or maybe it was him—all sexy, growly alpha male with a strong protective streak and a raftload of pain that he kept buried deep inside.

Whatever it was, she wanted more.

She started to throw the covers back and find something to slip into, but Brett appeared in the doorway holding two coffee cups. His hair was tousled, his chest was bare, and he wore a pair of sleep pants that hung low on his hips and emphasized those gorgeous grooves above his hipbones that exceptionally fit men had.

She wanted to lick him like a lollipop.

Their gazes met and he arched an eyebrow. Her thoughts must've shown on her face. She grinned. He did too. Then he walked over and handed her the coffee after she'd sat up in bed, tucking the covers around her chest.

"Morning, beautiful." He bent to kiss her cheek, then climbed into bed beside her. He picked up a remote and the television flared to life. An English-language news channel.

They sat in companionable silence. She thought she should feel awkward, but she didn't. Everything felt natural with Brett. Like it was meant to be.

Careful, girlfriend.

No sense indulging in fantastical thinking just because the sex was great and she felt comfortable with him.

"I don't remember coming upstairs last night," she said after she'd had the first sip. He made good coffee.

"You were out cold. And I couldn't take another entire night on the couch or the floor, so I brought us up here. Is it warm enough?"

"Definitely." She was toasty under the covers. And while the air had a hint of coolness to it where it hit her bare shoulders, the radiators in this room worked fine. She could hear them creaking from time to time.

Sunlight beamed across the bed just then, breaking free from the clouds of yesterday. She imagined it must be gorgeous out there with the sun sparkling on fresh snow. The mountains would be glorious in the sunshine too. She couldn't wait to see them, but right now she wanted to stay under the covers with Brett and drink her coffee.

"Got a phone call from the boss this morning," Brett said casually.

"Oh yeah? Good news?"

Brett nodded as he sipped his coffee. "We're headed back to the States."

Tallie's heart did a flip. "Really? I get to go home?"

"Not yet—but soon. We're flying to Washington. A couple of days in a safe house there and then you'll be home."

Ridiculously, her eyes filled with tears. Because she'd thought she'd never really get home again? Or because she didn't want to go quite so soon now that she and Brett had gotten naked together?

One night of blissful fun and it was time to pack up and head home. What did that mean for them?

"I can't wait," she said, though she wasn't sure she meant it nearly as much as she would have only a couple of days ago.

"I thought that might make you happy."

It did, but so did he. Not that she needed to tell him that. They barely knew each other after all. But some things you just knew. Some things felt right because they *were* right. And whatever this thing with Brett was, it definitely felt right. It might only be temporary, sure—but she wanted to see where it went. Even though the idea scared her.

"Of course," she said carefully. "But I'm kinda happy right now too."

She said it casually, coolly. Brett arched an eyebrow and her heart throbbed.

"Oh yeah?"

She smiled. "Well… yeah. Remember the desire to yodel at the mountains? And the window shopping? It's beautiful here."

He grinned. "Is that all that's got you feeling happy?"

She tilted her head to look at him. Handsome. Sexy. And wow did he know what to do with that tongue. "Yep, that's about it," she teased. "Mountains and shopping. Nothing else interesting going on around here."

He took her coffee from her and set it on the bedside table along with his. Then he tugged her down into the mattress and propped himself on his elbows above her. His dick was already hard and she pulled in a breath, barely able to contain a moan of excitement.

"Think I better give you another demonstration, babe. See if a couple orgasms jog your memory about what's making you feel so happy this morning."

She wrapped her arms around him and arched her breasts up to meet his bare chest. "I definitely think you should. I have a terrible memory. I might need a lot of demonstrating to remind me."

Brett dropped his mouth to hers. The world faded to the room around them—and the passion between them.

Chapter Nineteen

IT TOOK TWO HOURS TO GET TO MUNICH. BRETT LEFT the car in long-term parking, left the keys inside, and knew someone would be there to get it before too long. Tallie was still wearing the contacts, but her passport turned out to be the real deal.

Tallulah Margaret Grant of Williamsburg, Virginia.

He'd picked it up at the Delta counter along with their boarding passes. Tallie hadn't said anything but he knew she'd been impressed. Ian had many contacts, in many different places, and he used them to his advantage.

Black Defense International was global, and its ties were myriad. Which is how Brett picked up passports and got first class seats all in one stop. The woman behind the counter was brisk and efficient and gave nothing away, but she handed over the passports as if they'd given them to her for identification in the first place.

"Have a nice flight, Mr. Taylor. Miss Grant," she'd said.

They'd strolled through passport control like it was a walk in the park, had a beer and split a sandwich at a restaurant near the gate, and now they were on the plane in the first class section, with pods of their own where they could stretch out if they wanted.

It was an overnight flight, not typical for Europe to the States, but it meant they'd arrive in the evening in Washington. Tallie poked at the screen in front of her, probably searching for a good movie.

Brett sat back and closed his eyes, thinking about this morning when she'd said she was happy and then teased him by saying it was the mountains and the shopping, not him or the orgasms he'd given her.

He'd known better. And it hadn't concerned him that maybe she was getting too attached.

God she was cute. And sweet and sexy and so damned hot in bed that he'd worried the sheets might combust.

He liked that she wasn't shy with him after what they'd done, and that she was confident enough to tease him about it too. When he'd handed her the coffee this morning, he'd had a vision of handing her coffee in bed every morning—and it hadn't scared him. He'd liked the idea of having someone to wake up with whenever he was home.

But how would that work? He lived in Maryland, when he wasn't traveling, and she lived in Williamsburg. Not exactly a recipe for casual dating and getting to know each other, much less sleeping together every night.

They landed at Washington Dulles some fourteen hours later, after a stop in Atlanta to change planes. Brett took Tallie's hand as they walked down the concourse. All they had were their carryon bags, so no waiting at baggage claim. Most of the winter clothes had stayed behind at the house in Bavaria. Everything would be donated to a shelter so nothing went to waste.

Tallie had her Italian clothing, and Brett had what he'd left Italy with. He'd entered Italy as Carter Walker, arriving on a private jet. His wardrobe would be returned to HQ where he'd pick it up later. Or maybe it was already there. Not that it mattered just now.

When they exited the secure area, Brett spotted a familiar face. Tyler Scott was leaning against a pillar, watching the arrivals as they emerged. Ty straightened and sauntered toward them.

"Hey, Brett," he said.

"Ty."

Ty's gaze slipped appreciatively over Tallie. He smiled at her. Wolfishly, Brett thought.

"And this is Tallie," Brett said, his throat just a little bit tight. "Tallie, this is my coworker, Tyler."

"You can call me Ty, ma'am," Ty said smoothly.

"Hello, Ty."

"Colt's waiting with the SUV," Ty said to Brett.

They followed him through the airport and

outside where Colt pulled up a second later in a black Yukon. Ty took their bags and slung them in the back while Brett opened Tallie's door for her and then went around to join her on the other side. Ty got in and Colt eased into traffic.

"Hi again, Tallie," Colt said as he glanced into the rearview. "I trust you've been okay with this madman?"

Tallie smiled. "Hi, Colt. I'm fine, thanks. We had a lovely drive to Bavaria and Brett was a perfect gentleman."

"Excellent. Always glad to hear he was on his best behavior."

"What's the plan?" Brett asked as they merged onto the highway.

"Taking you to a safe house near HQ for the night. Boss will see you in the morning."

Brett let out a breath. He was glad to hear it. It was early morning in Europe but late here. Tallie's eyes were drooping. The pods on the plane were great, but it wasn't the most restful sleep imaginable. He thought she was probably also excited about being back in the States and so near her family, and that had kept her awake when she should have been sleeping.

He'd slept, but in short stretches. If he could lie down for a while, he'd be a lot fresher when it was time to see Ian and discuss Tallie's immediate future and any potential danger to her.

After almost an hour on the road, Colt pulled up to a plain ranch house on a plain street in a plain neighborhood in a Maryland suburb. There was a truck under the carport and the lights were on inside.

Tallie opened her eyes as the SUV came to a stop and looked around a little bewilderedly. Then her gaze met Brett's and she smiled. He smiled back.

Colt and Ty swung their doors open. Brett told Tallie to wait and then he joined them.

"You two staying here tonight?" he asked as they walked up to the house.

"Nope, just dropping you both off. Gonna clear the place again, then we'll get out of here. Keys to the truck are inside."

Brett went back to the SUV to get Tallie while Colt and Ty checked the house for a breach. It was probably overkill, but that was what the job required. What made them professionals.

When they returned to give the all clear, Brett helped Tallie from the Yukon. She wobbled a little when her feet hit the ground and he put an arm around her to steady her. She leaned into him like she belonged there.

Colt and Ty exchanged a look. Brett shot them both a *fuck you* look in return.

Ty handed over the house keys. "Here you go, man. Sleep well. House is stocked. Weapons and ammo are in the bag on the table."

Brett nodded. His Sig would show up tomorrow, having been shipped home through one of Ian's contacts. They had an entire system for getting weapons into and out of the places they traveled since they couldn't fly armed on commercial flights.

Brett ushered Tallie inside, then locked the door behind them. A glance out the window told him that Colt and Ty had backed onto the street. He turned to find Tallie standing in the middle of the room, peering at everything. She had her arms wrapped around her body. Brett went over to the range bag and took out a Glock 19. There were extra magazines and boxes of ammo as well as another Glock and a knife.

"Are we expecting trouble?" Tallie asked softly.

He looked at her. She seemed a little frightened, a little overwhelmed.

"No, not really. It's a habit, that's all." He wasn't expecting trouble, but even if he was he'd have said the same thing. "Are you tired? Hungry?"

"Maybe a little of both."

"Want a sandwich?"

"How do you know there's anything to make a sandwich?"

"Because I do. This is a safe house, stocked like all safe houses. I'm guessing we've got ham and cheese and roast beef in there. White bread, a toaster. Bet there are cans of soup too. We could recreate our first Bavarian meal."

She smiled. "Would you think I'm crazy if I said I miss that place?"

"No."

He kind of missed it too. Was it just last night—or

the night before?—that he'd stripped her naked and fucked her in front of that fire? Aside from the incident with the damned teenager and his pot stash, their stay in Bavaria had been wonderful. He'd never forget the intimacy of listening to her talk about her parents, about how her dad fixed hot chocolate to help her sleep, and about her dad's death.

Brett didn't usually trade confessions with anyone, but lying on the floor in that living room while she drank cocoa and asked him questions had loosened his tongue in ways that still surprised him. There were still things he hadn't told her yet, but he could almost imagine himself doing so.

"I wish we could have stayed longer," she said. "Just a couple days more."

He set the pistol down and went over to take her into his arms. She came easily, wrapping her arms around his waist and laying her cheek against his shirt. A wave of protectiveness washed over him.

"Maybe we'll go back there one day."

She tipped her head back to gaze up at him. "Careful, Brett, or I'll think you plan to keep seeing me once this is over. Or maybe you're just saying it to make me think so."

He threaded a hand through her hair, cupping the back of her head. He liked touching her. Just touching her. It didn't have to be sexual, though he didn't mind that either.

"Would that be a bad thing? Seeing me once this is over?"

"A few nights ago you told me not to expect a relationship if we had sex."

He swallowed. "I know. But I like you. I like the way I feel with you. And I don't know if it'd work out, because I still have this crazy job, but maybe we can leave it open instead of closing the book when you go home again."

She arched an eyebrow and grinned at him suddenly. "If that's your way of asking me out on a real date, then it's no wonder you don't do relationships. But I accept your request for a date, Brett Wheeler. Because I like you too."

TALLIE'S SLEEP was all screwed up, but it didn't much matter because when she was awake, Brett was awake too. Which meant they spent that time exploring all the ways in which they could make each other mindless with pleasure.

She'd felt nostalgic for the chalet in Bavaria, but they'd had sex in the shower and the bed in this house and, memorably, on the kitchen counter. That had been just like a porn movie, but way better because it wasn't about silly screwing positions for a camera. No, whenever Brett did anything to her body, he did it with the express intention of making her beg him for more.

When she woke up again, it was after ten and the bed was empty beside her. She yawned and stretched and went to take another shower. Only after she'd dressed and fixed her hair did she walk out into the small living room.

Brett was there with Colt and Ty. She'd heard talking after she'd gotten out of the shower so she wasn't surprised they were there.

"Good morning, gentlemen," she said brightly.

All three looked up. All three wore appreciative expressions on their faces, which bolstered her ego, but it was only Brett who looked at her with a knowing expression on his. It was intimacy and a care that went deeper than just the job of protecting her, and her heart thumped.

He meant so much to her. Already.

Was it possible to love someone this quickly? Or was it simply the power of their physical connection that made her all warm and tingly inside?

"Morning, Tallie," Colt said. "You sleep okay?"

She felt herself blushing. "It wasn't bad."

Ty was studying her carefully. It took her aback for a moment but then she remembered she hadn't put the contacts in this morning. Her eyes were unveiled in all their craziness today. She'd hated growing up with such an obvious physical difference, but she didn't feel that way anymore. It was a thing she shared with her dad, a connection that no one could take away.

Tallie arched an eyebrow at Ty and he looked sheepish. "I'm sorry for staring," he said. "I bet that happens a lot."

"It does. And it's okay. You don't see two different colored eyes everyday."

"No, definitely not."

"If you're done staring, Ty," Brett began.

"I'm done. I already apologized."

Tallie came over and sank onto the couch beside Brett. She didn't touch him, though. What was between them was private. Besides, these were his coworkers. Friends too, she thought. But coworkers nonetheless. What he chose to tell them was his business.

Brett picked up a phone from the coffee table and held it out to her. "All your contacts are restored. The number is new, though. Your suitcase is beside that chair." He nodded toward it. "You'll have to let us know if anything is missing."

Tallie glanced in surprise at the black suitcase sitting next to an empty chair. She hadn't even noticed it until he pointed it out. She took the phone. "Thank you," she said past the tightness in her throat.

She'd wanted her phone so badly when she'd woken without it in the palazzo. She'd felt lost without it. And now she stared at it like it was a foreign thing. A thing she didn't know how to use or if she even wanted to.

But Mom was on the other end of this phone. And Sharon. Bill, too. All the people she knew and cared for.

She hit the contacts and scrolled through her favorites. Even Josie.

Tallie teared up at her sister's name and picture. It was a pic of Josie with a huge grin on her face. Tallie had taken it on their last trip together. Josie was dead, but Tallie couldn't erase her from her phone.

"Hey," Brett said, dropping an arm around her. She turned into his shoulder and breathed him in, trying not to cry.

"It's okay. I'm okay," she said, her voice muffled.

His other hand came up to stroke her hair. She could hear his voice, pitched low just for her.

"I'm sorry, babe. I didn't know it would upset you to get your phone back. I should have waited until we were alone."

She turned the phone so he could see precisely what had upset her. He squeezed her tighter then. She heard movement and then the door opened and closed. Colt and Ty were gone. She knew it without raising her head to look.

She pushed herself back and met Brett's concerned gaze as she swiped away a tear. "I shouldn't have looked at my contacts. I don't know why I did. I just—I couldn't erase her name and picture, you know? I'm not sure I ever will."

"It's okay. You don't have to, honey."

Tallie sniffled. "I chased them away, didn't I?"

"Nah, they're big boys. They can handle a lady crying. They went outside to give us some privacy."

"I'm sorry."

"Don't be."

"I wasn't sure… I didn't think you'd want them to know about, uh, us. And now they must."

"I don't care if they do. Did you think I was planning to hide it?"

"I don't know. Maybe."

He frowned. Then he threaded his fingers through hers and raised her hand to his mouth, pressing a kiss to it. "You're thoughtful and sweet, Tallie Grant. But any man who wants to hide that he's dating you doesn't deserve you."

She gave him a tremulous smile. "Thank you." Tallie pulled in a calming breath as she held up the phone again. "Does this mean I can call my mother now?"

"Soon."

"Is the danger over then?"

"We're reasonably certain it is. The people who took you are in the business of selling women for profit. They got their profit and they have no desire to risk their operation by coming after you again. You were grabbed because you were convenient, and unusual enough to fetch a high price."

"What about going home?"

"Later today. We're going to HQ first. Ian wants to meet you."

Chapter Twenty

The place Brett and the others called HQ didn't look like anything other than an office building. It was a black building with black windows, and it was located in the vicinity of a few government agencies on a northeast corridor between DC and Baltimore.

It was much smaller than the government agencies they passed, but Tallie quickly realized that it would be a mistake to think it wasn't a state of the art facility.

Colt and Ty had gone ahead of them and were waiting in the parking garage when Brett pulled in. Tallie had her phone in the purse that had been inside her suitcase.

She often took a smaller crossbody bag, like the one she'd been wearing when she'd been abducted, for the days walking through the markets. She left her bigger purse in the hotel because it was heavier, but that was the one she carried most days. Her credit cards were inside, her library card, her grocery store card.

She'd had her passport and driver's license in the crossbody, along with a comb, lipstick, and her pen and small notebook.

It was, in many ways, a relief to have her things back. It was also weird. Unsettling, like she'd stepped into a time machine and didn't quite recognize who she used to be now that she'd returned.

Brett was her link to normalcy. Hard to believe given that a few days ago he'd been the connection to the bad things that had happened.

She'd already put on a white button down shirt and black pants from the Italian clothing Brett had bought her, but she added a scarf of her own. She kept the Italian ankle boots on, however, because she'd taken one pair of shoes with her to France and those had disappeared when she'd been abducted.

It was a process to get inside the building, but once inside they passed down a sleek hallway with gray walls and tiled floors until they reached a conference room. The chairs were plush black leather, and the table was a beautiful zebra wood with a high gloss finish. Tallie thought perhaps an ornate French cabinet at one end and some modern art would complete the look, but she wasn't here to decorate.

Colt and Ty left them and it was just her and Brett alone in the room. "Want something to drink?" he asked as she stood at one end and looked at her surroundings.

"No, I'm fine. Thanks."

Soon, another door opened and a tall, strikingly handsome man dressed in a fitted black shirt, black combat boots and urban camouflage pants walked in. He had dark hair and blue eyes and he smiled at her as he came over and offered his hand.

"Hello, Miss Grant. I'm Ian Black."

"Mr. Black. Thank you for all you've done for me."

He smiled and jerked his head toward Brett. "It's all Brett's doing, I assure you."

"I've already thanked him. And I know there are things he couldn't have done without your help, so I really do appreciate everything. I know it's cost a lot of money and time to get me home."

"It's what we do, Miss Grant."

"Please call me Tallie."

"Tallie then. You can call me Ian." He motioned to a chair. "Please."

Tallie sat down and Brett sat beside her. Ian took the chair at the end of the table and leaned back to fold his hands over his flat stomach. "I'm sure you're aware that you shouldn't talk about what happened," he began.

"It's been mentioned. But how does keeping silent about being abducted and sold into slavery help anyone? Shouldn't women know it's possible? That just because they're educated or have money doesn't mean they won't be targeted?"

"They should know, absolutely," Ian said. "But

this is an active operation, Tallie. We want to catch the organizers of this terrible auction, and we want to stop them. Not just stop them, but make it impossible for them to do business ever again. If you tell your story, you do two things. You draw their attention to you again—and you draw attention to them. They'll go even farther underground than they already are."

"Then I won't talk about it." She hadn't been sure she wanted to anyway, but she'd been thinking—what if talking helped others? Didn't she owe it to people to do so? That raised another question in her mind. "What have you told my mother about what happened? What am I supposed to tell her?"

"Your mother believes you were kidnapped, along with other tourists, and held for ransom by a radical group operating in the south of France. The demand went through the embassy, and we were called in to negotiate. You have spent the past few days being debriefed and checked out medically."

Tallie arched an eyebrow. "And my mother just accepted that she couldn't speak to me? Or see me?"

Ian flashed white teeth in a smile. "It wasn't quite that easy, but she was persuaded in the end. She's had continual updates on you and a liaison she could reach at any time of day or night."

"You've certainly thought of everything."

"That's our job."

Tallie wanted to glance at Brett for support but she didn't. "And do I go home now?"

"When we're done here, yes. Brett will drive you

back to Williamsburg. You should call your mother and let her know you're coming. Hearing your voice will go a long way toward relieving her."

Tallie knew what Ian was going to say next so she jumped in before he could. "If you plan to tell me not to talk about a certain woman I met in the Brenner Pass, then you're wasting your breath. I've already been told and I'm not going to say a word about her. She didn't strike me as a terrible person, but I suppose I'm not much of a judge of people anyway. I hope you find her and she gets what she wants from you."

Ian looked mildly amused at this little speech. Then he laughed. "In fact, I *was* going to ask you not to mention Natasha to anyone. As dangerous as the people who took you are, she's a hundred times more lethal. Best not to draw her attention to you."

"She knew who I was."

"She did. But she has no reason to seek you out. Unless you start talking about her."

"Not happening."

"Excellent." Ian glanced over at Brett, who hadn't said anything at all during their conversation. "I'm sending you home with one of my best operatives, Tallie. But you already know Brett is good as what he does. He'll be with you for a few days, in your home, in order to make sure all is well. We've upgraded your security system, and he'll show you how to use it."

"Thank you."

Ian stood. "If you'll excuse us, I need to talk to Brett alone for a few minutes. Then you'll be free to go. Now would be a good time to call your mother, by the way."

Brett got up to follow Ian. Before he did, he gave her shoulder a squeeze. Tallie waited until they were gone and then took out her phone. She stared at it for a while before she sent the first text to her mother, Sharon, and Bill.

Hey, everyone. I'm coming home.

IT TOOK a little over three hours to get to Williamsburg, and that was with moderate traffic. Brett hated to think how much time it would take if the traffic was bad.

It was a pretty city with a throwback feel, especially in the historic area. Tallie's house wasn't far from the town center, though it wasn't technically in the historic district. Still, she could walk to the main parts of the historic area if she desired.

He first took her to her mother's business because that's where she wanted to go. Mary Claire Grant Interiors was located in the historic district. He could tell it was pricey the instant they walked inside. It was packed with French antiques artfully arranged with fabrics and knickknacks.

In spite of being a guy and not giving much of a shit about decorating, even he had to admit the vignettes in the shop were pretty and inviting. They spoke to people, told them it would be great to sit in this chair and read a book, or lie in that bed and eat breakfast off the bone china dishes arranged on a pretty tray. He imagined people opened their wallets quite easily once they spent time in the shop.

The reunion with Tallie's mother was tearful and fraught. It was obvious that her mother loved her. It was also obvious that the woman was a control freak and a perfectionist. Brett thought of Tallie's pained admission that she wasn't her mother's favorite, and then her regret at saying it.

He didn't know what a relationship with a parent was like, not really, so he had no wisdom to offer. Still, he didn't think her mother had a clue how overbearing she could be. Mary Claire Grant wanted to take charge and make everything just so. That Tallie didn't really need her interference probably hadn't occurred to her.

Brett suspected that rather than Josie being the perfect daughter, she'd been the one least likely to go her own way. Another observation he wasn't making to Tallie just yet. Maybe never. Depended on if she asked him, or if it came up ever again.

Tallie introduced Brett as her friend. They'd agreed on the way down that returning home for Tallie would be hard enough without adding the element of a relationship with Brett. That could wait until another day—except that her mother was a shrewd lady and she kept eyeing Brett suspiciously.

Still, he'd left it to Tallie to decide when the time was right. After everything she'd been through, he wasn't about to insist that she tell her mother they were dating the minute they arrived in Williamsburg —not when it was still new to them both and they didn't know where it was going.

After an hour in her mother's company, Brett could see the strain in the tightness around Tallie's mouth. She was ready to go home.

She pasted on a bright smile and set her teacup on the table that perched between the plush couches in her mother's beautifully appointed office.

"Well, Mom—I think we should be going. I want to get home and get settled."

Mrs. Grant set her cup down. "Yes, I completely understand. I have a client scheduled soon anyway. You go home and rest, Tallulah. Take as much time as you need before you return to work."

Tallie's smile was brittle. "Thank you, but I think I'll be coming in for a little bit tomorrow. When will the French shipment arrive? Did they give you a window?"

"Another two weeks, I think."

"Good. I think you'll like the pieces. I've recreated an inventory for you. I'll email it a bit later."

"That sounds good, darling." Mrs. Grant's gaze strayed to him. Brett didn't twitch a muscle. "Where will you be staying, Mr. Wheeler?"

"He's staying at my house, Mom," Tallie interjected before he could answer. "In the guest room."

Tallie got to her feet. Brett followed. Her mother sat on the couch and stared up at them both. "Well," she drawled in her cultured tones, "I thought he might be staying in a hotel."

"No," Tallie replied. "Brett is a friend, and I have a guest room for friends."

Mrs. Grant lifted an eyebrow. "Very well." She stood and held out a hand to Brett. He took it, but he didn't squeeze. "It was nice to meet you."

"It's been a pleasure meeting you, ma'am."

Mrs. Grant hugged Tallie hard, in spite of the apparent strain, and then Brett and Tallie went outside. Brett opened the car door to let Tallie inside, then went around and got into the driver's seat. He started the car and backed out of the parking space.

"I'm sorry," Tallie said. "She can be a bit much sometimes."

"It's fine, Tallie. She's protective of you. Understandable."

Tallie shook her head and covered her face with her palms. "I should have told her I was seeing you. She clearly thinks I am anyway. You must think I'm ashamed of you or something."

"I don't. I think you've had a rough couple of weeks and you don't owe anyone an explanation for how you ease back into your life. Not even me."

She lifted her head to look at him. "You really are amazing, you know that?"

He shot her a grin. "I aim to please."

"You do, Brett. You definitely do." She sighed. "I know she didn't believe me, but the questions would have been even worse if I'd admitted we were seeing each other. I just didn't want to deal with it."

"Baby, I get it. I honestly do."

She lay her head back on the seat. "Thank you."

When they got to her place, Brett went inside first to turn off the alarm. Tallie stood just inside the entry and watched him. He couldn't get an idea how she was feeling so he returned and put his hands on her shoulders.

"You okay?"

She looked up at him. "Yes. Fine. It just feels strange to be here after everything. I swear I feel like I was abducted by aliens and they just dropped me off again with no explanation."

"Those feelings will pass. It'll take a little time."

"You didn't make me wait while you walked through the house with your gun," she said as she looked around her entryway.

"Didn't need to. You have a new alarm system, remember?"

"Oh. Yes. I guess that makes a difference."

"I'll show you how to use it. There are cameras too. Nobody's getting in here without you knowing about it."

"That's good." She nibbled her bottom lip. "You're definitely staying for a while, right?"

He and Ian had discussed it when they'd left Tallie in the conference room. Heinrich Von Kassel was currently in Monaco enjoying the casinos. There was no indication he was still offering a bounty for Tallie or that he intended to. There was no bounty even being talked about in the soldier-for-hire community right now. As far as they could tell, Tallie was safe. But he was still staying to make sure.

"Yes," he said. "I'll be here."

Tallie's eyes twinkled suddenly and he felt like a weight lifted from him. He hated seeing her worry. "Bodyguard with benefits?" she purred.

He put his hands on her hips and dragged her against him. Wouldn't take long for his dick to harden if she stayed there. "All the benefits you want, honey."

"Lucky me," she said. Then she stood on tiptoe and kissed him.

Chapter Twenty-One

Sharon: *ARE YOU SURE YOU'RE OKAY?*

Tallie smiled as she picked up her phone. She'd been home for three hours now and she was starting to get used to being here. She'd missed her little house with its pretty backyard and all the items she'd selected that decorated the rooms and made everything nice and welcoming.

Her house was *her.* Even though her mother thought she leaned too hard toward old-world style, she didn't think so. She loved her carved cabinets and oriental rugs, and she loved the modern touches she sprinkled in like salt.

Brett had said her house felt like the kind of place anyone would be thrilled to come home to. That made her happy. Then he'd pulled her down on the chaise that looked out on the garden and kissed her into a quivering bundle of need.

They might have gotten naked then, but her

grocery order arrived. She'd placed it right before they reached her mother's shop and nearly forgot about it until the doorbell rang. Then she'd had to clean out the refrigerator from all the stuff that had rotted over the past couple of weeks and put everything away. Brett helped her.

Right now he was outside raking her leaves. She watched him work, a warm feeling glowing inside her. Calvin had never raked her leaves. Or done anything domestic, come to think of it. He'd always told her to hire people for that.

Tallie: *I'm fine. It's over now and I'm home.*

Sharon: *I want to come see you. Make sure for myself.*

Tallie: *Come for dinner. 7ish? I want you to meet someone anyway.*

What was she doing, inviting Sharon for dinner when she'd only just gotten home again? She hadn't even cleared it with Brett. What if he didn't want to meet anyone tonight?

The muscles in his shoulders bunched and flexed as he raked. She'd told him he didn't have to do it, but she had many trees surrounding her small yard and the leaves had seriously piled up. She would have hired someone, but Brett said that was ridiculous when he could take care of it.

Sharon: *Seriously? Hang on a sec.*

Tallie waited for Sharon to return from whatever she was doing and finish the thought but her phone rang instead. "I should have known you'd call," Tallie said with a laugh.

"Well, hell, I should have called you in the first place. But I didn't know if you'd be asleep or something. And now you want to cook dinner and have me meet somebody? Your mother said you were held hostage with a group of tourists. I kind of thought I should come over and take care of *you*."

"You know that's not common knowledge, right? About the hostage situation, I mean."

"I know. She had to tell me because you weren't answering my texts or calls. I was worried about you."

Tallie sighed. She hated lying to her best friend, but she understood why she had to do it. "It wasn't pleasant, but I'm fine. I just want to forget about it."

"But you want me to meet someone. Someone you met while you were a hostage?"

"Yes, someone I met. He's a personal security expert and he's, um, staying with me for a few days. I met him after the hostage thing. During the, um, rescue and stuff."

"Oh my God—staying with you? Like *with* you? Or with you? And isn't that awfully fast if it's *with* you?"

Tallie laughed. Only Sharon could complicate the situation and make everything sound somewhat confusing at the same time. "Well, I don't know which of those withs is which—but he's staying in my bedroom. With me."

Because she'd never been able to hide stuff like that from Sharon and she wasn't going to try now. Sharon would see straight through her.

"Not that my mother needs to know that," she added. "She thinks he's a friend who's here to help set up my alarm system and make sure I feel safe."

"And she bought that?"

Tallie laughed. "Not really, but I wasn't ready to admit the truth to her. She never liked Calvin. I'm not letting her chase this one away before we've even gotten good and started."

"And he's a bodyguard?"

"Yes."

"Is he there to bodyguard you?"

"Um, he's here to make sure everything's okay."

"Why wouldn't it be, Tallie?"

Oooh, Sharon was too shrewd sometimes. "I don't know. I just know he's here and I feel safer for it."

"Okay, okay. Don't get your panties in a twist. Does this bodyguard have a name?"

"His name is Brett. He's from Texas, but he lives and works in DC."

"Oh dear. That's a little far—unless he lives on the Virginia side, maybe?"

"The Maryland side."

"Well it's not the West Coast, so at least there's that."

Tallie didn't want to think about how far away Brett lived. "So will you come? It'll just be something simple. Wine and pasta and a salad, maybe."

"Of course I'll come. But are you really sure? You just got home. And you've been through a lot."

Tallie's throat tightened. Sharon had no idea how

true that was. "I'm sure. Yes, it was an ordeal and I'll probably have nightmares and stuff—but I feel like I have to get back to normal. Because I'm afraid if I don't, it'll start to get into my head and then I'll feel worse, not better."

"Can I bring anything?"

"Just your sunny smile. I missed you."

"Aw, that's sweet. I'll be there. But I can't come empty-handed. I'll pick up a chocolate cake at Spencer's. I know how much you love them. No arguing."

Tallie couldn't help but smile. "Fine, no arguing. See you later."

"See you! Can't wait to meet the bodyguard!"

Sharon hung up and Tallie shook her head. That's why they were friends. Whatever Tallie threw at her bestie, she went with it. She was always supportive, no matter how crazy the idea—and Sharon probably thought Tallie was crazy for shacking up with a man she'd only known for a few days.

Hell, maybe she was. But life was too short and uncertain to not go after what you wanted. If Tallie had learned anything the past couple of weeks, that was the most glaring.

———

BRETT ENJOYED HAVING dinner with Tallie and her friend. Watching her in her own environment, he appreciated her even more than he had before. She was graceful and beautiful and so full of life and energy.

Tallie glowed when she was taking care of others. She liked fixing food and sitting at her round kitchen table. She'd set it with a white tablecloth, fresh flowers, and simple white plates that she placed on top of silver chargers. She added polished silverware and crisp white napkins. The whole thing was elegant and welcoming.

Just like her house. He'd thought her mother's shop was inviting, but Tallie's house was more so. He'd spent the first part of his life in rundown trailer parks, and then he'd spent time moving around to different foster homes, some nice and homey, others kind of rundown and crappy. He had never, not once, thought about decorating anywhere he lived with anything more than the basics. Couch, chairs, bed, tables, television. Preferably a big television.

But Tallie's surroundings were designed to make a person feel cared for and interested. That was how she designed her dinner party, too, even though it was a party of three and not dozens.

Crystal, china, silver, nice wine and simple food that she prepared with ease. She'd confessed, while he chopped onions for her, that she had a couple of favorite go to recipes and those were the ones she trotted out when she needed something on short notice.

Which is how he found himself sitting down with two women, eating fettuccine primavera in a white cream sauce, garlic bread, and a salad of greens, ripe tomatoes, and feta cheese that she drizzled with a honey vinaigrette. For dessert, there was coffee and a chocolate cake that Sharon had brought with her.

Brett liked Sharon. She was taller than Tallie and quite a bit fuller figured, with dark hair and intelligent eyes. When Tallie had answered the door, the two women hugged and sniffled before Tallie finally broke off and said, "Sharon, I want you to meet Brett."

Sharon had asked a few pointed questions about Tallie's captivity and rescue, but she accepted it when Brett told her there were things he wasn't authorized to talk about. Once she seemed to understand that her friend was doing well and adjusting, she left the topic and moved on to other things.

"Anything interesting at work?" Tallie asked as she twisted pasta onto her fork. "Sharon is a real estate agent," she added in an aside to Brett.

Sharon swallowed the bite of food she'd taken. "Oh my gosh, the crazy shit that happens sometimes. I took a listing for a house just last week where I had to get the photographer to *not* take photos of the dungeon in the basement. I mean that thing was unreal. When I told the couple they might need to put some of that stuff in storage until we sold the house, you'd have thought I asked them to renovate the kitchen or something. All I said was, hey, could we take down the sex swing and gothic punishment table with straps and maybe put the whips and chains away for a while? You know, nothing unreasonable." She shook her head. "Nope, they didn't want to do it. I think they will once they realize no one is making an offer with those things there. I mean somebody might, but most people can't see past that stuff."

"Oh my goodness," Tallie said.

"Right?" Sharon replied. "I don't care if they want to get kinky with each other. I just care that some of those things could be off-putting to buyers! Just pack it away for a while. That's all. Tuck the butt plugs into the bedside table for heaven's sake and enjoy all you want. But maybe lay off the dungeon until you get to the new place."

"Takes all kinds," Tallie said.

"Sure does. Oh by the way," she added casually, twisting her fork into the pasta. "I met a guy."

Tallie dropped her fork. "What? You should have led with that! What guy? What does he do? Do I know him?"

Sharon laughed as she held up a hand. "Whoa there, Tal. I just met him a couple of days ago. He came into the office looking for a house, and we hit it off. He took me to coffee yesterday at the Williamsburg Inn. That's where he's staying. He's moving to the area from New York."

"The Williamsburg Inn is a very nice place," Tallie told Brett. "Expensive. The Queen of England and Prince Phillip have stayed there. Twice."

"Yes, it's definitely expensive," Sharon said, looking sort of pleased.

"Who is this guy?"

"His name is Robert and he has his own business. I don't know precisely what he does yet. There's only so much prying a girl can do on the first date."

Tallie lifted her wine glass in a salute. "That is very true. I just hope he's a great guy. He needs to be if he's going to date you."

"I hope so too. I mean so far he's fabulous, but that's a couple of afternoons of house hunting and a coffee date. I'm taking him to some houses tomorrow as well. He's, uh, looking at some pretty fabulous properties. Two mil and up."

"Oh wow." Tallie leaned forward, a grin on her face. "Is he going to need a decorator?"

Sharon laughed. "If he buys one of these houses, I'll bet he does."

They talked about other things after that. Brett mostly listened, though Tallie tried to make him a part of the conversation. But he was used to observing so that's what he did.

And what he observed were two friends who genuinely adored each other. He was happy for Tallie that she had that, especially since she'd lost her sister nearly a year ago.

After a couple of hours, Sharon insisted she had to go. They'd had cake and coffee and Brett had quietly cleaned up while Tallie entertained. When she'd realized he was doing it, she jumped up to help him but he told her to sit back down and enjoy her friend.

Sharon stared at him as if he'd materialized on

the spot while riding a unicorn or something, but then she smiled and winked at him before turning back to Tallie and their conversation. He took that as approval.

Once Sharon was gone and he'd locked up for the night, Tallie looked at him shyly. They hadn't made love in her house yet, mostly because they'd gotten interrupted earlier, and he thought she might be feeling somewhat like she'd landed in the Twilight Zone.

The return to normal life after a mission was sometimes hell. It was a full stop where everything was suddenly ordinary, and you wanted to scream at everyone that they were being complacent because the big bad scary world was out there waiting to eat them alive.

Brett went over and gathered her to him. She was small and perfect in his arms. He liked having her there. She slipped her arms around him and lay her cheek against his chest. He kissed the top of her head.

"I'm not expecting anything, Tallie. In fact, just holding you while we sleep will be enough."

Was he going soft? Colt and Ty would rib the hell out of him if they could see him now. Jace, however, would probably smirk knowingly.

"Let's go to bed and see what happens, shall we?"

He scooped her into his arms and carried her upstairs to the master bedroom. He really did intend to sleep, but when he set Tallie down, she went to work on his clothes, ripping his shirt over his head, unbuttoning his jeans and shoving them down his hips. When she dropped to her knees and took him in her mouth, he thought he'd die.

Fortunately, he didn't. He didn't let her make him come, either. When he was getting close, he dragged her up and stripped her while she protested that she wanted to finish.

Only when he had her naked did he let her touch him again. He pulled her onto the bed, urged her up to straddle his face, then went to work making her come while she sucked his cock.

When it was over, when they'd both come apart and pieced themselves back together again, she lay in his arms and fell asleep.

Brett wanted to sleep, too. But it wouldn't happen. He lay awake and thought about a lot of things. But mostly, he thought about Tallie and the way he felt. There were things going on inside him, things he didn't understand.

He'd known her a little over a week, but it felt like a lifetime. It felt… *right.*

But he had to be mistaken because he'd thought he'd felt this way before—and he'd been seriously, seriously wrong that time. How could he trust himself to know for sure?

Chapter Twenty-Two

It took some time, but life slowly got back to normal. Tallie returned to work, though she found herself daydreaming a lot more than usual about what it might be like to have her own design studio. The kind of place where she took on big clients but also rose to the challenges of smaller budgets.

And then there were the buying trips overseas. She didn't want to go alone, though it wasn't time to consider it anyway. The buying trips would start again in the spring, but that was a few months away. That gave her time to talk to her mother about organizing trips where she took clients with her and they learned how to shop the markets.

The biggest change in her life was Brett. He stayed with her for five days, and then he announced one morning that he had to get back to Black Defense International's headquarters in Maryland. Her heart fell and then started to beat very hard.

Brett tipped her head back with his fingers beneath her chin—those long, perfect fingers that knew just how to strum her body into quivering orgasms—and looked at her very seriously.

"We aren't done, Tallie. I have to go back to work, but I'll be down here whenever I have time. And you can come see me if you want to. You'll like my house, I think. Well, you'll like the view anyway. You'll probably shriek at the decorating."

She put her hand on his wrist, felt his pulse. He meant something to her. It hurt to see him go. "I'd like to see your house."

"We'll talk every night, and I'll be back as soon as I can."

"Are you sure, Brett? I mean you've done your job where I'm concerned. You don't have to keep coming back if you don't want to."

He kissed her, hard and swift. Her lips stung. She welcomed it. "I want to," he whispered against her mouth. "I'm going to."

"Okay."

She hated that he was leaving even though it meant that everything was back to normal. Her life was hers again, and she was no longer in danger. Yet she'd been changed by what happened to her and she couldn't pretend she hadn't been.

"Thanksgiving is next week," she said, heart thrumming. "Will you come?"

"I will if I can."

"It's at Mom's. I'll understand if you don't want to."

"I want to."

He kissed her again and then he picked up his bag and went out to his truck. She stood in the doorway, watching him toss his stuff inside and then turn to her. He put his fingers to his lips and blew her a kiss.

Tallie stood in the door as he backed out of the driveway, her heart beating so hard she thought she might pass out. She didn't want him to go. She didn't know if he'd ever come back, no matter what he said.

If they were a couple. If they were in love with each other—

Tallie clutched her hand over her heart, stunned at the idea of it. But her eyes stung and her heart ached and she knew it was what she wanted. They hadn't said those words, but she felt them in her soul.

Not even a month with him. Not even two full weeks.

And she was in love.

THE DRIVE back to Maryland felt worse with every mile. Brett hated leaving Tallie in Williamsburg but he'd been there five days and there was absolutely no sign of Heinrich von Kassel or anyone else coming to take her away. She'd been in the wrong place at the wrong time, and she'd paid a high price for it.

But it was over. She was safe and it was time to get

back to what he did best.

He reached HQ late that afternoon and went up to the operations center. Ian was in his office—not the one that he greeted potential clients in, but the one inside the ops center—when Brett used his palm print to gain entry to the secure area and walked inside.

The boss looked up as Brett strode into the heartbeat of ops, smiling as he approached. Ian stood and waited for him to walk into the glassed-in office.

"The prodigal son returns. How's Miss Grant doing in Colonial Williamsburg?"

Brett had a flash of Tallie standing in her door, watching him drive away with her heart in her eyes. He hadn't wanted to leave her, and his gut had churned with chaotic feelings as he did so.

"Her house is secure. She's back to work at her mother's business and all seems normal."

"Excellent." Ian's brow furrowed. "I liked her. Tougher than she looks."

"Tallie Grant is definitely not an idiot."

Ian looked speculative. "She speaks fluent French. Knows where to find antique treasures in France. She has connections—she could be useful to us."

"No," Brett said coldly.

Ian arched an eyebrow. "Ah, I see."

"See what?"

Shit.

"Nothing, kid."

Ian called them all kid sometimes, even though he wasn't much older than they were. Ten years max,

Brett thought, which would put him at thirty-eight. But even then Brett wasn't sure he was right about that.

Brett backpedaled. "She could give us information, maybe. If she returns to France. She won't go alone, but she's thinking of taking clients on buying tours. And if she does, she might have some observations."

Ian seemed to consider it. "That would be enough. You didn't think I wanted her to engage in ops did you?"

Brett had no idea what the boss wanted sometimes. "No. She's not trained. Or suited to the work."

"No, she's not."

Brett's heart ached suddenly. He was here and Tallie was three hours away. No more Bavarian chalets and snowy walks together. "What do you have for me?"

Ian returned to his desk and sat. He flipped through some papers. "Heinrich von Kassel is still in Monaco, losing a mint at the tables. He seems to have had an infusion of cash from somewhere, but I think he's moved on from the idea of finding Tallie. He doesn't seem to know her identity anyway. I've been paying close attention to that. The only people who know her real name are those who work for the Syndicate. And they aren't about to risk stealing her away from her life in America."

"They got their money," Brett said bitterly. "Any luck on tracing it?"

Ian shook his head. "None yet. I've got Lane Jordan on it. He's the best IT person we've got so if there's any way to do it, he'll get it done."

Brett felt marginally better, though he still didn't like that there were people out there—criminals—who knew Tallie's identity.

"Don't worry," Ian said, seeming to sense his turmoil. "It's really not in the Syndicate's best interest to snatch her again."

Brett rubbed his forehead. "No, I know it's not."

Still, he was unsettled at the idea of leaving her. But what was he supposed to do? Move to Williamsburg and follow her everywhere she went?

His mind flashed to his mother then. She'd been in the next room and he hadn't been able to save her. She'd been killed with him lying only a few feet away and he'd had no idea it was happening.

Brett gritted his teeth. Where the fuck had that come from?

"Everything okay?" Ian asked.

"Yeah. Just thinking about something. Old memory."

His mother had nothing to do with Tallie. Nothing. Why think of the memory at all?

Because it made him feel lost and out of control, that's why. He'd left Tallie in Williamsburg because there was no reason to stay, but he still wanted to be there with her. Protecting her.

Jace Kaiser walked into the ops center then, looking about a million times happier than he had a few months ago. Jace had always had a closed off, secretive look about him. Now he looked like a kid who'd gotten a pony nearly every time Brett saw him. The dude *glowed* with happiness.

"Hey, Brett. How was Europe?" he asked when he got close enough.

"European."

Jace snorted. "Heard you saw my sister in Austria." His expression turned serious. Brett was one of the few who knew that Calypso was Jace's sister. "How'd she look?"

"Determined," Brett said. "Otherwise, she looked fine. She was nice to Tallie. Not nice to me."

"I don't think she entirely trusts us," Jace said, glancing at Ian.

"She will eventually," Ian said. "That's the goal anyway."

"Yeah, but I don't know if we should trust *her*," Jace added.

Brett couldn't say that he disagreed with that statement. Calypso—Natasha—was a loose cannon in the broadest sense of the word. She worked for the Gemini Syndicate and she had a string of kills that would put the best military snipers to shame. She hadn't lived as long as she had by being trusting or trustworthy. She was a woman who took her opportunities as they came.

Ian's phone rang then. He glanced at it before picking it up. "Gotta take this, ladies."

Jace and Brett stepped outside the office and

pulled the door closed.

"Hey, Jace?"

"Yeah?"

"Can I ask you something?"

Jace shrugged. "Sure. I may not give you an answer though."

"Nah, it's nothing like that." Brett gazed at the heads bent over desks in the ops center, the giant screens that took up an entire wall and showed the hot spots where Ian had Bandits engaged. It was a military operation, but on a broader scale. The rules were different for them than for the military—meaning there often were no rules.

This was his life, the life he loved—and yet, he felt a strange kind of emptiness in being here too. One he hadn't felt before.

"When did you know that Maddy was the one? That it wasn't just the newness of being with her that turned you on and made you crazy for her?"

Jace's eyebrows climbed his forehead. Then he grinned. "Oh man, never thought I'd see the day when you of all people would ask me that."

"I know, I know," Brett grumbled. "I was married to the mega-bitch from hell and I swore I wasn't ever getting serious about another woman again. But this thing with Tallie doesn't feel like that did. It's… *different.* Tallie is different. And I don't know if it's *because* she's different that I like her—or if there's something more."

Jace slung an arm around Brett's shoulders.

"Look, I can't tell you if you're in love with this woman or not. I can't tell you what that feels like for you. I knew I loved Maddy because I couldn't imagine life without her, because my life was better with her in it and the idea of being without her made me utterly fucking miserable. I was going to give her up, because I thought it was safer for her if I did—but turned out that wasn't my choice to make. Not alone anyway. And Maddy decided that I was full of shit and she wasn't giving up easily. So here we are, living together and making it work. And you know what?"

"What?"

"I'd give this—" He waved his hand around the ops center to encompass it all. "—Shit up in a heart-beat before I'd ever give Maddy up. I'd dig ditches if I had to. I'd shovel shit at the racetrack and call myself lucky. That, my friend, is how you know what you're feeling. What are you willing to give up?"

"Yeah, but you didn't give it up."

"No, I didn't have to. But I would. Without a second thought. You have to ask yourself, if push came to shove, which could you live without? Tallie or BDI?"

"I don't know yet."

Jace patted his shoulder and then let him go. "Figure it out, my friend. Before someone else figures it out for you."

Brett didn't quite know what that meant. But he knew Jace was right. He had to figure it out. And then he had to do something about it.

Chapter Twenty-Three

Tallie's phone rang and she snatched it up when she saw who it was. Brett had been gone for eight days now and she missed him like crazy. He hadn't been able to come for Thanksgiving, much to her disappointment. She might have thought he was letting her down easy, but he kept calling and texting her so she decided if he really didn't want to see her, he had a weird way of going about it.

Sharon had told her to stop overthinking it and imagining the worst. Brett lived three hours away and had a demanding job, so she had to give the guy a break in Sharon's words.

And that's what she was doing—even if it wasn't easy.

"Hey," she said happily. "I was wondering if you'd call."

"Hi, Tallie. You thought I wouldn't call?"

Tallie felt the heat blooming in her cheeks. She

settled into her bed and picked up the cup of tea she'd made. Chamomile to help her go to sleep. It'd been a busy day at work and she was feeling a little blue because tomorrow was the anniversary of Josie's death, but hearing from Brett made her feel better.

"I know you're busy. I wondered if you'd have time."

"As long as I'm not out of pocket and unable to call, I always have time for you, Tallie."

His words made her glow inside. "Thank you, Brett."

"How was your day? Did you design anything spectacular today?"

Tallie smiled. "I had a consultation with a newly married couple who want to decorate their first house." Her kind of customers because they had a limited budget and needed the most bang for the buck. Flea markets, bargain shopping, that kind of thing. No custom pieces. Her mother had frowned imperiously but hadn't said anything. "Oh, and Sharon's new boyfriend is buying a house that needs some renovations, so he wants a design plan."

He was planning to spend some serious coin, and her mother was happy about that—though apparently concerned that he'd insisted on Tallie doing the work, thanks to Sharon.

"Have you met him yet?"

"Not yet. He was out of town on business, apparently. But he'll be back soon. I'm going with Sharon to the house tomorrow to make some initial measurements and get an idea what needs doing."

"Sounds like fun."

Tallie laughed. "For me, yes. For you, probably not. There's not a bad guy in sight."

He snorted. "That's not always a bad thing."

"No, I suppose not."

"What time are you doing this measuring? I thought I'd head down tomorrow and spend a couple of days with you."

Tallie's heart skipped. "Really? Oh, that would be great. I've missed you," she added shyly. She'd been thinking about her feelings since the minute he'd left and she was positive that she'd never quite felt like this before. She was miserable without him, but she didn't want to admit it to him.

Because she didn't know if he felt the same way and she wasn't going to put herself out there just to be crushed when he backed off. Far better to act cool about the whole thing and see what happened.

"I've missed you too, Tallie."

Heat flooded her, warming her from head to toe. If he was here right now, she'd wrap her arms around him and kiss him senseless. Then she'd lead him to the bedroom and unbuckle his belt before sliding his zipper down and…

Tallie shook herself. He'd asked her a question. "Oh, you asked what time we're measuring. I'm meeting Sharon at three. It shouldn't take more than an hour."

"Then I'll be there around four. Why don't I take you both to dinner?"

Tallie smiled. "That would be great. I don't know if Sharon can go, but I'll ask her. I'm happy you're coming, Brett."

"I'm sorry I couldn't make it for Thanksgiving, but I wasn't planning to let you get through tomorrow without me."

Her stomach flipped. "You know what tomorrow is?"

"You told me. In Bavaria. Yes, I know. And I'm sorry, Tallie. But I'll be there with you."

Tears pricked her eyes. "Thank you. I can't believe it's been a year. It still seems like I should wake up and find out it was all a bad dream." She pulled in a breath. "We won't go to the cemetery tomorrow. Mom wants to go next week. On the day we buried her."

"I'll be there for that too, if you want me to."

"That would be nice. Thank you." She sniffed. "Ian won't mind?"

"He won't mind. I've got the time."

"How's work for you? Nab any bad guys this week?"

He laughed. "Work is fine. And we're always nabbing bad guys. That's pretty much the definition of what we do."

"I worry about you." The words slipped out and she nearly groaned. Way to go, sounding like a needy girlfriend.

"Don't worry about me, Tallie. I'm fine."

"I know that," she said, trying to sound light-hearted about the whole thing. "But I also know that you carry a big gun and you don't appear to be the sort of man who slinks in the other direction at the first sign of danger."

She was thinking of the chalet when they'd returned from the village that day. He'd known something was wrong—and he'd gone toward it, not away.

"Babe, wouldn't you rather talk about something else?"

"Like what?"

As if she didn't know. Whenever he called at night like this, they invariably ended up having phone sex. It wasn't nearly the same feeling when she stroked herself into orgasm, but with his voice in her ear, it was still pretty hot.

"I'm lying in bed with my hand on my cock. And what I want, more than anything, is to watch you sink down on me, taking me inside your sweet pussy while your eyes dilate and your mouth drops open. But since I can't have that, I want to talk about it."

"So you can jerk off," she said, her voice turning all sultry and heated.

"That's right. I want to jerk off, Tallie Grant, with your sweet voice in my ear. And I want you to fuck yourself with your fingers as if I were there doing it. I want to hear you gasping when you come, and I want to know it's because of me."

Tallie set the tea down and flipped off the covers.

Her hand drifted down, beneath her pajama bottoms, until she slipped a finger into her hot, wet folds. Her breath hissed in.

"I'm ready," she whispered. "So ready."

"So am I, baby. You make me hard."

"You make me wet."

"Touch yourself, Tallie. Slide your finger around your clit and pretend it's my tongue."

She closed her eyes and did what he said. "Oh," she gasped. "Oh Brett."

"Yes, baby. Just like that. You taste so good. So sweet and perfect. Faster, baby. Faster."

She obeyed, rubbing herself faster, wishing it was him. She spread her legs wide, brought her knees up to her chest, and stroked herself.

"Brett—I'm going to come," she gasped.

"Come, Tallie. Come for me."

She wanted to drag it out, make it last, but when he commanded her over the edge, she went. "Brett! Oh, God. Oh, fuck—ooooohhhhh…."

Tallie's body jerked with the force of her orgasm. Her inner walls clenched tight, but without him inside her it just wasn't as good. Still, it was good enough to make her moan.

"Shit," he said on a groan and she knew he was coming too. "Too fast," he told her after they'd both drifted back down to earth. "I wanted it to last longer."

"Oh Brett," she said. "I love—" Tallie's heart

squeezed. "This," she said quickly. "I love this. Doing this with you."

He chuckled. "I love it too. But I love it with you even more."

"Then hurry up and get down here. Because tomorrow night, I want to do this again—but with you inside me."

"Babydoll, I want that too. More than you realize."

They talked a little while more and Tallie started to yawn. Brett heard it.

"Go to sleep, Tallulah Margaret. I'll see you tomorrow."

"Okay, Brett. Night."

His voice was warm in her ear. "Night, honey. Sleep well—because I'm not letting you sleep at all tomorrow night."

She smiled, even though she was half asleep. "Mmm, sounds good…."

TALLIE WOKE up feeling both rested and restless. She'd slept well, thanks to Brett and his kinky phone call, but she was also restless because of what the day signified.

One year ago today, Josie had been hit by a distracted driver and lost her life. So many people thought that texting behind the wheel was no big deal, but it was a big deal to Tallie. Not everyone who texted while driving would die, or hit someone and kill them, but why take that chance? Why couldn't the text wait until they reached their destination? What was so all-fire important that it couldn't wait?

In the case of the woman who'd hit Josie, it wasn't important at all. She'd been texting her friends to tell them she was running late but she'd be there soon. And since she was paying more attention to her phone than the road, she'd run a stop sign and plowed into the driver's side of Josie's car at fifty miles an hour.

Josie'd had the right of way, but in the end it didn't matter. She'd been t-boned and, in spite of wearing her seatbelt and obeying the rules of the road, she'd been the one who died.

It wasn't fair. The woman who'd hit her was still alive, having served an absolute pittance of time for involuntary manslaughter, but she was out and she'd presumably just enjoyed Thanksgiving with her family. A thing Josie would never do again.

Tallie got into the shower and scrubbed her body vigorously before dressing in a sweater and leggings with ankle boots. She blow-dried and tousled her hair, slicked on lipstick and a bit of eyeliner and mascara, then stared at herself in the mirror before heading downstairs to grab a yogurt.

Her phone buzzed and she looked at the text.

Brett: *Thinking of you today.*

Warmth flooded her at his thoughtful text. *Thinking of you, too. And thank you.*

Brett: *See you around four.*

Tallie: *I can't wait.*

Her fingers hovered over the little keyboard. She wanted to type three more words, but that was sheer insanity. If she told him she loved him, he'd probably freak out. And rightfully so since they'd known each other less than a month.

It was too fast—and yet she knew it was how she felt. But he didn't feel the same, so it was best to keep it to herself for now.

Tallie drove to her mother's shop, parked in the designated lot behind the store, and went inside to start her day. There were client meetings, design consultations, orders to complete, and shipments to check in. She'd recreated, as much as she was able, the record of the things she'd bought in France. The crate was on its way and would arrive in the next week or two, after a delay at the port.

Around two, Tallie met Sharon for lunch. They were planning to eat at a little café near the historic area of Colonial Williamsburg and then proceed to the house once they were finished.

Tallie arrived first. Sharon breezed in ten minutes later, looking excited. "Sorry I'm late," she said as she took her seat. "Robert called to tell me he was at the airport and he'll meet us at the house a little after three."

Tallie blinked. "Wow. I admit I wasn't expecting that. I mean I'm not really prepared to offer him any ideas just yet. Not until I've seen the house."

Sharon reached out and put her hand on top of Tallie's. Squeezed. "It's okay, Tal. He doesn't expect a complete design plan today. I've told him you and your mother are the best there is and he's completely set on using Mary Claire Grant Interiors—and you. He's a terrific guy. You're really going to like him."

Tallie smiled. She loved seeing her friend excited over a man. Sharon didn't trust easily after her last boyfriend had cheated on her, but she had a big heart and she needed a man who would be patient and give her time. Tallie hoped Robert was that man.

"Okay. Brett is coming down around four. I'll text him the address in case we're still there. Maybe Robert can join us for dinner."

Sharon smiled. "Maybe so."

Tallie sent a quick text to Brett. He sent back a thumbs up. She told herself not to waste any time wishing it was a heart, but of course she spent time wondering why it wasn't. *Stop.*

"Hold up," Sharon said after they'd ordered. "What's got you so preoccupied."

Tallie blinked. Was it that obvious? "I'm thinking about Brett. I haven't seen him in nine days now—and I miss him like crazy."

Sharon looked smug. "I know you do."

"You know?"

"Well of course. You're in love with him."

Tallie sat back against her chair, jaw hanging open. "How do you know that?"

"Because you talk about him a lot. And when you don't talk about him, you're daydreaming about him."

"But that doesn't mean I'm in love," Tallie protested.

"Of course not. But I know you, and I haven't seen you this worked up over a guy since, well, *ever.* You weren't even this worked up about Calvin."

"Calvin and I just sort of fell into a relationship. It was comfortable, but not exciting."

"Exactly. Brett is exciting. He's tall and dark and dangerous. You're turned on by all that danger."

Tallie wished she could tell her friend everything, but she was conscious of the fact she wasn't supposed to. Not while Ian and Brett and all the people at BDI were working to find the money behind the operation that had abducted and sold her.

"Who wouldn't be?"

Sharon picked up her water glass. "Some people want quiet, dull lives."

Tallie gave her a look. "Quiet and dull and *rich*, perhaps?"

Sharon laughed. "Guilty. I'm attracted to Robert anyway, but the money doesn't hurt."

"What does he do? Did you ever figure that out?"

Sharon nodded as she set her glass down. "Medical equipment. He's a doctor and his company is working on a lens that's supposed to help blind people regain some of their sight. It's all very high tech."

"Good lord, that's incredible."

"Yep. He pioneered some sort of surgical technique, which is where the money comes from, but it's the company's work on vision technology that drives him now."

"Why Williamsburg?"

"He wants to be somewhere near major airports, but also far enough removed from the bustle of a big city to get some relaxation. His parents emigrated from Spain when he was five, which is why he has a slight accent, but he loves American colonial history. Makes our city a huge draw for him."

Their food arrived and they waited for the waitress to get everything settled and walk away again. Tallie picked up her spoon and dipped it into the crab soup she'd ordered.

"I told Robert about your heterochromia. He's seen it before, but I think he's looking forward to meeting you at least partly for your eyes," Sharon said with a laugh.

Tallie's belly squeezed. She was used to people staring at her eyes and asking questions about them. She'd lived with it long enough. But since her experience in Europe, and the knowledge that her eyes were at least partially responsible for her abduction, she felt sort of funny about any attention they got her lately.

She'd put her contacts in this morning but then had to remove them when she got dust in her eyes while unpacking a shipment. She'd cleaned them but her eyes had felt so scratchy she hadn't put them back. She thought about doing it before they reached the house, but Sharon would probably be insulted if she did.

"Wait," Sharon said when Tallie didn't say anything. "Are you upset by that? You never seemed bothered before. Not since we were kids, I mean."

Tallie rushed to soothe her. "No, not at all. I'm sorry. It's just that I've felt a little self-conscious about any attention since everything that happened in France. When we were being held, well, it wasn't a good idea to draw the terrorists' notice."

Her cheeks heated at the lie, but it was the closest she could come to explaining herself without telling the truth. Sharon frowned and shook her head.

"Oh Tallie, I'm sorry. I didn't think about any of that. It's just that Robert, well, he's a doctor and when I told him about you, he was interested when I mentioned your different colored eyes. I wouldn't have done it if I'd known it would make you uncomfortable."

Tallie reached out and grabbed her friend's wrist. "It's fine. Don't worry about it, okay? Brett told me it would take time to readjust to everyday life, and I think this is one of those things. I'm overly sensitive. And I have to get back to normal, so I'll be pleased to meet Doctor Robert and let him view my eyes. It's not like he wouldn't have noticed, so at least now he's prepared, right?"

Sharon nodded. "I don't really know what you went through in France. If you ever want to talk about it…"

"Thank you, sweetie. But I'm fine right now. I'm having lunch with my bestie and we have work to do together."

"I also haven't forgotten what day it is. I should have been a little more sensitive to how you might be feeling. I think I was just trying to distract you a bit."

"And I love you for it, but it's okay to talk about it. I'm feeling a little raw inside, to be honest, but I think that's to be expected."

"Of course it is. How's your mom today?"

Tallie thought of her mother this morning. Cool, collected, the quintessential steel magnolia. Mary Claire hadn't mentioned the anniversary at all. She was no doubt saving herself for the visit to the cemetery next week.

"You know Mom. Focused on work. Strong as steel. I expect she'll have a quiet breakdown tonight, and then she'll put it behind her. She'll be stoic and controlled at the cemetery and no one will ever know what she's feeling inside. Not even Bill."

Sharon signaled the waitress. "Let's get a bottle of champagne and toast Josie. We can Uber to the house and Brett or Robert can bring us back for our cars."

Tallie started to refuse but then she thought, *why not?* A couple of glasses of champagne wasn't going to hurt. And she wanted to do something to mark today that wasn't work and wasn't just her going about her normal life.

"Let's do it," she said. "For Josie."

Chapter Twenty-Four

Brett found the house where he was meeting Tallie and Sharon easily enough. It was a big house set on about five acres of land, with a long driveway that turned into a circle in front of the house.

The house was two stories, brick, with two smaller wings that perched on either side of the central portion. There was a bronze statue at the center of the circular drive, with a fountain feature, and a motor court off to one side of the house with wrought iron gates that stood open. There were no cars in either the circular drive or around the side of the house where the six-car garage sat inside the motor court with doors lowered.

Brett checked his watch. It was twenty after four. He'd gotten stuck in traffic, but he'd sent Tallie a text to let her know he'd be along. She might have already left, though. He picked up his phone to check his texts in case she'd replied and he'd missed hearing it. There was nothing.

Brett sat in the truck, one hand hanging over the wheel, one holding his phone, and stared at the house. An uneasy feeling chipped away at his gut, but he told himself there was no reason for it. There was absolutely nothing out of the ordinary here, other than Tallie's car was missing. But since he was late, she'd probably already left and she'd be texting him soon enough to tell him where to meet her.

He decided to call her, in case she was driving and couldn't answer texts. He dialed her number and waited.

It went to voicemail.

Brett lowered his phone and frowned. Then he opened the door and got out of his truck. He didn't know why he did it, other than that feeling digging away at him, knocking on the foundations of his calm.

He checked the garage doors first, peering through the glass at the top of the wooden doors. The garage was empty so he strode over to look in the windows along the back of the house.

The first room he saw was a mudroom. There was nothing there. He moved along the rear of the structure and looked into the next window. It gave way to a large kitchen with a huge island, white cabinets, and a massive professional grade stove perched beneath a custom hood.

There was a table at one end with at least twelve

chairs. It sat on a huge oriental rug. Brett peered at it. Something wasn't quite right—

There were feet at one end of the table, the far end, lying on the carpet.

Fuck!

The unease in Brett's gut flared into full blown panic. He sprinted for the door and twisted the handle—but nothing happened.

It was possible the house was alarmed, but he didn't give a shit. He shoved his phone into his jeans pocket, withdrew his Sig, and smashed the glass with the barrel, then reached inside and twisted the locks until he could yank the door open.

He entered the house, sweeping the pistol left and right, looking for an intruder. No one emerged to threaten him and he made it around the table and dropped to his knees beside Sharon.

There was tape on her mouth, and her arms and legs were bound. A chair lay on the floor and he could see that her legs were tied to it. Her eyes were closed.

"Sharon?" Brett said, smoothing her dark hair from her face. "Honey, are you okay?"

Her eyelids fluttered and then snapped open, fear evident in the wide-eyed look she shot him.

"It's Brett, Sharon. You're safe now. I'm going to peel the tape off, okay?"

She nodded as her eyes filled with tears. He peeled the tape slowly. As badly as he wanted to rip if off so he could find out if Tallie had been with her, he had to be gentle.

Brett eased the tape from her mouth and a sob escaped her. "Brett—he took Tallie. It's all my fault. He took her," she wailed.

Brett's blood turned to ice. But as much as he wanted to leap up and go after Tallie, he had to take care of Sharon. And he had to find out what she knew.

"Who took her?"

"Robert. His chauffeur pulled a gun on us and then they made me sit in that chair while Robert bound me. He seemed to know Tallie, but I don't see how that's possible. She didn't know him."

Rage and fear boiled in Brett's gut as he slipped his pocket knife free and cut into the zip ties that bound Sharon's hands. Then he cut through the ones binding her to the chair and helped her sit up. There was the beginnings of a bruise on the side of her face where she'd hit the floor when she fell over. She lifted her hand to gingerly touch it.

"Look at me, Sharon."

She did and he asked her a couple of quick questions to test for concussion. She didn't hesitate to answer about the date and her name and who was president, but he still wanted her checked out.

First, he had to ask her about the man who'd taken Tallie.

"I need you to tell me everything you know about Robert. His name, his address, where he works, where he lives—everything, Sharon."

Tears rolled down her cheeks. He smelled a hint wine on her breath, but she wasn't drunk. "I thought he was interested in *me.* I should have known. Oh God, I should have known something was wrong. He was too good to be true—the money, the houses, the interest. He was so concerned about getting a decorator and he wanted my recommendations—I should have known."

Brett put his hands on her shoulders to steady her. "You couldn't know, honey. He tricked you. But right now, I need to know what you know. It's the only chance we have to save Tallie. You have to calm down and tell me everything from the moment you met him until now."

She nodded, her sobs turning to hiccoughs. Brett took his phone out and dialed a number that he knew would get an immediate answer.

Ian picked up on the first ring. "What's up, kid?"

"Someone took Tallie. I've just found her friend tied up in a house this guy was buying. They were supposed to measure it for a decorating job."

"Fuck. Okay, I'll get a response team together. Anything else?"

"I'm questioning her friend right now. I'll let you know."

"Roger. Call me as soon as you're done."

"Copy."

The call ended and Brett stood, helping Sharon up with him. Inside, he was anything but calm. Outside, he did his job. Because that's how you found people. You focused on the work and you performed coolly and calmly.

He sat Sharon gently in a chair and dragged another out to face her.

"Shouldn't we call the police?" she asked. "They've been gone a while. It feels like I've been here for hours, though it can't be, can it? An hour, maybe. I was trying to scoot over to where I'd left my purse on the bar, but I fell. I don't know how long I lay there."

"It's four-thirty. I just called for help, and the man I called is better than the police. Just tell me everything you know. Everything you can think of. Everything he ever said to you."

Sharon closed her eyes and took a deep breath. She was trying to focus and be calm, and that was a direct result of his being calm with her.

"Okay, I can do this. I *can.*"

"You definitely can."

Sharon had a methodical mind that catalogued facts and recited them in order. Brett appreciated that more than he could say at the moment. She made it easy for him to pull the necessary information from what she said. When she was done, he called Ian, desperately pushing down the panic and focusing on the facts as he did so.

"I want you to stay in Williamsburg until we know more," Ian said. "If he's still in the vicinity, I need you ready to lead a team to capture him and free Tallie."

"Copy that, boss."

"When I know more, I'll call."

Sharon had stood and was hugging herself, waiting patiently for Brett to finish his call. When Ian hung up, Brett felt lost. Empty.

"There were no French terrorists, were there?" Sharon asked.

Brett focused on her. "No."

"Tell me, Brett," she forced out. "You aren't telling me everything."

He hesitated. And then he decided that she deserved to know. Without her, they wouldn't know who'd taken Tallie. They didn't know Robert Cortes's true identity yet, but they had enough to look for him. Thanks to Sharon.

"Tallie was abducted by a human trafficking organization and sold into sexual slavery. Fortunately, I'm the one who bought her as part of an undercover operation. We thought she was clear of it, but I think Robert must be involved with the group who took her."

Sharon made a sound of horror that moved Brett into action. He went over and caught her shoulders, squeezed reassuringly. "It's not your fault, Sharon. You couldn't have known."

Her eyes filled with fresh tears. "I delivered her to him."

"No, you were doing your job and she was doing hers. He used you to get to her."

Sharon's eyes widened. "Oh my god—I have a picture of him, Brett!" She rushed over to her purse where it sat on the counter and dumped it out, scattering everything until she found her phone. "I almost forgot because he didn't want me to take any pictures of us together, but I was snapping the restaurant's decor when he took me to dinner last week and his profile was reflected in the mirror. I didn't tell him he was in it because I thought he'd make me delete it. It's not a great picture, but it's something."

She pulled it up with trembling fingers and thrust it at him. Brett stared at half of a shadowed face, a knot forming in his gut as he remembered the last time he'd seen that profile.

The night he'd spent one million dollars to buy Tallie. His competition had been Heinrich von Kassel —and this man.

"WHERE ARE YOU TAKING ME?" Tallie asked, trying to be calm, though inside she was a mess. She kept thinking of Brett and how coolly he'd charged into danger back in Bavaria. Or how he'd faced Natasha across a table when he'd thought she had a gun pointed at him. He'd stayed rational and cool and everything turned out okay.

Tallie's heart hammered in her chest. She didn't know how this could turn out okay. Her wrists were cuffed in front of her body, limiting movement. Robert had slapped tape over Sharon's mouth, but he hadn't taped Tallie's.

Yet.

Robert lifted a thin eyebrow. He sat across from her in the limo. He was wearing dark trousers and a crisp button-down. He looked rich even without the limo. He was a good-looking man—not as handsome as Brett—but there was something creepy about him. The way he looked at her made her skin crawl. It had done so even before his chauffeur entered the house with a gun.

When that happened, Tallie had known in her gut what her mind refused to acknowledge. That Robert knew who she was and had romanced Sharon specifically to get to her. He had to be a part of the group that had abducted her in France.

"I am taking you to my laboratory, Miss Grant."

Tallie shivered and clasped her hands tighter. "Laboratory? Why?"

An unholy light lit his face. "Because you are interesting, and I like to study interesting things."

"Are you really a doctor?"

"Oh yes. I can give you bigger breasts. Plumper buttocks. A trimmer waist. Even a new face."

"I don't want any of those things," Tallie said, her throat tight.

"We shall see."

Her heart flipped. Her belly sank. "Do no harm. Isn't that part of your oath?"

He laughed but he didn't answer.

They reached the airport then, pulling up to a guard shack before driving through a gate and toward a jet that sat on the tarmac. Tallie berated herself for not screaming when the driver talked to the guard, but it happened so fast that she hadn't realized what was going on until they were through the barrier and the window was up again.

The driver parked at the foot of the stairs. Tallie's heart squeezed. She could see men working in the distance, loading luggage onto another plane, and she decided to scream the instant the door opened.

She didn't get the chance. Robert picked up the roll of tape he'd used on Sharon and tore off a strip, then pressed it over her mouth. Hard.

Harder than necessary because her jaw ached where he pinched. His dark eyes glittered. He *liked* causing pain.

"I can see your thoughts, Miss Grant. Every one of them. We're going to have fun together, you and I. By the end, you'll beg me to ease your suffering. You'll beg for my touch, and for the comfort I can give you."

The door opened and Robert dragged her out of the car, then up the steps. He thrust her into the plane and toward the rear of the cabin, past a flight attendant who didn't glance twice at Tallie.

It was a small plane in the sense it wasn't like a commercial jet, but it was spacious and long. There were four club chairs that sat on either side of the cabin and faced each other, with tables in between, and there was a couch with a television that was mounted on a long console. There was another section to the interior, behind walls that cut it off from the first section, and Robert pushed her back there and thrust her into a chair beside a round porthole.

He didn't take off the tape or the handcuffs as he sat across from her and smiled. It wasn't a friendly smile. In fact, it chilled her to the bone—as if his words hadn't done that job already. He seemed to be studying her eyes.

"I want to see how these eyes look when they are in pain. And I want to see them dilate with pleasure, too. We will experiment with it all by the time we're done. We might have already had our fun if not for your interfering boyfriend. He isn't what he pretended to be that night, is he?"

Tallie's gut twisted. What if he'd sent someone to hurt Brett too?

Robert ran his fingers down her cheek. She shrank from him because she couldn't stop herself.

"Such strange eyes. Rare eyes. I'm going to enjoy studying them and all the emotions they reflect." He lifted his chin as he looked down at her. "Right now, they reflect fear. I wonder how many ways they can do that? How many variations there are to the fear response."

Tallie glared at him—and then she closed her eyes because she didn't want him to look into them for a single moment more. She thought he might get angry with her, but he only laughed. She heard him stand, the leather creaking and squeaking as his weight left it. Then he walked away. She felt it more than heard it, but she still didn't open her eyes to look.

Tears pressed hard against the backs of her eyelids. She let them fall because holding them in wasn't going to work. It took her a second to realize that she could peel the tape off if she wanted—but her hands arrested in the act of trying to find the corner.

What if removing the tape angered him? Did she really want to bring his attention to her any more than necessary?

Tallie dropped her hands to her lap and leaned back in the seat. She was sick at heart, and angry and scared. She was a prisoner, but she wasn't going to be helpless. She would look for an opportunity—to escape, to inflict damage to Robert, whatever it took.

Despair filled her at the slim possibility she'd get to do either of those things.

She prayed that Brett was alive and well—and that he was already looking for her. She had to hold onto his image in her head, tight, and she had to believe that Brett would find her.

Because if he didn't, she'd probably never see him again.

Chapter Twenty-Five

Brett paced the floor of the ops center, ready to tear his fucking hair out by the roots. Tallie had been gone for six hours. And they still had no idea where she was. Where *Robert* had taken her.

Brett had returned to HQ by helicopter two hours ago, but they still had nothing to go on. Nowhere to go.

The man had given Sharon a fake name, of course, because there was no Robert Cortes who owned a medical research company and lived in New York City. Sharon, bless her, was physically okay even if she was feeling mentally knocked for a loop. She'd gotten checked out at the hospital and sent home to rest. Brett had promised to keep in touch with updates. And she'd promised not to tell anyone about what had happened at the house. Not until they had Tallie back safely.

Ian had sent someone to fix the glass Brett broke,

and everything would be put back to the way it'd been. No one would ever know anything had happened there.

Right now, Brett's body felt like it was encased in ice. Pure, hard, cold ice. He'd shut down his emotions hours ago. He was operating on instinct and training right now. It was all he could do.

But beneath the ice, the scared kid who'd sat vigil beside his dead mother's body was crying out in fear. Crying that he couldn't go through it again.

Ian was on the phone, pacing back and forth. He'd been working the phones since Brett had phoned to tell him Tallie was missing. Ian had a hand on his head and the other held the phone to his ear when he suddenly swore explosively.

Brett's senses went on high alert as Ian finished the call and dropped the phone to his side.

"His name is Roberto Cortes Broussard," Ian said. "He holds dual Spanish and French citizenship, and he *is* a doctor. A plastic surgeon of some renown who has a very exclusive practice in Barcelona and Geneva. He is also, unfortunately, a collector of curiosities. Like Von Kassel—except his curiosities seem to be exclusively human."

"How did he learn her identity when Von Kassel didn't seem to know it? Only the Syndicate knew."

Ian was frowning. "I'm afraid that's the answer. He could have paid someone to get the information, but I think it's more likely he's a member. He has a fortune of his own and skills that are desired by the Syndicate. I've been told he's made notorious criminals disappear entirely by giving them new faces and new identities. It's rumored he experiments on patients at a hidden location—but I don't know where."

Brett's blood ran cold.

"Where the fuck is he then?" Colt asked. He and Ty and Jace were all there. Waiting for a destination so they could break Tallie free.

Ian's jaw worked. "He has a practice in Geneva and a house there, as well as a home near Chamonix and a house in Barcelona, where he has another office."

"Do we have addresses?" Jace growled.

"We do."

"Then we need to go," Brett said. "He has a fucking six hour head start on us."

"I know that," Ian bit out. "But which location? That's what I don't know yet."

Brett exploded. "We can't just sit here, Ian! We've got to find her. Before he does something—"

His voice choked off, the bile swiftly rising in his throat. He thought of that night when he was eight, when the trailer was fucking freezing and his mother brought home a john so they could eat and maybe have some heat again.

He hadn't done anything to stop it and she'd died. While he lay mere feet away, under his blankets, his mother's life was snuffed out and his life had changed irrevocably. He wasn't going to sit by and let it happen again.

Because his life *would* change. He knew it would. Without Tallie in it, without her sweet smile and her gentle touch, he'd lose the best thing that had ever happened to him.

He slumped heavily against a table and forced himself to breathe in and out.

She *was* the best thing that had ever happened to him. He could roll it around in his head forever, second guessing himself, but somehow he knew that the answer wasn't going to change no matter how long he thought about it. Tallie Grant was *the one.*

She just was, and there was nothing he wouldn't do to bring her back again.

Ian's hand clamped his shoulder. "We're going, kid. He's at one of those locations. I don't know which one yet, but we'll figure out which one before we get there. The plane is ready to go, so grab your gear and let's move."

"We, boss?" Jace asked as they started for the armory located deep inside the bowels of the building.

"That's right," Ian said. "I'm going with you."

They went into the armory, loaded up on weapons, ammunition, and assault gear, and then drove to the private airport where one of Ian's planes waited for them. As soon as they were onboard, the plane started to move. They fell into their seats and buckled in mere moments before the pilot opened the throttle and began his takeoff roll.

Once they were airborne and had climbed past the ten-thousand feet threshold, they unbuckled and headed for the ops center where technicians were working on satellite-connected computers.

Ian picked up a phone—a red one, naturally—and barked into it, "Do you have a location for me yet?" He paused. "Keep working. Send it as soon as you have anything."

Ground ops and airborne ops would work together to locate Broussard's destination. Until then, there was nothing they could do except wait.

Brett returned to the main cabin, threw himself into a seat, and buckled in. It was going to be a long flight. Worse than that, it was going to be a torturous one.

Ian appeared at his side, glass in hand. "Here."

"What is it?"

Ian didn't say anything, just held the glass out. Jace, Colt, and Ty appeared with glasses as well. Brett took it and sniffed.

"Vodka." He set the glass on the table between the rows of seats. "I need to keep a clear head."

Ian sat down across from him with his own glass. "We've got six hours in the air at least. I think a couple of drinks aren't going to hurt anybody. And you need to take the edge off."

Jace said something in Russian. Ian replied and laughed. Ty grinned, which meant he'd understood it too. Colt shrugged. Apparently, they were the only two who didn't speak Russian.

"Drink up, kid. At least have one," Ian said.

Brett slid the glass toward the edge of the table. Then he picked it up and drained it. The vodka burned going down.

But not enough to numb the pain in his heart.

THE DRINKING HAD SUBSIDED and they were each sitting around with their thoughts when the ops center door opened and one of the technicians peered out.

"Sir, it's HQ calling. They've got something you should hear."

Ian got up. Brett went with him. The others stayed, because they knew they'd hear it soon enough, but Brett wasn't waiting.

Inside airborne ops, the IT crew worked to keep communications smooth and information flowing. There were three techs, two of whom were women. Brett knew one of them. Mandy Parker was former Air Force and had flown with the president on Air Force One.

He hadn't paid any attention when he'd been in here earlier, because he'd been keyed up, but now he gave her a nod. "Mandy."

She nodded back. "Brett." Then she turned to Ian and handed him the phone.

"This is Black." His expression tightened for a

second. Then his eyebrows went up. "You sure about that? Okay, yeah, thanks. Good work. Keep coordinating with Mandy. Anything else you find out, let us know."

"What is it?" Brett asked when Ian put the phone down.

Ian's dark eyes—they'd been blue earlier today—sparked with anger and determination. "Broussard has a house in Barcelona. But he also has a mountain home nearby. And not just any home, but a former monastery—one of those carved out of solid rock jobbies at the pinnacle of what appears to be an inaccessible mountaintop. It isn't listed under his name, but that of a shell company. It's where he keeps his acquisitions."

"And performs his experiments?" Brett's stomach churned.

Ian's expression filled with rage. "It would seem so."

"And he's taking Tallie there."

"It's the most likely destination. It's impenetrable for the most part. The kind of place you go when you don't want anyone sneaking up on you. HQ tracked down the flight information. He had a private jet waiting in Richmond. They filed a flight plan for Barcelona. He *could* take her to his home there, but the monastery seems more likely."

"We need to plan a mountain assault."

"Indeed." Ian rubbed his hands together and headed for the conference room at the other end of the plane. "Go get the girls from their little tea party in the main cabin and let's plan how we're getting Tallie back."

TALLIE'S EMOTIONS had run the gamut over the past few hours. They'd ranged from abject fear to utmost terror to white-hot anger. She'd experienced exhaustion and hunger and nausea and she'd cried copious tears. But now?

Now she was fighting resignation to her fate. She kept telling herself that Brett would come for her. But as the hours ticked by and he didn't arrive, hope started to fade. How would he know where to find her?

They'd arrived at this place by helicopter shortly after dawn. What she'd seen of their surroundings hadn't given her much hope. It was all sheer mountain—and no other dwellings besides a fortress that looked like it was fairly old. Medieval, maybe.

The helicopter had dropped down into a central courtyard where a man waited for them. Robert had climbed out of the helicopter and dragged her with him, uncaring that she stumbled and fell on the cobblestones because she couldn't get her footing. She'd ripped her leggings wide open at the knee, scraping her skin until it bled.

"Get up," he'd ordered, clasping her arm hard. He squeezed until she gasped but she managed to get up and trot along beside him. They passed inside and she had an impression of medieval stone and dark timbers as he hustled her through the corridors and up a set of curving stairs. They passed people on the way, but none of them seemed surprised by the way he treated her.

None of them would help her. She knew that now.

Robert opened a door and shoved her inside, closing it behind them. He took out a key and unlocked the handcuffs and she'd thrown herself backward, away from him, to press her body to the wall as she rubbed the feeling back into her sore wrists.

"Enjoy your day, Miss Grant. I'll be back tonight, and we will begin our experiments. I suggest you rest for what is to come."

Tallie watched him go, listened to the lock twisting behind him, and nearly fainted with relief. She didn't want to dwell on what he'd said, but she knew he said it to provoke terror.

He was the kind of person who enjoyed causing pain. She'd watched him on the plane, watched as he twisted his fingers into the flesh of the flight attendant and the expression of agony on the woman's face. She hadn't said anything to him because he was her boss, but Tallie had seen the fear in the woman's eyes.

Now that Robert was gone, Tallie peeled off the tape, cursing softly whenever it pulled her skin too hard. She wondered that he hadn't yanked it off himself so he could enjoy her pain, but he was probably anticipating the things he would do later.

Tallie had all day, when she wasn't sleeping off her jet lag, to stare at the barren rock and worry about Robert's return. She'd heard the helicopter leaving earlier, so she knew he'd left the fortress entirely. The view made it clear they were very high up on the side of a mountain. It was the most savagely beautiful landscape she'd ever seen.

Tallie thought about breaking a window and climbing out. But then she pressed her cheek to the glass in an attempt to see what was down there—and encountered nothing but a sheer drop into blackness even before the sun disappeared over the horizon at the end of the day.

Eventually, a small woman arrived with food while another stood in the door and watched. Tallie glared defiantly and peppered them with questions. They didn't respond.

Tallie was starved, but she didn't eat the soup in case it was drugged. She ate the bread, however, after sniffing it for anything that seemed off. Unless they'd baked drugs into the bread, it was a lot harder to tamper with it. Or so she hoped.

She dozed in stretches, but then she jerked awake from time to time and looked around fearfully. Now, she pushed herself up and made another circuit of the room and the bathroom, just in case she'd missed anything she could use to break free—or fight off Robert when he returned.

There were small bottles of toiletries in the bath. A toothbrush and comb. She looked for a hair dryer. The cord could be wrapped around someone's neck and tugged tight.

But there wasn't a hair dryer, just like there hadn't been the several times before that she'd looked.

The toiletry bottles were small and plastic. Not heavy enough to do any damage. The toothbrush was blunt. The toilet paper wouldn't harm anyone.

Tallie exited the bath and cast around the room again. There was a bed, a chair—plastic, nothing that would do any damage—and a table that had been bolted to the floor. The bed was a four-poster, with draperies on three sides and a heavy-looking canopy. But she couldn't figure out how to get up there and hide long enough to push it down on someone. Someone who just so happened to climb onto the bed to look for her.

Tallie frowned and pushed her hands through her hair. She was tired, frustrated, scared, still hungry—and losing hope. It was after dark now, and he could return at any minute. What would she do when he inflicted more pain on her?

She climbed onto the bed and pressed herself against the headboard, trying to make herself invisible. Then she stared at the windows and their reflection of the room, and she prayed for rescue.

Chapter Twenty-Six

Tallie awoke with a start. Panic flooded her as she tried to hear again the sound that had jolted her. Was it a helicopter? Had Robert returned?

Or maybe it was just her dreams that startled her awake. She'd been running from a giant monster with dripping red fangs. Every time she thought she was free, she'd round a corner and the monster would be before her. So she'd turn and run the other way.

She'd round a corner and, again, there he was. A tall, hairy, slavering beast with those dripping fangs and yellow eyes. He shuffled toward her, never running, but always he looked like he was about to pounce.

Like Robert had looked when he'd left her here earlier.

A key rattled in the lock on her door and Tallie's blood ran cold. She jumped off the bed and dropped beside it, willing herself to stay calm and wait for an opportunity. If she was lucky, maybe she could disable whoever it was and dart out the door.

She could run through this dank, dark place and outside—where she would do what?

Stop. Don't overthink it.

The door glided open. Tallie's muscles coiled. She prayed it wasn't Robert…

It was a woman.

Relief flooded Tallie, making her knees shake. Not that the woman was a friend, but at least it wasn't Robert and his experiments.

The woman appeared to be average height, slim build, with dark hair coiled on her head in a sleek bun, and a seeking gaze. She was wearing black. A black jumpsuit maybe.

"Hello, Tallie Grant," she said as she strolled into the room.

Tallie continued to crouch on the other side of the bed.

"I know you are here. It's no use hiding."

Tallie didn't move or speak, but the woman came around the end of the bed and frowned. She was wearing a holster around her slender hips with guns on either side. Unlike a cowboy holster, this one was also tied around her thighs.

She looked like Lara Croft, tomb raider, and Tallie's brain tickled in recognition.

"I know you," she said, and then wanted to bite her tongue when she remembered what Brett had told her.

Forget you ever met her. Forget her name, forget her.

"Ah, so you do remember me."

Tallie's heart pounded. She wondered if the woman would draw one of the weapons and fire. But why? Robert hadn't brought her here for this woman to shoot her and end the misery before it began.

"I, um, could be mistaken."

Natasha came over and lifted Tallie up with a firm hand beneath her elbow.

"You could be. But you are not."

Tallie studied her. "You don't look the same."

Natasha smiled. "That is the entire point. Now come. We're getting out of here."

"I—what? Did Brett send you?"

Natasha snorted. "Send me. No, dear girl, he did not send me. Those boys couldn't find their asses with flashlights and a map, I dare say. Or at least not soon enough to make a difference."

"How do I know I can trust you?"

Natasha leaned in, putting her pretty face in Tallie's. Anger flashed across her features.

"There are some who will tell you I am the monster—and I am, Tallie Grant. I definitely am. But the people I've killed have deserved it. I've never killed an innocent, no matter what others say. Not ever. But that is what will happen to you if you do not come with me." She shrugged. "It is up to you, however. If you wish to wait for Roberto Broussard, I will not stop you. But you must decide quick, because he is on his way home."

BROUSSARD'S mountaintop monastery was in a remote area of the Catalan Pyrenees. It had once belonged to the Benedictine order, but had fallen into disuse and disrepair decades before and was sold. Broussard had gotten it from a Madrid businessman who'd gotten it from a businessman before him. There'd been plans to turn it into a hotel retreat at one point, but those had never come to fruition.

For Broussard, it served a dual purpose. First, it was a place where members of the Gemini Syndicate could hold secret meetings when necessary. And second, it housed the men and women that Broussard took there for his own disgusting reasons.

Brett gripped his assault rifle as BDI's stealth helicopter winged its way toward the mountain. They'd considered HALO-ing in, but decided that stealth was the way to go. There was no such thing as a completely silent helicopter, but this wasn't a military mission and Broussard didn't have a command center with 24/7 ops on the watch for an invasion.

He was a wealthy surgeon with a mountain retreat where it was rumored he did dirty things. That wasn't typically the kind of place likely to be assaulted by a team of commandos.

Until now.

BDI had managed to get a schematic of the fortress. There was a central courtyard surrounded on all sides by wings of the structure. There were four towers as well, one at each corner, and a church that had been deconsecrated. Leading up to the monastery, there was a twisty road that made its way along torturous switchbacks to a spot about two hundred feet below the gates.

There was also a medieval bolt hole that wound down through the mountain and came out on the road below. They'd considered the tunnel and discarded it. It would take too long, and they didn't know whether or not it was in good repair. They'd also considered the road, but they'd need headlights and they might be noticed at some point before they arrived.

Finally, they'd decided that dropping out of the sky onto the roof was their best and fastest option. The commandos would rappel down to the roof and the helicopter would lift away. Then they'd skirt the roof until they could enter one of the towers. They'd make their way systematically through the structure, checking wings and towers as they went.

It wasn't a military target, but that didn't matter. This is what Black Defense International did.

The hard jobs. The dirty jobs. The jobs the military wasn't going to get involved in because targeting a civilian wasn't what they did.

Brett gazed at his teammates on this op. Ian, Colt, Jace, and Ty were all quiet, all thinking. They wore black assault suits and they'd grease-painted their faces. They were armed for bear and willing to use those weapons to achieve their objective—and then some. There was no messy paperwork involved for mercenaries, no justifying what they did to a military commander.

The only person they had to answer to was sitting across from Brett, and Ian Black was as determined to rescue Tallie as any of them. By whatever means necessary.

Brett didn't know what lay in Ian's past, but whatever it was, it made him extra angry when human trafficking was involved.

"Drop zone approaching," the pilot said into their earpieces. "Prepare for jump."

It wasn't technically a jump, but he was still dropping them high above the structure. They stood and slung their rifles behind them as the craft descended.

Ian watched the pilot and co-pilot. When the co-pilot flashed a thumbs up, Ian turned and threw a line out. "Go time, kids," he said, his teeth flashing white in his dark face as he shot them a crazy grin. The kind of grin that said he loved this kind of shit, even if he didn't love the reason for it.

Jace threw the other line out the opposite door and they rappelled down to the roof until all five of them were standing on the terra-cotta.

It was cold in the Pyrenees after dark in early December, and there was frost on the roof that made the terra-cotta slick in spots. They'd have to pick their way carefully over to the tower where they'd drop over the edge of the roof and onto the second-floor colonnaded walkway that ringed the buildings.

From there, they'd breach the tower and enter the interior.

They reached the tower without incident and Ian sent a hand signal. Jace dropped over the edge first. Colt was next, then Brett, then Ian and then Tyler. The tower was before them, the medieval doors darkened from centuries of exposure. Jace reached the doors first and pushed the handle.

The door creaked open on ancient hinges, thankfully. No need to pick the lock. They stood, listening for any sound, and then Ian took point and motioned them all in.

The tower wasn't a small structure with a single stairway leading up or a room at the top that housed the princess. It was a large tower with one staircase leading up and rooms on each floor. It'd been modernized with electric lighting, at least.

Brett had half expected guttering torches.

They moved silently through the tower, checking the rooms for occupants. Whenever they found anyone, they immobilized them with steel-toothed zip ties and tape over their mouths. They herded four people—three women and one man—into a room on the first floor.

"Where is Roberto Broussard?" Ian asked.

Eyes darted back and forth. Ian peeled the tape off one of the women. "Señora? Where is Broussard? And where is the woman he brought here today? Small, blond hair. Shoulder length," he added, tapping the edge of his hand against his shoulder.

The woman darted a glance at the other three. They all looked scared. Maybe a little ill.

"No lady," the woman spat. "Señor Broussard not here either."

"She's lying," Brett growled.

"I am aware of that," Ian said mildly. "Señora, if you wish to survive this night, you'd best tell me how many people are being held against their will and where they are. Because I'm getting them all out of here—and then I'm blowing this whole rotten facility to kingdom come. If you don't want to blow with it, you'll tell me what I want to know. Understand?"

Her eyes had widened as Ian spoke. She nodded her head emphatically.

"Now start with the blond lady. Where is she?"

Chapter Twenty-Seven

There was never really any doubt that Tallie was going with Natasha. She'd met Natasha once before, and the woman had been nice to her even if she'd managed to set Brett's hackles on end.

Roberto Broussard, however, had creeped her out from the beginning. Even before she knew he was planning to abduct her.

"Smart girl," Natasha said to Tallie before she led them from the room and back toward the stairwell that Robert—*Roberto*—had dragged her up hours ago.

Natasha moved on silent feet while Tallie felt like she was clomping her way through the echoing hallway with its old marble tiles and mosaics.

She was still wearing the low-heeled boots, torn leggings, and sweater she'd been wearing when she'd met Sharon for lunch yesterday—or was it the day before? She had no idea what time it was, or what time it was supposed to be. Her purse and phone had been left behind in the house with Sharon. Her coat was there too.

She noticed the lack of a coat the instant they stepped out onto the colonnaded walkway ringing the interior of the fortress. It was utterly dark out, but there were lights in the courtyard below. In the distance, she heard a sound. A steady, thumping sound. She stopped to listen.

Natasha must have noticed it too because she halted, turning, a hand straying to one of the guns on her hip.

"It is a helicopter," she said. "Broussard is returning. We have to get to the tunnel."

"Tunnel?" Tallie's heart hammered a million miles an hour. She remembered walking through a tunnel with Brett in Venice. That seemed like a lifetime ago now.

"You heard me. Now move, Tallie—unless you want to be caught?"

Tallie's feet started to move of their own accord. Natasha jogged down the long walkway, Tallie on her heels. Her knee was sore from the fall, but she wasn't going to let that stop her from keeping up.

They reached another stairwell and Natasha took the stairs two at a time. Tallie scrambled after her, nearly plowing into her back when she hit the bottom and discovered Natasha at a standstill, both weapons drawn and pointing at a group of black-clad men who'd drawn their own weapons and were aiming at her in return.

One of the men dropped the barrel of his rifle as he looked past Natasha. Directly at *her.* But who was he, with his dark face and his eyes hidden behind what seemed to be night vision goggles?

"Tallie?"

Oh, god. She knew that voice.

"Brett," she said on a half-sob, unable to keep the emotion from her own voice. "You're here."

He shoved the goggles up. "I'm here, baby."

Her heart slammed her ribs. The blood threatened to rush from her head and make her faint. It *was* him. Brett had come for her.

Natasha suddenly grabbed her as Brett took a step toward them, wrapping an arm around her throat, one gun pointing at the men, the other held loosely against Tallie's body. Tallie should have fought, maybe, but she was so stunned she couldn't move.

Someone spoke in what Tallie thought might be Russian.

"No, you put yours down, Mr. Ian Black," Natasha answered in English.

"Tasha," one of the other men said. "Please."

Tallie didn't think she'd met this one yet. But he clearly knew Natasha as well.

"Hello, brother," Natasha said, and Tallie blinked. Brother? Natasha's arm around her neck wasn't all that tight. It was almost as if she were playing the part that was expected of her.

Tallie didn't really think Natasha wanted to hurt her. She remembered what the woman had said about not ever hurting an innocent, no matter what anyone thought. But did Tallie fit her definition of innocent? That's what she didn't know for sure.

"I swear to God," Brett growled, "If you hurt her, I'll kill you myself. Even if I have to hunt you to the ends of the earth to do it."

Natasha trembled, but Tallie didn't think it was fear. Excitement maybe. Natasha was like a stick of dynamite. The primer cord was burning its way to the source. If it got there, Natasha would explode.

"Please," Natasha said dismissively. "I am the one who found her, you moron. But I will not be taken by you people. Not tonight. Not ever again. Miss Grant and I are walking out of here, boys. Alone. I'll release her when I'm sure you aren't on my tail."

Ian took a step forward. He dropped the barrel of his rifle and motioned the others to do the same. "We're on the same side, Natasha. But why are you here?"

Her grip on Tallie's neck loosened even more. Tallie wasn't going to break away though. She was positive that Natasha meant her no harm. And positive that any fast movements on her part would put them both in danger as Natasha and the men reacted to each other.

"Because I owe Señor Broussard a thing or two. And I have come to pay up."

Ian frowned. "What did he do to you?"

"To me?"

Tallie felt Natasha tremble again. It wasn't excitement this time. It was fear. Or rage.

"He did nothing to *me.* It is what he has done to others."

The helicopter was drawing closer, the beating of the rotors echoing through the mountains.

"There is a tunnel," Natasha said. "Unless perhaps that is your helicopter coming to pick you up?"

"Not ours," Ian said.

"Then it is Broussard, returning from Barcelona."

"The tunnel is passable?" Ian asked.

"Yes. You know where it is?"

"We do," he said.

"Then perhaps you should go, Mr. Black." She unwrapped her arm from Tallie's neck and pushed her toward the men. "And take her with you."

Tallie stumbled toward the men, toward Brett's outstretched arms, but then she stopped and turned to look at Natasha.

Natasha stood there proudly, exposed, but she held both guns trained on the five men who outgunned her and outweighed her, daring them to attack.

Brett swept Tallie back into his embrace, tugging her out of the path of the bullets.

"No," Tallie said, fighting him. "Don't hurt her. Don't you dare."

Natasha must have heard her because she

laughed, but it wasn't a derisive sound. Was it the laugh of a friend?

"Tallie Grant," she said, "You have heart and beauty and brains. Go with your man and have many babies together. You will not be in danger from the people who took you and sold you. Not ever again. I promise it."

She backed away from them slowly, guns up, ready to fire—and then she whirled away and disappeared into the darkness.

"You can't leave her here," Tallie said as they started to move away from the direction that Natasha had gone. "She helped me."

The helicopter grew louder still. Brett looked up. They were still beneath the colonnade.

"We have to get you out of here, Tallie."

"I know that. But get her too. Take her with us."

"She doesn't want to go," the man Natasha had called brother said. "She has her own mission. And we have ours."

Colt snorted. "Besides, you can't trust her. She fucking shot me. If she comes with us, I might be tempted to shoot her in return."

"In twenty minutes, this mountain is going to be crawling with commandos," Brett said in her ear as he hustled her toward the opposite side of the fortress. "Spanish special forces, coming to rescue the people Dr. Broussard has trapped inside. And when they do, they will arrest him and everyone who works here with him. It's best if we aren't around when it happens. Too much explaining."

Behind them, Ian swore. They stopped moving and turned as one to look at him.

"Boss?" Brett asked.

"I'm going after her," Ian replied. "Get the fuck off this mountain, kiddos. I'll join you soon."

IAN SLIPPED toward the courtyard as the helicopter began its descent.

He must be crazy. Natasha Orlova was perfectly capable of taking care of herself—and she wasn't in the least bit interested in anyone helping her. But if she was still here when the Spanish commandos arrived, she'd get swept up in the raid —or killed outright because she wasn't the type to surrender.

He'd told Broussard's servants that he was going to blow the mountain, but that wasn't true. The monastery, no matter what disgusting purposes it'd been used for in the past few years, dated to the sixth century. Parts of it did, anyway. And Ian wasn't the sort to destroy historical sites.

No, he'd used his connections to get the Spanish commandos involved. They were incorruptible, and Dr. Broussard wasn't going to disentangle himself easily. Oh, Ian didn't think he'd spend any real time paying for his crimes. But that was okay because Ian would make sure he went down permanently when the time came.

The helicopter touched down and the door opened. A man in a tuxedo stepped onto the cobbles. He hesitated, no doubt confused at the lack of servants, but he started for the entrance to the monastery when it was apparent no one was coming.

Ian could see him in the light. Roberto Broussard was about six-foot, his hair slicked back, his tuxedo shiny and expensive, his watch glinting gold in the lamplight. He'd been to a function in Barcelona that was designed to raise money for children who needed cleft palate surgery. The man was a monster and a hypocrite and Ian hoped like hell he got a taste of his own medicine when he ended up in a Spanish prison for the night. If there was any justice in this world, he'd spend a few nights there before he got released.

Broussard was almost to the doors when he stopped suddenly. The helicopter was still perched in the courtyard, the rotors slowing as the pilot shut it down for the night.

Ian edged around the perimeter, trying to see what had made Broussard stop suddenly. As if he couldn't guess.

He didn't have long to wait before she came into view. Natasha Orlova, looking like Lara Croft, two long pistols with silencers pointed at Broussard's heart. Or maybe it was his head.

Ian didn't know what she planned—but he didn't have long to wait. Roberto Broussard dropped before

Ian heard the shots. Silencers weren't entirely silent, after all. The pilot must have noticed because the rotors spooled up again as he started the engine, no doubt intending to make his escape.

Ian started for the helicopter. The pilot was busy watching Natasha as she strode toward him and he didn't see Ian approach from the other side. The man reached down, grabbing a pistol and aiming it at Natasha as she got closer.

She shot him in the head and he slumped over the controls. Then she jumped into the helicopter and shoved him out the door.

Ian swore as he sprinted toward the helo.

But he wasn't fast enough.

Their eyes met—and then Natasha grinned. She pulled the collective control up and the helicopter lifted off. Ian stood beneath it and watched in frustration as it flew higher, eventually disappearing into the pitch black of night.

He waited for a long moment, heart in his throat as he listened for an explosion. It was tricky flying this territory at night and he didn't know if she was capable of it. Hell, he hadn't even known she could fly.

He kept expecting her to crash into a mountainside, but nothing happened. No explosion came.

Ian strode over to where Roberto Broussard lay. His eyes were open wide and there was a neat hole in the center of his forehead. It took Ian a moment to notice that the doctor had also been shot in the crotch. Right in his balls.

"Fuck," Ian whispered.

Another helicopter sounded in the distance, only this one was bigger and filled with commandos.

Ian didn't want to be here when they arrived. He didn't want to explain the dead men, and he didn't want to spend hours giving statements. He damned sure didn't want to explain himself to Phoenix, his handler in the CIA.

No, it was time get the hell out of here. There was nothing more he could do.

Ian sprinted for the tunnel.

Chapter Twenty-Eight

TALLIE SAT WITH HER LEGS CURLED BENEATH HER, sipping hot tea to warm her frozen bones. She was tucked into a plush seat on the private airplane that belonged to Black Defense International. The journey home was going much better than the journey over had.

For one thing, she wasn't bound or gagged, and five big strapping men tiptoed around her as if she were made of glass.

She wasn't, but she didn't tell them that. She was tired and cold and enjoying that they were concerned with her comfort. It was a nice change from the past day.

It had been a hard trip down the mountain. After negotiating the tunnel beneath the monastery, they'd emerged into a wooded area and then had to hike through the forest for a couple of miles. When they came to a clearing, a big black helicopter dropped out of the sky and picked them up.

Ian Black caught up to them just in time to jump onto the helicopter too—but Natasha wasn't with him. Tallie hadn't really expected that she would be, but she'd hoped.

"She commandeered a helicopter and flew away," Ian had said in explanation.

The man Tallie now knew was called Jace had looked as if he'd been thumped between the eyes with a two-by-four. "She can fly?"

"Apparently."

After a quick trip to the airport, they'd boarded the BDI jet and taken off. Tallie's head was still spinning at the speed with which everything had happened.

Brett sat down beside her and Tallie's entire body heated at his nearness. Emotions she'd been holding in check wanted to spill from her lips, but she didn't let them. He'd come for her, but that didn't mean anything by itself. It just meant that he was one of the good guys.

He took her hand and pulled it to his lips, pressing a kiss to the back of it. A lump formed in her throat. She deliberately didn't look at him so she didn't lose control.

"I'm sorry, Tallie," he said. "So fucking sorry I wasn't there to stop him."

She turned. He'd washed off the greasepaint and was once again the handsome, sexy man she loved.

The look on his face was tinged with so much anger and sorrow that she nearly cried out. Instead, she lifted a shaky hand and caressed his stubbled jaw. His green eyes blazed at her touch, and an answering fire began to pulse inside her.

"I don't understand any of this, Brett—but I know for a fact you couldn't have known what was going to happen. Robert—Roberto—used Sharon to get to me. How could you have known he'd do that?"

"I should have anticipated it."

He would insist on blaming himself, but she knew it wasn't his fault. It wasn't anyone's fault except Roberto's. He was the sick fucker who'd orchestrated everything. She'd told Brett what Roberto had said to her, what he'd intended. But he hadn't actually hurt her, other than the small hurts when he'd abducted her.

"How is Sharon?" She knew that her friend was safe, but she didn't know her mental state—and she'd been afraid to ask.

"Angry. Confused. Feeling guilty. She's at home now, resting. I texted her to let her know you were safe. She knows about the auction, Tallie. I had to tell her."

Tallie nodded. It was actually a relief that her best friend knew what had happened. Because she was going to need someone to talk to about it all.

"It's okay. But what happened with Roberto is not your fault and it's not hers either." She pulled in a breath. Let it out. "You're both stubborn. So stubborn."

"She loves you."

Do you? She wouldn't ask it, though. She sniffed and pushed away thoughts of unrequited love.

"Who is Roberto Broussard really? He told Sharon his name was Robert Cortes."

"Dr. Roberto Cortes Broussard. A prominent plastic surgeon who was at the auction that night I rescued you. He bid on you, and he lost."

"He's not really trying to pioneer any vision technology for blind people, is he?"

Brett shook his head. "No. He lied to Sharon about that. About everything other than the fact he's a doctor. He is rich, but his fortune comes from an inheritance and from being a criminal as well as from his practice."

Tallie shuddered. "What will happen to him now? Will the Spaniards arrest him?"

Brett frowned. She could tell he was thinking about what to say.

"Tell me," she said. "I think I deserve to know."

He nodded. "Broussard is dead."

She blinked. Was it awful to feel relief over a man's death?

"I can't say that bothers me even a little bit." She snorted softly. "Is this what happens? You just get used to death and violence and then you start feeling like it's justified?"

"Sometimes. It's okay to be glad he's dead, Tallie.

Broussard was a monster. The world hasn't lost much now that he's gone."

Tallie shivered. "Do you think Natasha was right?"

Brett frowned. "About what?"

"When she said I wouldn't be in danger again. Do you think she was right?"

He stared at her for a long moment. "Yeah," he said. "I think she was."

She nodded and closed her eyes. But she wasn't sure she was ready to believe it.

ONCE THEY LANDED IN DC, Brett took Tallie to his place on the Eastern Shore because it was much closer. Ian probably would have given them a helicopter to return to Williamsburg, but Brett hadn't asked. Because he was selfish enough to want Tallie to himself for a while, which he would not get if he took her home.

Things weren't settled between them, and he wanted them to be. He just didn't know how to go about telling her what he felt. It hadn't seemed right to tell her while they were running from the monastery, or when they were on the plane and everyone else was there too.

But he needed to tell her, and soon. Maybe she didn't feel the same way he did. That was something he dreaded knowing, but also something he needed to know. Because he couldn't move forward until he did.

It terrified him to say the words to her. For now, he could at least pretend they were on the same page.

He drove them over the Chesapeake Bay Bridge and to the small town where he'd bought a house on a creek that spilled into the bay. It was peaceful and quiet and he hoped she would appreciate it like he did.

They didn't say a lot during the trip. He pointed out the sights and they discussed superficial topics. He felt like one of those water bugs, skating along on the surface of something that was much deeper and more treacherous than he knew.

Brett was uncharacteristically nervous when he finally pulled into the driveway of his little white house with the timeworn wood siding. What if she didn't like it? What if she hated everything about it?

She was a decorator. A woman with impeccable taste who lived in a home that looked like it fell out of a magazine.

"What a beautiful setting," Tallie said when the house came into view. He drove around to the side-entry garage, but didn't enter it.

Tallie was gazing at the yard where it sloped down to the water. The creek was small but pretty and there was a short dock that Brett liked to sit on sometimes. He'd take a couple of beers, sit in one of the Adirondack chairs, and just watch the birds flying and the fish jumping. It was relaxing.

"I think it is," he told her, wishing it was a sunny day instead of a gray one. "Wait there."

He got out and went around to her side of the vehicle to open the door. She smiled as she put her hand in his, and his heart flipped in his chest. It was chilly, but nowhere near as chilly as Spain had been. She was wearing a new quilted jacket and fresh clothing because BDI kept entire wardrobes of clothes on hand for various purposes.

He'd planned to take her inside and show her the house first, but that wasn't what he did. He led her down the sloping green grass to the wooden dock. They stepped onto it and ambled to the end where the chairs sat. A blue heron stood on the opposite bank, in the marsh grass, one foot up as it waited for an opportunity to strike.

The air was fresh and cold and the setting was beautiful. It was as if they were the only two people in the world right now.

Brett turned to face Tallie, his heart ready to beat right out of his chest. She smiled up at him. She looked happy, and for that he was thankful. She'd been through so much. Too much.

If he had his way, she'd never experience another moment of fear so long as she lived. Probably a tall order, but it was what he wanted for her.

He didn't let go of her hand, and she didn't pull it away.

"Thank you for bringing me here," Tallie said, breaking the silence. "I wasn't ready to go home."

He squeezed her hand. "Are you afraid to go home again?"

She drew in a breath. Then she shook her head. "No, I'm not. No one broke into my house. A man who pretended to be interested in my best friend used that relationship to get to me. It happens to women all the time, in some form or another. Stalkers, abusive husbands, jealous lovers. I refuse to let it change me, Brett. I don't want to be scared all the time."

She was strong. Brave. "I'll protect you, Tallie. I swear it."

"You won't always be there though, will you? Which means I need to learn to protect myself. I'm going to take some self-defense classes. Apply for my pistol permit. I should have done that long ago. Because the world is a dangerous place, especially for women."

He hated that she felt that way but he knew she was right. He'd seen firsthand, at a young age, just how dangerous it was for women who were alone. He'd feel better if Tallie knew how to protect herself when he wasn't around.

"I need to tell you something," he said.

A little line formed on her forehead. "Okay."

"I told you my mother died when I was eight. But I didn't tell you that she was murdered, or that I was the one who found her."

Tallie gasped, her fingers curling harder into his. "Oh, Brett. I'm so sorry. That had to be terrifying for you. You were just a little boy."

"It was. I didn't realize she was dead at first. She'd been strangled. It was cold and dark because we didn't have any electricity. I heard her bring the man home, but he didn't know I was there. I was hiding beneath blankets in the living room, trying to stay warm. He—"

His throat closed up as he remembered. Tallie slipped her arms around him and held him tight, her head tilted back to look up at him.

"It's okay," she said. "You don't have to tell me."

"I need to," he forced out. "I've never told anyone. The police knew. It's in my record so I'm sure the fosters knew whenever they got me. But I've never told anyone, never said the words myself. My mother was murdered and I found her. And I swore I'd do everything I could to keep it from happening to anyone else."

"Oh, Brett. You're one man. You can't stop all the evil in the world—but you've made a difference. You made a huge difference for me. Without you…"

Her eyes were shining. She dropped her chin, hiding those beautiful eyes from him. He put his finger beneath her chin and tipped it up again. A tear broke free, slid down her cheek.

"I love you, Tallulah Margaret Grant," he said, the words spilling from him even though he didn't want them to. Because he was afraid. Afraid of her reaction. Afraid it would change everything between them and they'd never get it back again.

"You do?" Her voice sounded full of wonder.

His heart had stopped after he'd said the words, but now it started beating with renewed hope. "Yes. I didn't think there was such a thing as destiny and finding *the one.* Knowing in your soul that you've found her. But there is, and I have. I've been waiting for you, Tallie. All my life, I've been waiting."

Her jaw had dropped during his little speech. She laughed, a watery, sobby laugh that caught at his soul.

"I love you too, Brett Stone Wheeler. Like for realz and forever and all that stuff. But I'm not strong or brave like you. Or like Natasha—she's so magnificent and tough, and I'm not."

He put his fingers over her lips, softly hushing her. "You're one of the strongest people I know, Tallie. There are men who wouldn't survive what you've survived this past month. Natasha is a fighter—but so are you. You may not wear guns and fight battles, but you're strong. Never doubt it."

"Wow," she said. "You really mean it."

"Hell yeah, I mean it." He put his arms around her, tugged her close. "You're soft where you need to be soft, and strong where it counts, and I think you're perfect."

"I'm not perfect. You'll see."

"Whatever you say, baby. You can spend a lifetime trying to prove me wrong, but you aren't going to. I'm stubborn like that."

She wrapped her arms around his neck, laughing. "Fine, be stubborn. I can be stubborn too. Right now, for instance, I stubbornly want you to kiss me. Then I want you to take me inside and undress me and make love to me. I am feeling *very* stubborn about it."

Brett laughed. "If that's your definition of stubborn, then I'm all over it, honey."

"So long as you're all over me, we're good."

Tallie grinned up at him. Brett grinned back. Then he kissed her, his heart full of love and his soul feeling free for the first time in twenty years. He'd finally found the key that clicked into place and said, *Home.*

The key was Tallie. He was hers forever.

He picked her up and took her inside where he undressed her tenderly, then pushed his way into her body while she begged him to go faster. But he didn't want to. He wanted to enjoy every moment, every stroke, every single sizzle of sensation as he built the pleasure to a peak.

He built it until Tallie was practically sobbing with need. Until his balls ached and his throat was tight and his love for her threatened to burn him alive. Then he let her fly free, and he flew with her until they were both spent, until they came back down, entwined together, blissfully happy in the knowledge that all their lonely yesterdays were gone.

Epilogue

Christmas Eve…

BRETT WALKED from his kitchen to his living room and stopped, as stunned as he'd been the first several times at the transformation Tallie had wrought in his home. She looked up from where she sat on the couch in front of the fireplace and smiled at him.

She was still dressed in the deep berry-colored gown she'd worn to the gala tonight and he was still in his tuxedo. He'd had to restrain himself from ripping her clothes off and making love to her the minute they walked in the door, but he'd wanted to spend time in the living room, staring at the Christmas tree and all the beauty that Tallie had created for him.

He carried a bottle of wine and two glasses and he set the glasses on the table so he could pour. Then he handed Tallie her glass and clinked it with his before he sat back and lifted his arm so she could snuggle in beside him.

The Christmas tree twinkled with white lights and the fire blazed merrily while carols played in the background. It felt like the kind of Christmas he'd always longed for. He never decorated, but Tallie had insisted. She knew what he'd gone through as a child and she'd said that he needed to experience the magic of the season in his own home, with the woman who loved him.

"You were right," he told her as he sipped the wine.

"Of course I was. What was I right about?"

He snorted. "Christmas decorations. They're gorgeous and so are you. I'm happy."

She squeezed him. "I'm happy too."

"I'm grateful to you for this, Tallie. But I want you to understand that I don't expect you to move to Maryland. I can move to Williamsburg just as easily."

They'd told her mother they were dating, and she seemed to like him. They were going to her house for Christmas dinner tomorrow.

"Oh, I don't know," Tallie said in that tone that told him she was planning something. "I've been exploring the local area and I think maybe they might need a Tallie Grant Interiors and Antique Tours."

He blinked. Then he turned to stare down at her. She grinned up at him. "Are you serious?" he asked.

"Why not? I'll never open my own place in Williamsburg. I can't compete with my mother. I don't want to, either. Besides, I like it here. I love the view and I can envision so many projects to make this house really shine. The bones are here—it just needs the vision."

God, he wanted her here with him so badly. But he didn't want to take her from her life in Williamsburg. Her mother. Sharon, who'd bounced back from the experience with Broussard and been a rock for Tallie. Even Bill, who Brett liked a lot. Bill was a no nonsense kind of guy who loved to hunt and fish and wanted to make Mary Claire Grant his wife. That she wouldn't say yes hadn't phased him yet. He wasn't giving up, and Brett thought he'd wear her down one of these days.

"Tallie, if you want to tear it down and rebuild it, I'm on your side. Whatever you want."

She laughed. "We don't need to go that far."

"What about your mom? What will she say?"

Tallie shrugged. "I already told her I was thinking about it. She was a little shocked at first. But she came around. She likes you a lot. And I think maybe she's realized that I need to do my own thing and not try to emulate her. I won't ever be her, or Josie."

"Baby, we've talked about that. You know that you're perfect the way you are."

"Not perfect, but yes, I know now that Josie basically did whatever Mom wanted so she was easier for

Mom to deal with. I was always a little too independent, I guess." She pushed herself upright to meet his gaze evenly. "Do you know that she told me just yesterday that she loved every stick of furniture I bought in France? Even the pieces I didn't tell her about before I did it? She said I had a great eye. The shipment's been in the warehouse for two weeks, so I wasn't expecting her to say anything now. But she did."

Brett was happy for her. "You do have a great eye. I wandered around Bavaria with you, remember? Hey, think we can get one of those painted pieces you liked?"

"We are definitely getting one of those painted pieces. In fact, I was hoping maybe we could go back there, sometime next spring or summer, and find it together."

"You know I'm a guy with zero taste in furnishings, right?"

"I do know that. But I also know I want to see those mountains again. *With you.* I want to yodel."

"You do not want to yodel."

She giggled and snuggled back into his side. "Okay, maybe I won't yodel. But I want to spend more than two nights there this time, and I want to hike the mountains."

"We'll go then." It was an easy thing to give her.

"I want to go to Venice, too." She frowned fiercely. "I want to replace all the bad memories with good ones. You said those people weren't a threat anymore, though Natasha said it first."

"She did say it first. But Ian confirmed it."

In reality, Lane Jordan had finally managed to break the encryption and trace the money to the source. The Gemini Syndicate wasn't responsible for the auctions, but they had definitely taken a cut. The organizers were Chinese mafia, and Paloma Bruni was the connection between them and the Syndicate. The whole thing had gotten too hot to handle and the mafia was shutting it down. For now.

Paloma had gone to ground after Roberto Broussard was killed, but she'd been sighted in Brazil recently. Brett had a hunch that Natasha Orlova would soon take care of her. He didn't feel a shred of disgust over it either.

Natasha remained a mystery, but he was beginning to think there was method to her madness. She'd shot her own brother, and she'd shot Colt—but Brett couldn't hate her the way he might once have done. Maybe she'd had ulterior motives, but she'd helped Tallie—and he would always be grateful for that.

"Did you find the other women who were on the stage that night?" Tallie asked, her pretty eyes filled with concern.

"We did. They've all been freed. Except those who didn't want to be."

Tallie blinked. "There were women who didn't want to be freed?"

"Believe it or not, there are some lonely billionaires in this world with shitty dating skills. And they attend bachelorette auctions to find a woman. At least one of the ladies is engaged to her man, and a couple of others are living in the lap of luxury."

Tallie's mouth had dropped open. "Wow."

He pressed a quick kiss to those cherry lips. "Hey, don't be so skeptical. You're in love with the man who bought you, aren't you?"

She laughed and set her wine down to wrap her arms around his neck. "Well, yes, I am, Mr. Big Bucks."

"Best money I ever spent," he said. "The most, too."

"I'm worth it. You'll see."

He set his wine down and tugged her across his lap. "I already see, baby. Every minute with you is worth a million bucks. Every second."

"You are so romantic, Brett Stone Wheeler. And handsome as hell in that black-tie get up. Now kiss me."

He didn't stop at kissing her. After they'd stripped and made love in front of the fireplace, with the Christmas lights twinkling and soft carols playing in the background, he dragged a blanket over them as they lay together and stared at the fire.

"I love you, Tallie."

"I love you, too."

"What do you think about getting a puppy together?" He'd save the marriage and kids for another day, but he wanted those with her too.

"I think I'd love that. Can we get a kitten as well?"

"We can get anything you want, baby."

"Even a pony?" she teased.

He dropped his mouth to her neck, licked her skin. "If a pony makes you happy, we'll get one of those too."

She turned in his arms, caressed his cheek. "You make me happiest of all."

"That's the plan. For the rest of my life."

NEW YEAR'S EVE...

COLT THOUGHT about skipping Jace and Maddy's New Year's Eve party, but in the end he decided to go. Angelica Turner would probably be there, but he could deal with it. The girl turned him on, no doubt about it, but that didn't mean a thing. Not since she wouldn't let him get close to her.

She hadn't texted him since that day on the plane. He hadn't texted her either.

He walked into Jace and Maddy's house, which was packed with BDI operatives as well as other friends of theirs, and accepted the beer someone handed him.

He circulated, talking to people as he went, scanning the crowd for Angie. When he spotted her, his heart did a flip and his balls started to ache. She had her long red hair pulled back in a pony tail and she was wearing a black dress that hugged her curves. Strappy heels helped to showed off miles of leg. Not that she was very tall, probably five-six or so, but the heels made her seem taller and leggier.

She looked up then and her gaze met his. Her lips were painted red and her blue eyes sparked with emotion. He decided to make his way toward her, but before he got there someone else started to talk to her and she turned away.

As the night wore on, he talked to a lot of different people, but he never approached Angie. And she didn't approach him.

"Hey, it's time," Jace announced.

Everyone began to shout the countdown along with Ryan Seacrest on the television. "Three, two, one—Happy New Year!"

Colt shouted it out with everyone else. Horns blew and people kissed. Colt watched his friends kissing their women. He lifted his beer, prepared to kiss that instead, when someone tapped him on the shoulder.

He turned around. Angie stood there, looking up at him with soft eyes. Then she went up on tiptoe and pressed her mouth to his. It was a quick kiss, yet it rocked him to his toes.

She pulled away, frowning at him. "Happy New Year, Colt."

"Happy New Year. Angie, I—"

She put her hand over his mouth, stopping him from saying another word. Then she turned and slipped into the press of bodies in Jace and Maddy's living room.

He didn't follow her. He knew she didn't want him to.

One day, she'd be ready. He hoped it was soon.

Books by Lynn Raye Harris

HOT Heroes for Hire: Mercenaries

Black's Bandits

Book 1: BLACK LIST - Jace & Maddy

Book 2: BLACK TIE - Brett & Tallie

Book 3: BLACK OUT - Colt & Angie - Coming Soon!

The Hostile Operations Team ® Books

Book 0: RECKLESS HEAT

Book 1: HOT PURSUIT - Matt & Evie

Book 2: HOT MESS - Sam & Georgie

Book 3: HOT PACKAGE - Billy & Olivia

Book 4: DANGEROUSLY HOT - Kev & Lucky

Book 5: HOT SHOT - Jack & Gina

Book 6: HOT REBEL - Nick & Victoria

Book 7: HOT ICE - Garrett & Grace

Book 8: HOT & BOTHERED - Ryan & Emily

Book 9: HOT PROTECTOR - Chase & Sophie

Book 10: HOT ADDICTION - Dex & Annabelle

Book 11: HOT VALOR - Mendez & Kat

Book 12: HOT ANGEL - Cade & Brooke

Book 13: HOT SECRETS - Sky & Bliss

Book 14: HOT JUSTICE - Wolf & Haylee

Book 15: HOT STORM - Mal ~ Coming Soon!

The HOT SEAL Team Books

Book 1: HOT SEAL - Dane & Ivy

Book 2: HOT SEAL Lover - Remy & Christina

Book 3: HOT SEAL Rescue - Cody & Miranda

Book 4: HOT SEAL BRIDE - Cash & Ella

Book 5: HOT SEAL REDEMPTION - Alex & Bailey

Book 6: HOT SEAL TARGET - Blade & Quinn

Book 7: HOT SEAL HERO - Ryan & Chloe

Book 8: HOT SEAL DEVOTION - Zach & Kayla

The HOT Novella in Liliana Hart's MacKenzie Family Series

HOT WITNESS - Jake & Eva

---

7 Brides for 7 Brothers

MAX (Book 5) - Max & Ellie

7 Brides for 7 Soldiers

WYATT (Book 4) - Max & Ellie

7 Brides for 7 Blackthornes

ROSS (Book 3) - Ross & Holly

Who's HOT?

Alpha Squad

Matt "Richie Rich" Girard (Book 0 & 1)
Sam "Knight Rider" McKnight (Book 2)
Kev "Big Mac" MacDonald (Book 3)
Billy "the Kid" Blake (Book 4)
Jack "Hawk" Hunter (Book 5)
Nick "Brandy" Brandon (Book 6)
Garrett "Iceman" Spencer (Book 7)
Ryan "Flash" Gordon (Book 8)
Chase "Fiddler" Daniels (Book 9)
Dex "Double Dee" Davidson (Book 10)

Commander

John "Viper" Mendez (Book 11)

Deputy Commander

Alex "Ghost" Bishop

Echo Squad

Cade "Saint" Rodgers (Book 12)
Sky "Hacker" Kelley (Book 13)
Dean "Wolf" Garner (Book 14)
Malcom "Mal" McCoy (Book 15)
Jake "Harley" Ryan (HOT WITNESS)
Jax "Gem" Stone
Noah "Easy" Cross
Ryder "Muffin" Hanson

SEAL Team

Dane "Viking" Erikson (Book 1)
Remy "Cage" Marchand (Book 2)
Cody "Cowboy" McCormick (Book 3)
Cash "Money" McQuaid (Book 4)
Alexei "Camel" Kamarov (Book 5)
Adam "Blade" Garrison (Book 6)
Ryan "Dirty Harry" Callahan (Book 7)
Zach "Neo" Anderson (Book 8)
Corey "Shade" Vance

Black's Bandits

Jace Kaiser (Book 1)
Brett Wheeler (Book 2)
Colton Duchaine (Book 3)
Tyler Scott
Ian Black
Jared
Rascal
? Unnamed Team Members

Freelance Contractors

Lucinda "Lucky" San Ramos, now MacDonald (Book 3)

Victoria "Vee" Royal, now Brandon (Book 6)

Emily Royal, now Gordon (Book 8)

Miranda Lockwood, now McCormick (SEAL Team Book 3)

Bliss Bennett, (Book 13)

About the Author

Lynn Raye Harris is the *New York Times* and *USA Today* bestselling author of the HOSTILE OPERATIONS TEAM ® SERIES of military romances as well as twenty books for Harlequin Presents. A former finalist for the Romance Writers of America's Golden Heart Award and the National Readers Choice Award, Lynn lives in Alabama with her handsome former-military husband, two crazy cats, and one spoiled American Saddlebred horse. Lynn's books have been called "exceptional and emotional," "intense," and "sizzling." Lynn's books have sold over 4.5 million copies worldwide.

To connect with Lynn online:

www.LynnRayeHarris.com
Lynn@LynnRayeHarris.com